THE HOLIDAY

INSPECTOR WEST

PETER MULRANEY

Cover image: Tobias Hüske on Unsplash

ISBN 13: 978-0-6481046-7-4

This edition published 2018.

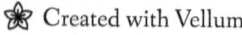 Created with Vellum

To those whose hearts are touched by the innocence of children.

CHAPTER 1

HELEN WOKE WITH A START. She looked at the alarm clock. It was nearly ten o'clock. She had slept in. Terry would be arriving any minute to pick up Toby to take him to the game.

She slid out of bed and went to see if Toby was ready. He rarely slept in on Saturdays. It was the only day she let him watch TV in the morning. He was always excited whenever Terry took him to the football. They were football mad and their team was having a great season, so she fully expected to find him ready and waiting to go.

She wondered why Toby hadn't come in to wake her.

There was no sign of him in the TV room. There were no dirty breakfast dishes on the table or in the sink. There was nobody in his bed. She was the only one in the house.

She looked into the backyard through the laundry window. There was no sign of him. She checked the back door. It was locked from the inside. She checked the front door. It wasn't locked, but the security door was locked from the outside. Maybe Terry had come while she was asleep. She went into the kitchen, to see if they had left her a note on the white board attached to the side of the fridge - nothing.

Typical bloody Terry, she thought. She went back into her bedroom to fish her mobile phone out of her handbag.

Before she could call him, she heard Terry's truck pull up in the driveway. When she opened the front door, he was standing there, alone.

'Hi, Helen. Is Toby ready?'

'I thought he was with you.'

Terry looked at her. He hadn't expected that response.

'How could he be with me? I only just got here.'

The colour drained from Helen's face, as it dawned on her that she didn't know where Toby was.

'If he's not with you, where is he?'

Terry managed to catch her, before she hit the tiles on the front veranda, and carried her inside. When she came out of the faint, he checked the house. He opened all the wardrobes that Toby could be hiding in and looked under the beds. He went out into the backyard and checked the small shed where the garden implements were stored. Toby was nowhere to be found.

When he returned to the living room, Helen told him that Toby's backpack and red parka, which he had left next to the front door before he went to bed last night, were gone. It looked like he'd taken off on his own. They looked at each other in disbelief.

'God, what if he's run away?'

Helen felt warm tears running down her face.

Terry did something he hadn't done in a long time. He hugged her. It felt so good she was reluctant to move out of his embrace.

'We'll find him,' he said softly, as he stroked her back, like he used to do when she was upset over something. 'There has to be a logical explanation.'

They called their parents to see if Toby had turned up at either of their houses. Toby spent a lot of time with his grandparents in the after school hours. While Terry asked the neighbours if they'd seen him leaving, Helen called the mothers of Toby's group of school friends. No-one had seen him.

Terry called the police to report him missing and then they waited, not knowing what to expect. This was so unlike Toby. He was such a good kid. He had never given them any trouble.

'What have we done to him?' Helen asked.

'What do you mean?'

'Think about it, Terry. What do you think our separation, and all the fighting that went before it, has done to Toby?'

'Hadn't thought about that.'

'You not thinking about things is half the problem.'

Terry reached over and held her hands. 'Let's not get into a fight?'

Helen glared at him. 'What if they can't find him?'

'Don't go there. He can't have gone too far. He's a ten-year old on foot. The police should be able to track him. They said they'd bring a dog.'

The twenty minutes it took the police to arrive seemed a lot longer to Helen and Terry. They were relieved when a patrol car pulled up in front of their house. Five minutes later a second patrol car with a police dog and its handler arrived. The dog was introduced to Toby's scent and immediately appeared to pick up his trail at the front doorway of the house. The dog crossed the front lawn and stopped at the kerb in front of the house next door. The trail ended there.

The policeman handling the dog spoke to the sergeant inter-viewing Helen and Terry, and then returned the dog to the back of his patrol car.

'Looks like your son probably got into a car in front of the house next door,' said the sergeant.

'What does that mean?' asked Helen.

'Means we have a bit of a problem, Mrs Moore. It looks like either your son has been taken or he had help.'

'If he got into a car, he could be anywhere by now.'

'Do you have a recent photo of Toby, Mrs Moore?'

'The school photos came last week. I haven't even paid for them yet.'

'Where are they?' asked Terry.

'On the TV,' said Helen.

Terry got up and went into the TV room off the kitchen. He wanted to have a look at the photos before they handed them over to the police. One of the downsides of living at his parents' place, while he and Helen were sorting themselves out, was missing out on things like seeing Toby's school photos when they arrived. He pulled out the large portrait of Toby and handed it to the sergeant.

'Nice looking lad,' said the sergeant.

'What happens now?' asked Terry.

'Two things. First, we'll distribute a copy of this photo to every patrol car in the State.'

'How do you do that?' asked Terry, thinking that could take forever.

'We'll scan this photo into the system in the car. It will appear on the screen of every other patrol car within seconds.'

The sergeant handed the photograph to her constable, who went out to the patrol car.

'Okay, and the second thing?

'When I get back to the station, I'll release details to the media so we can get Toby's picture and description out to the public. They're our eyes and ears. Hopefully, they'll help us locate him as soon as possible,' said the sergeant.

'And, what do we do?' asked Helen.

'Stay here in case he comes home. Give me a call if he does. If you come up with any ideas as to who he might have gone off with, call this number.' The sergeant handed Terry a card and stood up to leave. 'If you hear from anyone who claims to have taken him, call me. I'm sorry I can't make it any easier for you. This is going to be tough until we find him or he comes home.'

As the police were leaving Helen's parents arrived.

Kevin and Mary Sloan waited for the police car to leave before alighting from their silver Mercedes. The police car had been parked in Kevin's favourite parking spot in front of the house. He liked to look out through the front window and see his Mercedes in the street.

Mary waited for him to check that the electronic locks had engaged, and then she followed him across the small patch of lawn to the front door. Terry opened the door before they could knock or ring the doorbell.

'Any news?' said Kevin.

'No. They've only just left to start looking for him.'

'Where's Helen?' asked Mary.

'In the living room,' said Terry, stepping back to allow them to enter.

Mary pushed past Terry. Kevin stood on the veranda. 'What did the police have to say?'

'They think he got into a car in front of next door.'

'How'd they work that out?'

'They used a dog. It followed Toby's trail across the lawn and stopped at the kerb just over there, about a car's length in front of where your car's parked.'

'Any sign of forced entry?'

'No. It appears he let himself out the front door. Took his backpack with him. Helen thought he'd packed a few things for the football. Looks like he had other plans.'

'So, he's run away from home.' Kevin took one last look at the car and entered the house.

Terry closed the door and followed Kevin into the living room. If Helen hadn't been distressed before her mother arrived, she was now.

'Hello, darling,' said Kevin.

'Hello, Dad,' said Helen. 'Thanks for coming.'

'Terry, have you called Sean and Louise?' said Mary.

'I've talked to Dad. They'll be here once Mum gets home from the hairdresser.'

Louise Moore visited her hairdresser and manicurist every Saturday morning. It was a treat she gave herself as a reward for surviving another week picking up after Sean. She'd given up trying to change his habits after thirty years of marriage, and now simply used his credit card to compensate herself. She reasoned that if Sean could throw good money away on the horses, he could afford to look after her in the style of her choice.

He'd only protested her credit card bill once. A month of no sex had been enough to persuade Sean it was better to pay the monthly account, regardless of the balance, without asking questions.

Mary glared at Terry. She blamed him for everything. He was so much like his father - irresponsible and self-centred. Mary regretted ever having supported Kevin, when he insisted Helen marry Terry, once they had discovered she was pregnant with Toby. Helen would have been better off as a single mother, in Mary's opinion.

'You realise this wouldn't have happened if you two hadn't separated,' said Mary.

'For God's sake woman! Our grandson, their son, has run away from home and you want to blame them. Where's your compassion woman?' Kevin didn't particularly like Terry either, but he didn't see any point in inflaming an already strained relationship.

'It's okay, Kevin,' said Terry. 'She's probably right. We love Toby. I'd do anything to have him walk back through that door.'

'Would you grow up and accept some bloody responsibility as the boy's father?'

Everyone in the room stopped as Mary's outraged shout washed through them.

Terry looked at the floor. He knew Mary didn't think much of him. She wasn't all that good at hiding her feelings, especially when she was attacking him for what she regarded as his immature behaviour. She'd taken him to task several times over the years for his gambling and drinking. He looked at Helen. She was waiting for him to answer.

'Yes, Mary, I'd be willing to do that.'

The fight had gone from Terry. The three weeks he had been apart from Helen had been the longest three weeks of his life. At first, it had been a relief to have a break from their constant quarrelling. Then it had turned into agony. He missed being with her so much it hurt.

He'd planned to ask Helen if they could get back together this weekend. He'd already admitted, to himself, that it was his fault they had been fighting, especially after his mother had opened up and shared what is was like living with his father.

Louise had even advised him to find another job. Spending all day with his father, she'd told him, would not help, if he wanted to change his habits. Terry didn't know if he could do that, he enjoyed working with his father. They were a good team, and they were making good money. But he did know that for things to work out with Helen, he'd have to give up going to the pub and betting on the horses, for starters.

Helen smiled. She'd seen Terry beaten before, but there was something about his energy this time that suggested his perspective might have shifted. There was no fire in his response. She hoped he'd stay with her until Toby came back. She didn't want to have to cope with this on her own.

'What say we call a truce and have a coffee?' said Kevin.

Before anyone could answer, the doorbell rang. Terry opened the door to his parents, Sean and Louise Moore.

The stink of cigarettes wafted in with them as they entered. Sean had obviously had a quick smoke between the car and the door. Louise did not allow smoking in her car. Sean could smoke in his work truck if he wanted to, but she drew the line at the front door of the house and inside the family car, the one she regarded as her own.

At the time of Toby's birth, Louise and Helen had invested a lot of energy into persuading Terry to stop smoking. That was one victory that still gave Louise joy, and it had helped cement her relationship with Helen.

'We think we might know who he's with,' said Louise, breezing into the room, looking radiant with shining hair, highly polished nails, and firm breasts bouncing under a tight pink sweater, thanks to her Berlei lift and shape bra.

That got everyone's attention. Except for Kevin, who was momentarily distracted by the movement of Louise's pink sweater.

'Who?' said Mary.

'Kieran.'

'What makes you think he's gone off with Grandpa?' said Terry, who was having a few problems believing Toby would go off with the grumpy old man he knew as his grandfather.

'The two of them have spent a lot of time talking on Skype over the last couple of weeks. Kieran even dropped in to see Toby after school on Tuesday. First time I'd seen him since Martha died,' said Louise. 'They took the dog for a walk down to the park.'

'Any way you can contact Kieran?' said Kevin, now that he had tuned into the conversation.

'I've been trying to get him on his mobile ever since Louise joined the dots,' said Sean. 'He's either got it turned off or he's out of range. I've left him a message to call me.'

'Can't you go around to his place?' asked Helen.

'We called by his place on the way here. He wasn't home,' said Sean.

'His next door neighbour said he'd heard Kieran leaving around five thirty this morning,' said Louise, who wasn't shy about asking people for help.

'Wouldn't he have said something if he was taking Toby somewhere?' asked Mary. 'Surely, he wouldn't kidnap his own great-grandson, would he?'

Kieran was a mystery to Kevin and Mary. They'd only met him briefly at a couple of family events, and he hadn't been all that friendly. Mary had been repulsed by his tattoos. He was simply too taciturn for Kevin, who liked to engage people in conversation to see if they offered anything he could take advantage of, even if it was only a connection to someone else who might be interested in what he was selling.

'I'm pretty sure Kieran wouldn't see it as kidnapping,' said Louise. 'He probably thinks he's helping these two get their act together, giving them something to think about apart from themselves. He's a man of action. He does stuff and thinks about the consequences later.'

'We'd better call the police, Terry. The sergeant said to call if we thought of anything,' said Helen. 'Where'd you put that card she gave you?'

Terry took out his wallet, extracted the card the police sergeant had given him, and went into the kitchen to use the telephone attached to the wall above the sink. After a couple of minutes, he came back into the lounge and asked his father to come and talk to the sergeant. They all listened as Sean told the police Kieran's mobile phone number, described his van and told them where he lived.

'He's semi-retired. He's got a little courier business, does runs between here and the Riverland, two or three times a week. Okay, I'll ring as soon as I hear from him.'

Sean put the handset back into its cradle.

'She said they'd look up the registration number and send out an alert,' said Sean, as he rejoined the others in the living room.

'I hope you're right about him being with Grandpa,' said Terry.

'Let's hold on to that thought until we hear otherwise,' said Louise.

'What do we do now?' asked Helen.

'Well, we can sit around and starve or we can do something about lunch,' said Mary. 'Louise, why don't you and I go down to the shops and get some fresh rolls and cold meat?'

'Sounds good to me,' said Louise. 'Do you have any cheese, Helen?'

'You'd better get some of that, too,' said Helen.

'I'll put the kettle on,' said Kevin, who was dying for a coffee.

After an hour of polite conversation over lunch, Sean and Louise went home. Sean wanted to place some bets and Louise needed to have a lie down.

Shortly after, Kevin and Mary decided to go home as well, so that Kevin could prepare for the open inspections he had booked for Sunday.

'Are you two going to be alright here together, or do you want me to stay?' said Mary, as they were preparing to leave.

'We've been together for eleven years without killing each other, Mum. I think you can go,' said Helen, with a forced smile.

After her parents had gone, Helen turned to Terry. 'What are you planning on doing?'

'When today started, I was planning on asking if I could move back in with you and Toby. Now, I'm planning on staying.'

'I'd hoped you'd say that. I don't think I can do this on my own.'

They sat looking at each other across the kitchen table.

'I'm sorry, Helen. I'd like to start over.'

'Do you think we can?'

'I had a really long talk with Mum last night, when Dad was at the trots,' said Terry.

'You mean you didn't go with him?'

'No. Mum asked me to stay home and talk things over with her. She pointed out a few home truths. Some stuff, in fact a lot of stuff, I didn't want to hear.'

'What sort of stuff?'

Helen was starting to understand where the change in Terry's energy had come from. He'd been enlightened by his mother.

'For starters, she told me I was an idiot for the way I've been treating you. Then she told me that Toby needed a father, not a big brother.'

'How come it seems to mean something when she tells you? Isn't that what I've been telling you?'

'I don't know. I couldn't or didn't want to hear it before. She made me look, really look, at the way my Dad treats her.'

'And how is that?'

'He treats her like a slave. He doesn't even put his dirty undies in the washing. He just leaves them on the bathroom floor for her to pick up. He expects her to meet his needs, but he's not interested in knowing what her needs are. She said I was the only reason she stayed with him when I was growing up.'

'Why does she stay now?'

'Now she stays for the money and what it lets her do. It's become a game for her and Dad doesn't know the half of it.'

Helen wondered whether Louise had found herself a lover. That might explain why she spent so much money on clothes and beauty products, and the way she flaunted her body. Must be nice not to have to work, even if your husband is a jerk.

'So what does that mean for us?'

'I don't want to treat you the way he treats her.'

'Do you have any idea what that might mean?'

Terry looked her in the eyes. 'It means doing what your mother said - accepting my responsibilities as a husband and a father. It means being here for you, and not being in the pub. It means putting you and Toby first.'

'Do you want to do that? Do you think you can do that?'

'The other side of that coin is life without you. After the last few weeks, I don't want to do that.'

'Do you know how hard it is to break habits? We're talking some seriously addictive habits here. Do you think you can give up the horses and the pub, and your mates?'

'Ask Mum. I haven't had a drink or placed a bet for a week.'

'A week! I read somewhere the other day that it takes forty-two days to change a habit. You've got some way to go yet.'

Terry noticed she was smiling. 'At least I've started.'

Helen reached across the table and held his hands. 'I love you, Terry. Let's start again. I don't want to end up living like your parents, or mine.'

They were wrapped in the afterglow of their reconciliation when the telephone rang.

CHAPTER 2

CARL SAT in his reading chair, soaking up the winter sunlight streaming through the floor-to -ceiling windows of the sitting room of his two bedroom apartment, enjoying a quiet read of the weekend paper with a glass of red.

He put the paper down and let his thoughts drift to wondering how he was going to resolve his Nina problem. She had gotten closer to him than any other woman since the end of his failed marriage. He'd had a series of short relationships to get over Virginia, who had divorced him and married an accountant, someone who kept more respectable hours than a policeman. The last time he'd seen her, a couple of years back, she had presented herself as a happily married woman with three children, and a big house in the eastern suburbs. He let Virginia fade into the background. She wasn't his problem.

The previous afternoon, Chief Inspector Rankin, commander of the Major Crime Unit, had summoned Carl to his office to discuss, what the chief had referred to as, his 'Nina problem'. The chief inspector had been supportive. He'd told Carl he was relieved to see that he had settled into a stable relationship, which was a good thing, according to the chief. The chief inspector was a man who believed in stable relationships. He'd been married to Evelyn for thirty years.

The chief had also pointed out to Carl the potential conflict of interest between his professional and personal relationships.

Carl had been a little taken aback. He'd thought that he and Nina had been discrete. However, it seemed the chief had his sources. Carl hoped they didn't include Harry.

The upshot of the meeting was that, as of Monday, Detective Sergeant Nina Strong would be a member of DI Reid's team. The chief had wished him well with his relationship with Nina, and added that he thought they suited each other.

When he broke the news to Nina, she requested a week's leave and went to visit her parents, who had moved onto a small riverside property in the Riverland following her father's retirement. She wanted time to process being found out. The chief inspector's intervention meant a lot more people knew about them than they had believed. Their relationship being public knowledge within the force created a whole new dynamic she would have to live with.

Having heard the stories of his exploits in the years after his divorce, Nina wanted to know how committed Carl was to their relationship. She'd already had one bastard of a husband, a lawyer she had discovered screwing his secretary, in their matrimonial bed, after coming home early from an aborted night shift stake out. This time, she wanted someone she could trust, so she'd asked Carl to think about where he wanted the relationship to go.

In her mid-thirties, Nina also wanted to consider having children before it was too late, and she'd asked him if he was prepared for that, and given him until she returned to make up his mind.

Carl hadn't thought about children since his divorce. What sort of father would he be? Could he be a father? Did he want to be a father? His thoughts were interrupted by the ringing of his mobile phone.

'DI West.'

'Sorry to trouble you, Carl. I hope you haven't had too many reds,' the voice of Chief Inspector Rankin sounded in his ear.

'Only the one, so far, Chief.' If the Chief Inspector was calling him on a Saturday, when he was rostered off, something serious had happened. 'I guess this isn't a social call.'

'Get your travel bag, Carl, and make sure you pack a toothbrush. I'm sending you on a little holiday up the river. Harry should be there to pick you up in about half an hour,' said the Chief Inspector. 'We have a body and what looks like a kidnapping.'

That sounded like standard fare to Carl. There had to be more to it than that.

'Why can't the local boys handle it?'

'The body is Kieran Moore.'

'Oh. And the kidnapping?'

'Been listening to the radio or watching the TV today, Carl?'

'No, I've been reading the paper.'

'Yesterday's news, Carl. We've been looking for Kieran's great grandson since eleven o'clock this morning. Turns out he was with Kieran.'

'And now he's not.'

'Good to see your head is clearing. Give me a call when you've spoken to the local boys.' The Chief Inspector hung up.

Carl pulled the travel bag he kept prepared for these situations out of the closet in the hallway, collected his toiletries from the bathroom, and a suit from the wardrobe in his bedroom. By the time he was ready to leave, Detective Constable Harry Fuller was ringing his doorbell.

Carl settled in for the three hour drive from the city to the Riverland, a narrow zone of agricultural land and townships stretching along the river for three hundred kilometres, devoted to irrigation farming, mostly grapes and fruit trees, and tourism. He knew the place was dotted with riverfront shacks, hamlets, farmhouses and houseboats, because last winter he'd been one of the thousands of tourists attracted by the wild beauty of the region's national parks and abundant wildlife.

The arid, sparsely populated area outside the irrigation zone was a place he'd had cause to visit in the line of duty on several, less enjoyable, occasions. All sorts of things and people had disappeared into that vast empty space, and its network of roads provided a place for people to meet and transact all sorts of business, unobserved. The Riverland itself was also a place where interested parties grew illicit crops in among the legal ones, far from the prying eyes of the police. The force was thin on the ground outside the city, which was precisely why he and Harry were heading into the interior.

'Know anything about this Kieran Moore the Chief Inspector was so worked up about, Boss?'

'The thing to keep in mind, Harry, is that the Chief and Kieran Moore go back a long way. I'm fairly sure that Kieran Moore was the Chief's first big conviction, about thirty years ago, before I joined the force.'

'So why is his death such a big deal?'

'I guess we'll find out in due course. What I do know is that the Chief and Kieran Moore came to some sort of understanding while Kieran was doing his time. The Chief used to visit him in prison. I know they had meetings over the years after Kieran had done his time. In fact, the Chief introduced me to Kieran in a pub not long after I made sergeant. Big bloke, arms covered in tattoos. Intimidating, even though he was probably in his fifties at the time.'

'What was he done for?'

'Something to do with drugs. He'd be well into his seventies by now, so I guess he would have lost some of the intimidating physique. Let me have a look at the file.'

Harry concentrated on driving through the afternoon traffic, while Carl logged onto the on-board computer to see what information they had been provided with to introduce them to the case. Not much as it turned out.

'A conviction for dealing, the heavy stuff, back in the eighties. The leader of a local ring, and a Hells Angel to boot. Only the one conviction.' Carl scrolled through several screens. 'Going by his date of birth, he would have turned seventy-five this year.'

'Old enough to be well and truly retired. Wonder what he's been up to recently.'

'No details on that in here. Do you know anything about his great grandson being missing? Must admit I hadn't heard anything about it until the Chief mentioned it. Too busy with yesterday's news.'

Harry smiled, as he recalled Nina telling him how Carl got his weekend relaxation - with his head in a newspaper and a red in his hand.

'I heard the media briefing on the midday news. The boy's name is Toby, a ten-year old. Was gone when his mother woke up this morning. The Chief told me it wasn't until a couple of hours after he was reported missing that someone in the family realised he was probably with Kieran.'

Carl located the report on the computer and read the details, including the note stating that the boy's parents were separated.

'Tough being a kid these days, Harry. You ever thought about having any?'

'Haven't got to that part yet. Still working on finding someone willing to play the game.'

'Don't rush it, Harry. Being a policeman's wife is a big ask.'

'So my mother keeps reminding me. I think she's looking forward to the day my dad retires.'

PETER MULRANEY

'Your father's got it easy. Nice, cushy desk job down in the dungeon supervising all those girls in the call centre. Regular shift. What's your mother got to complain about?'

'I think my mum remembers the days when he was with the highway patrol, away for days, when I was a kid.'

'That why you became a detective, Harry?'

'Not really. I'm not into car chases or sitting around with radar guns. Too boring, if you ask me. I became a detective because I like to find out how things happen, and why people do them.'

'Yes. All that patrol work is not much fun. A lot more routine than some of the cases we get to work on.'

Winter days consume their daylight quota quickly. Harry was obliged to turn on the headlights an hour before they reached their destination.

Riverland Police Station had been a regional headquarters before the last restructure had seen its status downgraded. The Commissioner's new design for the region had moved the head-quarters two hundred kilometres down river, to where the crime statistics told him he needed the resources.

Inspector Bill Norris, the officer in charge of Riverland, wasn't happy that Major Crime's Chief Inspector Rankin had seen fit to interfere in his investigation. He didn't score many murders but that didn't mean he lacked the resources or the skills required to solve one.

Carl and Harry entered the station and introduced them-selves to the duty constable. He informed them that Inspector Norris was still at the crime scene with Forensics, who had arrived earlier in the afternoon. Carl called Bill Norris and arranged to meet with him later in the evening, as he couldn't see

18

any point in blundering around in the dark and getting in the way of Forensics' examination of the crime scene. There would be plenty of opportunities to look at the crime scene in broad daylight.

'We're staying at the Resort Hotel. We'll go and check-in and get something to eat while we're waiting for Inspector Norris.'

'Okay, Inspector. I'll tell the inspector where to find you when he gets back.'

Carl and Harry drove the short distance from the police station to the Resort Hotel. It took around ten minutes to complete the check-in process and locate their rooms. They were in the dining room, eating dinner, when Inspector Norris entered looking for them.

'Hello, Carl. Been a while,' said Inspector Norris, extending his hand.

Carl stood and shook hands with him.

Carl did the introductions. 'Inspector Norris, Detective Harry Fuller, my right-hand man.'

Harry stood and shook hands with the inspector.

'Why don't you join us, Bill? You look like you've had a long day,' said Carl.

As Inspector Norris took his seat, the waitress arrived with the chicken schnitzel and salad he had ordered on the way in.

They exchanged small talk about the weather, the state of the world and the recent federal elections while they ate, and waited for the tables around them to empty as people moved off to their Saturday night activities.

'What's so important about this one that Rankin thinks I need help from you, Carl?' Inspector Norris asked while they contemplated the dessert menu.

'What do you know about the victim, apart from his name?'

'Not much.'

'What about the missing boy? Any sign of him?'

'A backpack, full of clothes, with his name on it under the seat of the old man's van. And if that's not enough, the old man's girlfriend has disappeared as well. No luck with the dogs either.'

Harry was volunteered to place the dessert and coffee orders.

'How smart's your right-hand man, Carl? Is he a good apprentice?'

'One of the better ones I've had in a while. He actually thinks for himself.'

'What's your team like?'

'Decimated. I lost most of the good ones in the reshuffle.'

Harry came back to the table. He was followed by a waitress with their desserts and coffees. They waited for her to serve.

'I suspect the chief thinks this is not a local crime, and the boy is a complication that might not end well. That's why we're here, Bill,' said Carl.

'How do you want to play it?'

'I was going to suggest that your people focus on finding the boy. You have the local knowledge and contacts. Harry and I will work with Forensics on the murder. What do you think? It's your kingdom.'

'Might have been a kingdom once, Carl. I think it's more of a duchy these days,' said Inspector Norris with a wry smile. 'Anyway, that sounds like a plan. I have a meeting scheduled with the Forensics people at eight in the morning. Guess you had better be at that. There's not much point wandering around in the dark looking for the boy. We'll have to wait for first light for that. In fact, my sergeant is organising a search party for first thing in the morning in case he's gone to ground locally, if you want to join in.'

'We'd only get in the way, Bill. Besides, if the dogs couldn't pick up his trail, he probably didn't leave the scene on foot.'

'You're probably right, but we need to cover all bases, just in case.'

'Who's the girlfriend you mentioned?'

'Sally Arthur. She has a shack on the river about three kilo-metres out of town. Seems our Mr Moore stayed with her whenever he was in these parts. The body was found in the yard outside her place. She's in her mid-fifties, so maybe girlfriend isn't the right word.'

'What makes you think she has disappeared as well? Maybe she just isn't home.'

'Her car is still there.'

'Does she own a boat, Inspector?'

'That's something we have to find out, Harry. We know she doesn't have a registered boat but that doesn't mean she doesn't have a boat.'

'Any near neighbours?'

'Her shack is in a group of three but the other two are holiday homes. It was one of the other shack owners coming up for the weekend that found the body.' Inspector Norris stood up from the table. 'It's been a long day. I need some sleep. I'll see you boys in the morning.'

'Okay, Bill. We'll see you at eight.'

They watched in silence as Inspector Norris made his way out of the dining room.

'What do you think, Boss?'

'Just as well you like a puzzle, Harry.'

'Just off the top of my head, I'd say we have a few possibilities around the disappearance of the boy. The woman and the boy could be hiding. If the woman has access to a boat, say a canoe or a row boat, she and the boy could have escaped on the river. That sort of boat doesn't make any noise. Or maybe the woman had a role in both the murder and the kidnapping. Or maybe the boy didn't arrive with Kieran. He could have left the boy someplace between here and the city. And I haven't started on the murder yet.'

21

'Might be best to leave that until after tomorrow's meeting with Forensics.'

'Yes, we don't want my wild speculations to distort our thinking.' Harry laughed.

'I'm calling it a night. I'll see you in the morning for breakfast.'

When Carl got to his room he noticed there was a text message on his phone from Nina, telling him that she was thinking of him. He dialled her number.

'Where are you?' she asked, when she answered the call.

'I'm in the Riverland Resort Hotel.'

'If you miss me that much you could have come and stayed here. I'm only half an hour upriver from there.'

'I miss you but that's not why I'm here.'

'I thought Inspector Norris was handling the case. In fact, I saw him talking about it on the TV. I didn't see you.'

'The victim has a long history that involves our chief inspector.'

'What about the boy?'

'I'll know more about that in the morning. If he doesn't turn up, I'll have to make him my priority. The locals are conducting a ground search in the morning.'

'That might not suit Rankin.'

'The media will crucify him, if he makes solving the murder of a veteran Hells Angel the number one priority. Besides, solving one will probably solve the other, unless Harry is right about the old man dropping the boy off somewhere on the way here.'

'Better keep that in mind, sweetheart. Harry's hunches have been right before.'

'Anyway, I just wanted to hear your voice before I go to sleep. I love you.'

'I love you too, Carl. Have a good sleep. Call me if you need to talk anything over. Better still, come and see me. My parents are dying to meet you.'

'I'll call you tomorrow once I have a better picture of what's going on. Sweet dreams.'

Carl ended the call. He wished he was with her and not here in a hotel, with Harry in the next room.

CHAPTER 3

TOBY WAS SO excited about sneaking off with Grandpa Kieran that he was awake at 5.30 am. He had agreed to meet Grandpa Kieran out the front at 6.00 am. After quietly peeing in the toilet in the bathroom, he washed his face, collected his toothbrush and got dressed without turning on a light. He sat on his bed and waited for the clock on the dresser next to his bed to read 05:55. Then he crept, as silently as a ten-year old boy sneaking out of his house could, along the passageway past his mother's bedroom. Fortunately for Toby, Helen always closed her bedroom door, and concrete floors don't creak. He wasn't really worried that she would wake up. He knew she liked sleeping in on Saturdays, especially after staying up late studying.

When he got to the front door, he slipped on his parka and put his toothbrush into the front zip pocket of the backpack holding the change of clothes Grandpa Kieran had told him to bring. With the backpack on his back, he used his house keys to open the front door, and then the security door, and stepped out onto the veranda. He looked over in front of the house next door. Grandpa Kieran's van was parked where he said it would be. Toby closed the front door, locked the security door and walked over to the van.

Kieran opened the door for him as he approached the van.

'G'day, matey. Jump in and we'll get going.'

Toby pulled off his backpack, dropped it on the floor in front of the seat, climbed in and buckled up.

'Morning, Grandpa.'

Kieran didn't like being called Great-grandpa. It made him feel ancient as opposed to just old, so he had schooled Toby, his only great-grandson, to call him Grandpa or Grandpa Kieran, when there was the possibility of confusion. Besides, he had missed the opportunity when Terry was still a small boy of being called Grandpa. Apart from spending the first eight years of Terry's life in prison, he'd suffered years of Louise preventing him from spending time with Terry. He hadn't gotten to know Terry until he was a teenager. It wasn't until he had re-established his life after prison, kept out of trouble for five years and married Martha, that Louise had been persuaded that he was sufficiently reformed to no longer be a threat to the safety of her precious son.

Oh how he missed Martha. She had been twenty years his junior and the love of his life, but she had succumbed to breast cancer, after a long battle, earlier in the year. Kieran had thought being inside was lonely. It had nothing on being without Martha. He hardly ever thought of Susan, Sean's mother, who had overdosed and left him to bring up Sean on his own. Sean had been mothered by more women than Kieran could remember. If he was honest with himself, he couldn't remember much of what happened between the time Susan died and he ended up in court.

He often wondered what his life would have been like if he'd never met Susan and her drug dealing mates. Too bad he hadn't met someone like Martha instead way back at the start. The last seventeen years with Martha had been magic. He'd finally discovered what it was like to be appreciated for being himself, instead

of for being a muscle-bound thug on a big motorbike. Unfortunately, it had all come to an end way too soon. The last six
months had passed slowly. In a way, the bust up between Toby's
parents had helped him come out of his self-absorbed funk. It had
given him something and someone else to think about.

Kieran knew what it was like being the small boy caught
between quarrelling parents. His parents had split back in the
days when women had few rights, and men settled things with
violence or by disappearing and abandoning their wives and kids.
He'd passed through a string of foster homes after his father had
abandoned him and his mother, at the end of an alcohol fuelled
year of violence, when he was about Toby's age. His mother had
been so badly beaten that she'd died three months after his father
disappeared. He knew things were different these days, but he
didn't want Toby to suffer what he had suffered. When the boy
had opened up to him and shared his pain, Kieran had decided
that an unauthorised weekend holiday away from home would be
just the thing to get Terry and Helen back on the same page.

'Your mum still asleep?'

'Yes. She's going to get a surprise when she wakes up, isn't
she?'

'That's the plan.'

'You sure we aren't going to get into trouble?'

'We might but it will be worth it if we can get them back
together, won't it?'

'I hope this works. I hate it when they're fighting and
shouting at each other.'

'Well, shall we go?'

Toby nodded his assent. Kieran started the engine and they
drove off into the darkness of a cold winter morning.

Three hours sitting in a car was a long time for a small boy,
especially one that had spent half the night watching the clock.
Toby was asleep before they had reached the city limits. Kieran

let him sleep until he parked the van in the yard of Sally's riverside shack just before 9.00 am. Sally wasn't home. She'd let him know on Wednesday night, when he had called to tell her he was bringing Toby up for the weekend, and the circumstances under which the trip was being conducted, that she wouldn't be home when they got there. She said she'd keep his secret and make sure the larder was stocked, so they could have a quiet weekend without having to venture into town. Sally was good like that. She was a discrete operator and had been his partner in their little business venture over the last fifteen years. She was the only person alive that Kieran trusted. She had been Martha's closest friend from their school days.

Toby awoke as the van came to a stop.

'Are we there?'

Kieran reached over and tousled his hair. 'Yes, sleepyhead, we've arrived. Come on, let's go get some breakfast.'

They climbed out of the van and walked across the yard to the back door of the shack. Kieran inserted a key and opened the door into the main living room of the dwelling.

'See if you can find some eggs and bacon in the fridge, mate.'

Toby opened the fridge door and found a packet of bacon sitting on top of an egg carton full of eggs waiting for him. He carefully picked up the egg carton and carried it over to the bench.

After breakfast, as Kieran was explaining that a few people would be calling around to either pick up or drop off packages over the next few hours, a grey van pulled into the yard and parked next to Kieran's van. Two men dressed in black, one tall and muscular the other just as tall but slender in stature, got out of the van and waited.

Kieran looked out the window. He didn't recognise either of the men but, given the nature of his business, that was nothing new.

'How about you clean up the breakfast dishes while I sort these guys out?'

'Okay, Grandpa.'

Kieran walked out into the yard.

'Morning, boys. Picking up or dropping off?'

'Picking up,' said the slender one.

'Who for?' said Kieran.

There was no response apart from the big guy flexing his muscles.

Kieran stopped. He looked at the big one, who reminded him of himself in his younger days. Then he remembered that time had done things to his body, despite all the hours he spent in the gym. Being seventy-five had some disadvantages, one of them being he could no longer fight his way out of trouble.

The smaller one pointed towards the van. 'Open her up, we haven't got all day.'

Kieran noticed the smaller guy had something in his hand. One of those switch blade things, which Kieran knew had a very sharp pointy end. Kieran didn't like knives. He'd seen what could be done with a knife.

'Don't do anything stupid, old man, and you won't get hurt.'

Kieran had heard those words before. He'd used those words himself when he'd been an enforcer. He hoped Toby was doing the washing up and not looking out the window, because he knew that people who used those words didn't always tell the truth.

'What is it that you want?' he asked, as he walked up to his van and slid open the door to reveal a pile of small packages and three metal drums encased in wooden frames. He hoped they didn't want everything. Robberies were not good for business, and there were some things in his cargo, like the drums, that couldn't be insured.

The big guy transferred the three drums into their van while his partner stood next to Kieran. Although this wasn't the way the customer who ordered the drums on a regular basis usually conducted business, Kieran decided to act as if this was the normal pick up and not the theft it appeared to be.

'Do you have the return delivery?' Kieran asked. Usually he got a package in return for the drums.

The big guy smiled. He walked up to Kieran and said, 'Game over, old man.'

Kieran looked at him. He had no idea what he was talking about but, before he could respond, the big guy punched him in the stomach. As Kieran's body buckled under the force of the blow, his head came forward. The big guy lifted his knee.

Kieran jerked backwards away from his attacker and fell. His head hit the edge of the floor of the van as he went down. He crumpled onto the ground and lay still. The slender guy bent down and checked for a pulse. He slipped the knife into his pocket and stood up.

'That was easy, George. I thought I'd have to use the knife to finish him off.'

'Guess we got lucky.'

The back door of the shack banged shut. George looked up from the body at his feet. Toby had come out onto the veranda to see what Kieran was doing.

'Malcolm, there's a kid over there.'

'What's wrong with Grandpa?' Toby ran towards them.

George grabbed him as soon as he arrived where they were standing, next to Kieran's body.

'What's your name, boy?' asked George.

'Toby. What's wrong with Grandpa?' Toby squirmed trying to get to Kieran but couldn't break from George's hold.

'Your Grandpa tripped and hit his head,' said Malcolm.

'Are you going to call an ambulance?'

'Things aren't quite that simple, kid,' said Malcolm.

Toby looked at Malcolm and then at Kieran. A wet patch had

appeared in Kieran's jeans and the smell of fresh excrement wafted up to his nose. Toby had seen enough action movies on DVD with Terry to recognise those signs.

'He's dead, isn't he?' Toby stopped squirming.

Malcolm squatted down to look Toby in the face. 'What were you doing in the house?'

Toby didn't respond. He looked away from Malcolm down at Kieran's body on the ground.

George pulled him around to face Malcolm. 'Better answer him, kid. He gets pissed off when people ignore him.'

Toby sized up his position. He was clearly outnumbered and outgunned. 'Cleaning up the breakfast dishes.'

'Where's the woman that lives here?'

'I don't know. Grandpa didn't tell me anything about her.'

'What are you doing here anyway? We were told your grandpa would be on his own.'

'Grandpa brought me for a holiday.'

'A holiday? Well, we can't have you missing out on a holiday just because you grandpa fell down and died on you, can we?' Malcolm stood up. 'George, put him in the van. I'll check out the house to make sure there's no-one else in there.'

'For Christ's sake, don't touch anything!'

Malcolm pulled out a pair of leather workmen's gloves, the type tradesmen wear on building sites, and slipped them on as he walked over to the back door of the shack.

George's firm grip, as he led Toby to the van and opened the door, was a clear signal to Toby that he didn't have any say in what was happening. Toby did as he was told. He knew a bully when he saw one, and this one was a lot bigger than the bullies he usually encountered at school. As he climbed into the van, Toby told himself not to cry and to pay attention. He wasn't so sure Kieran had tripped and hit his head, and these men were acting like they had something to hide. He suspected they were taking him with them so that he couldn't tell anyone about them.

As George was securing Toby into the seatbelt over the seat between the two main seats in the front of the van, Malcolm reappeared with a red parka in his hand. Malcolm got in behind the wheel and handed the parka to Toby.

'You might need this.'

Malcolm started the engine and backed the van out of the yard onto the road. Then he drove off to begin Toby's second unauthorised holiday for the weekend.

CHAPTER 4

TERRY ANSWERED the telephone and listened in stunned silence as the caller explained the situation to him. He hung up without having said another word after his initial words of greeting.

Helen came into the kitchen from the bathroom as he was hanging up the phone. She'd slipped on a tee shirt but hadn't bothered with anything else.

She looked at Terry standing naked next to the fridge, with his shoulders slumped in line with the angle of droop of his spent member, and his face as white as the bench-top.

'What's happened?'

'They found Grandpa. He's dead.'

'What about Toby? Where's Toby?'

Helen's hands went to her face. It was just as well she'd had a pee, otherwise she would have wet herself while she waited for him to respond.

'She said they found his backpack in Grandpa's van but there's no sign of him. They're looking for him in the Riverland.'

'What's he doing there?'

'That's where they found Grandpa.'

'But he could be anywhere! Your grandfather could have dropped him off somewhere on the way.'

Terry walked over and wrapped his arms around her. 'They think Toby's been taken by whoever killed Grandpa.'

Helen broke from his embrace, ran into the bedroom and threw herself onto the bed screaming. 'Noooooooooo!'

Terry sat on the bed and tried to comfort her but she wouldn't listen to anything he said. It had been bad enough thinking that Toby had run off with his great grandfather to punish them, but now that he was really missing, abducted by murderers, she was inconsolable. Terry waited next to her on the bed.

When she calmed down he suggested they get dressed before anyone arrived, as he knew the police had called his father. The telephone rang again as they were dressing. It was his mother.

'This is not good, Terry. You know what sort of friends your grandfather used to have.'

'I thought he'd put all that behind him.'

'You realise it's all going to come out in the papers.'

'It's all been in the papers before, hasn't it?'

'That was a long time ago.'

'How did Dad take the news?'

'He went to the pub right after the police called.'

'You going to be alright tonight, then?'

'I know how to handle him. What about Helen? How is she?'

'How would you have been if I had been kidnapped by some of Grandpa's so called friends when I was little?'

'You'd better stay there, then.'

'Mum, there's no way I'm leaving her on her own. Not now, not ever.'

'Good. I hope they find Toby wandering around in the Riverland. I can't bear to think of him being kidnapped by some murderous thug. I hope he didn't have to watch Kieran being killed.'

'I hope you're right, Mum. Suppose we'd better let Helen's parents know.'

'Do you want me to do it?'

'No, I'd better do it. You heard Mary. I have to be the responsible parent. God, it's going to be fun when they find out about grandpa's past.'

'Good luck.'

His mother rang off.

Terry went into the bedroom to check on Helen. She had dressed but she was sitting on the bed staring blankly at her reflection in the mirrored wardrobe door.

'I'm going to ring your parents.'

'What was that you were saying to your mother about being in the papers a long time ago?'

Terry didn't know how to answer her. He hadn't ever really explained his grandfather's past. The incriminating part had happened a couple of years before he had been born. He decided he'd better tell her what he knew. It was going to be public knowledge soon enough.

'Mum was talking about Grandpa's past. Something that happened before I was born.'

Helen looked at him with those big wide eyes that had so captivated him when they first met. He knew there was no way out of it now.

'Grandpa did a ten year stretch in jail for drugs.'

'He was a drug dealer.' She stated it as a fact. Helen worked for a group of lawyers and was studying law. She knew what sort of crime a ten year sentence for drugs translated into.

'Not only was he a dealer, he was the leader of a gang of Hells Angels pushing heroin, according to Mum.'

'Guess that explains the tattoos. But I must admit, he never struck me as being a Hells Angel.'

'As far as I know he gave it all up when he got out of jail. He's been a courier driver ever since I was a kid. Driving all over the state and driving Martha mad with worry when he was away for days at a time. I've never even seen him on a motorbike.'

'Mum's going to be pretty shitty when she finds out. You sure you want to tell her?'

'Better she finds out from me than from the TV news, don't you think? She can't think any less of me than she already does. Anyway, it's not like I've committed a crime.'

'Why didn't you say anything about it before?'

'Honey, I was eight when he got out of jail. I don't really know any more about it than what I just told you. In any case, what difference would it have made? Your mother didn't want you to have anything to do with me without even knowing my grandfather was a criminal.'

'Yes, she keeps telling me the biggest mistake I ever made was having sex with you.'

'Do you think it was a mistake?'

'The mistake was thinking I could change you, and then getting angry when you wouldn't change. The mistake was all the fighting we've been doing over the last couple of years.' She stood up and took his hands. 'I don't know how I'm going to cope if anything has happened to Toby. I don't give a shit what my mother says. I decided to be with you. I need you to be here for me, can you do that? Will you promise me that you'll stay no matter what happens?'

'Yes.'

They held each other tightly for an intense moment.

'Come on. Let's go and tell my parents Toby really is missing.'

On the pretence of needing to complete some paperwork and make sure everything would be ready for the open inspections he had planned for Sunday, Kevin Sloan had gone to his office in the city. The truth of the matter, however, was he simply had to get out of Mary's presence before he hit her with something.

She was toxic company when she got worked up over an issue, and Terry Moore was an issue she had been working up to ever since Helen had told them she was pregnant with Terry's child. For the last three weeks, she'd been urging Helen to dump Terry and stop wanting to get back together with him. In Mary's eyes, Terry was a loser. Toby running off with Kieran, another dead loss of a life in Mary's opinion, only confirmed her view that they would all be better off without Terry Moore being around making a mess of their lives.

Mary had used the trip home from Terry and Helen's to repeat every judgmental thought she had ever had about Terry, and his Neanderthal of a father. Then, when Kevin thought she had exhausted her store of anti-Moore venom, she had accused him of being infatuated with Terry's flirt of a mother who, according to Mary, had been flaunting her 'silicon enhanced boobs' in her tight pink top as if she was some teenage sex symbol and not a mature woman in her fifties. Once they got home, Kevin couldn't get out of the house quick enough. God help her sister, he thought as he drove away in his pride and joy.

Kevin was enjoying a quiet whiskey in the Irish pub, three doors down from his office, and recalling the feel of Louise's definitely natural breasts, when Terry reached him on his mobile phone to tell him what the police had found out about Kieran and Toby.

Apparently, Terry had tried to tell Mary his news, but after finding her line continuously engaged, he'd decided to call Kevin. Lucky choice, Kevin thought to himself, as he listened.

When Terry told him about Kieran's criminal history, Kevin made a few notes. What Terry told him went some way towards explaining Kieran's tough, old man persona. Kevin didn't mention to Terry that he would be taking great delight in telling Mary all about Kieran - repayment for her accusation of his interest in Louise's boobs.

There were some moments a man wanted to relish on his own, especially ones involving Mary being so flabbergasted she wouldn't be able to speak. Kevin didn't have a big store of such moments, but he enjoyed replaying them privately, whenever he needed a boost. Just anticipating Mary's reaction lifted his spirits.

He ordered another shot of whiskey, and scolded himself for being caught enjoying the sight of Louise's bouncing boobs in that pink sweater. He hoped all the commotion caused by Toby's disappearance, and Kieran's death, wouldn't delay his next encounter with his sex goddess.

While Mary's sexual appetite had all but vanished, Louise's was insatiable, and Kevin took great pleasure in attempting to satisfy it at every opportunity.

When he finally made it back home, Mary was distraught. She had called Helen after spending most of the afternoon venting her spleen with Christine, her twin sister. She was beside herself with grief. Not for Kieran - she didn't give a shit about Kieran. He deserved whatever he got for being a drug dealer, even if it was more than thirty years ago. No, she had given up all hope that Toby would be found alive.

Kevin wished he'd met her sister first, before she'd met Robert. Christine was the polar opposite of Mary. The sisters looked alike but the similarity ended there. Christine was the Director of Nursing at University Hospital. Mary worked in the accounts department of the local council. Christine was still a nice person. Mary had been a sexy firebrand when they met but, over the years, under the weight of her disappointment at not being appreciated at work and the stress of, what she referred to as, the 'Terry and Helen disaster', she had morphed into a diffi-cult person to live with.

He tried to reason with her.

'Sweetheart, they're saying they haven't found him. No-one is saying that he's already dead. All they're saying is that they don't know where he is yet.'

'Don't be so stupid! Do you think whoever killed Kieran would leave a witness?'

The neighbours would have heard that outburst. Kevin tried his best to speak calmly.

'They don't even know if Toby was still with Kieran when he was killed. All they've said is that his backpack was in the van.'

'Then where is he? Why hasn't he called home?'

'Maybe someone is hiding him. Maybe he's been abducted.'

'Being abducted by a murderer is the same as being killed you dolt!'

She stormed out of the room. He heard the slam of a door as she retreated to her bedroom.

It hadn't turned out as he had envisaged after talking to Terry. Kevin was torn between wanting to comfort and punish her at the same time. Now he was the one that was exasperated. He hated it when she was like this. He didn't like irrational behaviour, unless it involved a buying decision when he was selling.

Knowing she'd be inconsolable for hours, he went into the kitchen to make himself something to eat. Then he sat down to watch the TV news. It was just as well Mary was sulking in her room, as the news bulletin had an extensive segment on the murder and kidnapping. There was even a photograph of a distraught looking Terry and Helen, standing next to that cute female police sergeant they had seen earlier in the day.

Kevin didn't know what to think. He hoped that Toby was still alive and that he would turn up safe and sound. Life would certainly get back to something like normal when he did. He didn't want to think about what life might be like if Toby didn't come home.

Sean told Louise he was going to the pub, and he planned to visit one on the way home, but that's not where he went. He drove to Kieran's place, to make sure it was clean before the police got a chance to search it, as he knew they would. The old man may have kept his record clean, and played Inspector Rankin for a fool, but the police would no doubt come looking.

Kieran had worked out a way of neutralising his nosey, elderly neighbour, who noted every movement in the street, and Sean used it now. He drove his truck into the driveway of the house directly behind Kieran's place.

According to the story Kieran had spread about, they'd bought the house with Martha's inheritance, the money realised from selling her parents' property up the river, following her mother's death about ten years ago. Sean knew that story wasn't the whole truth, because he'd contributed over half the purchase price through his money laundering operation. Now it was used as the office and storage yard for Moore's Garden Services, Sean's legitimate business.

The gate in the back fence between the properties provided Sean with a concealed entrance into the back of Kieran's shed, and from there, unseen access into Kieran's house. Once in the shed, Sean slipped on a pair of rubber gloves and used his key to let himself into the house. Fortunately, there was still enough daylight for him to see without having to turn on the lights. He went into Kieran's office and was relieved to see Kieran's laptop on the desk. He checked through the drawers of the desk to make sure Kieran hadn't kept any of his old manifest books, beyond the ones they had constructed for tax purposes. Then he lifted the carpet, opened the in-floor safe and removed the bag of banknotes Kieran kept there for a rainy day. Kieran only banked the money that could be traced to his legitimate customers, the ones listed in the set of books they kept for the taxman.

Once he had replaced the carpet, he took the laptop and the bag of money out to the shed. Then he went back into the house and quietly made a mess. He pulled clothes out of drawers. He up-ended furniture and scattered books. He spread the contents of Kieran's desk all over the floor of his office. Satisfied with his efforts, he returned to the shed, picked up the laptop and money and crossed back into the other yard. He decided that the best place to hide the laptop was in plain sight, so he slipped it onto a shelf in his office. As he did that he realised he'd left the door open. After dropping the money into his own in-floor safe, Sean headed back to Kieran's to lock the door. As he was about to open the gate in the back fence, he heard the sound of a motorbike pulling into the driveway behind him. That could only mean one thing. The man had heard the news and figured Sean would be here cleaning up. He walked around the shed back to the driveway.

The motorbike rider was taking off her helmet when Sean came around the side of his truck. He wondered why they'd sent the girl.

'Hello, Sean. I haven't seen you for a while. You haven't been hiding from me have you?'

'Hello, Clare. I guess this isn't a social call. Want to step inside?'

He didn't wait for her answer. He turned and walked to the back door of the house and held it open for her. She followed him to the door and they went inside, out of earshot of the neighbours, who no doubt had heard the motorbike. Sean caught a whiff of her perfume as she passed in front of him, as he held the door for her. The same scent he remembered from their last encounter.

He shook his head. There was no way he could touch Clare. The man would cut his balls off and she knew it.

'What's the man think?' Sean asked her, as they got comfortable in his office.

'I'm sorry about your dad, he was a really nice old man. I hope they find your grandson.' She paused for Sean to take that in. Then, getting back to business, she said, 'The man is pretty pissed off. Not only have we lost Kieran, we've lost three drums of the pure stuff, and it looks like someone has taken out the lab up the river.'

'Shit! That means we've lost our source.'

'We can replace the lab. What the man wants is the reserve supply.'

'It's not here. Kieran kept nothing here.' Sean could hear Kieran telling him keeping the stuff in the house was the biggest mistake he'd ever made. It had cost him ten years of his life and put that dickhead policeman around his neck like an albatross.

'So where is it?'

Sean thought about denying there was a reserve. Then he thought about what would happen to him if the man found out he'd been holding out. 'It's in a self-storage place down by the port. We change the box every couple of months.'

'When can you get it?'

'Whenever you want. I have the codes for the warehouse and the storage unit.'

'Let's go. The man wants it now.' Clare stood up. 'I'll follow you.'

Sean knew better than to argue, and besides, handing over the pills would put him in the clear. The police wouldn't be able to find anything on him when they came looking.

It took them thirty minutes to drive down to the port. It was dark by the time they arrived. Clare parked her motorbike next to Sean's truck, and they went into the second warehouse back from the street through the customers' entrance. They walked down a long corridor, with a door every three metres on both sides and automatic lighting that came on and switched itself off as they passed, until they reached an elevator. Sean pushed the button to go up.

'The unit's on the next level,' he said, as he waited for Clare to get into the elevator.

'Must be a shit-load of stuff stored here,' she said, as they rode up to the next level, where they walked down a second corridor similar to one on the floor below.

Sean stopped outside a door marked 215 and punched several numbers into the keypad that controlled the door lock.

'How do you remember that stuff? I have trouble with the PIN for my credit card,' said Clare as the door swung open.

'You should use it more often.'

They walked into a space three metres high by three metres wide and five metres deep, with a row of identical boxes stacked up along the wall facing the door. Sean pulled out a box from the middle row of the stack and opened it to show Clare the contents. She looked inside the box and then asked him to seal it back up, as she would have to carry it on her bike.

Sean placed the box on the floor and resealed it. When he looked up he was looking into the barrel of a large Glock pistol.

'Step back from the box, Sean.' Her voice was calm and businesslike.

Sean raised his hands and stepped back. 'What's going on?'

Clare used her foot to move the box to one side.

'Your contract's being terminated. Say Hi to Kieran for me.'

She squeezed the trigger. The round hit Sean in the chest and he fell back into the wall of boxes, before collapsing onto the floor. Clare stepped over the boxes and put a round between his eyes. When she was sure he was dead, she slipped the Glock back into its holster, in the padded section of her leather jacket below the breast line. Then she searched Sean's pockets for his keys. When she had transferred them to a pocket in her jacket, she picked up the box containing the pills, walked out and shut the door. Before leaving she gave the door a tug. It was locked.

Clare retraced the journey back to the door they had entered by and let herself out. When she reached the parking area, she called in on her mobile phone and waited for Malcolm to arrive.

Two minutes later a large black car, without lights, stopped long enough on the street outside the warehouse to drop Malcolm off, then it slowly disappeared into the night. When Malcolm walked into the parking area, Clare gave him the box and Sean's keys.

'You got the combination to the safe?' she asked him.

'Got it.'

'Make sure you leave it somewhere in his desk, not too obvious, but so they'll find it. I'll catch you later.'

Clare started the bike and slowly rode out into the night.

Malcolm climbed into Sean's truck and drove it back to Sean's yard.

CHAPTER 5

CARL AND HARRY arrived at the station shortly before eight, after a hot breakfast in the same dining room they had eaten in the night before.

The duty constable directed them into a conference room with a heavily scratched wooden table taking up most of the available space. The chairs around the table looked like they'd been reclaimed from salvage. The walls of the room had the dull glow of a surface that hadn't seen a fresh coat of paint in living memory. Inspector Norris and the sergeant from Forensics were seated at the end of the table under the window opposite the door, the only bright spot in the room.

After exchanging greetings, they got down to the briefing.

'The pathologist reckons he was dead before midday, yesterday. Maybe as early as ten o'clock,' said the sergeant from Forensics.

'That's a bit ironic, isn't it?' said Harry.

They all looked at him.

'He was dead before the boy was reported missing.'

'It takes three hours or so to drive here from the city, so he must have picked up the boy around six.' Carl made a note on his iPad mini. Even though the Force couldn't afford to upgrade its furniture, it had gone high tech.

'What else have you got?' Carl asked the sergeant opposite him.

'The fatal blow appears to have been delivered to the back of the head, but the body has a large abdominal bruise and a broken nose. It looks like someone hit him pretty hard and he fell back and hit his head on the van. There's blood on the edge of the floor, and the side door of the van was open.'

'Any idea how many people might have been involved?' asked Inspector Norris.

'I can tell you there are multiple sets of footprints at the scene, Inspector. I can't tell you how many were involved.'

'How many sets of footprints?'

'There are four sets of adult sized footprints, and one set about the right size for a ten-year old boy. One of the adult sets matches the victim's boots, another set matches the shoes of the neighbour that found the body. What I can tell you about the others is that they come from Rossi work boots. One set's about a size nine and other set is a size eleven or twelve.'

Carl looked at him. 'Rossi work books. That's fairly specific, Sergeant.'

'They make it easy for us sometimes, Inspector.'

The sergeant took a photograph from his folder and turned it towards Carl. The Rossi imprint was clearly visible in several footprints left at the scene.

'Any fingerprints?'

'The only prints on the van appear to belong to the victim and the boy. We found the same prints in the kitchen. It looks like the boy washed up the breakfast dishes. The only other prints in the house appear to belong to the woman that lives there, they're everywhere. One set of Rossi footprints suggests one of the boot wearers went into the house.'

'Any sign of anything being taken from the house?' asked Carl.

'Not that we could see, Inspector. You can check that with the owner when she turns up.'

'Any news on her, Bill?'

Inspector Norris shook his head, and then asked, 'What can you tell us about the vehicle used by the killers?'

'It's bigger than the Mitsubishi sitting in the yard. Going by the wheel base dimensions, I'd say it's probably a Ford transit,' replied the sergeant. 'It's got new tyres. We have a nice Goodyear G26 tread pattern.'

'Can you tell if the boy got into that van?' asked Carl.

The sergeant handed him another photograph and pointed to a set of small footprints that ended abruptly next to the tyre marks on the ground. 'I'd say he got into the van that left the scene, Inspector.'

'I wonder why he didn't take his backpack,' said Harry.

'What else was in the van besides the boy's backpack?' asked Carl.

'Most of the stuff that was on his manifest. Several boxes of spare parts for Riverland Motors and a couple of boxes of art supplies for a local artist called May Butterfield. The only items on the list that are not in the van are three drums of something called white river oil for a customer listed as BB.'

'That mean anything to you, Bill?' Carl asked.

'I've got no idea what white river oil is and BB could mean anything,' said Inspector Norris, shrugging his shoulders.

'If the three drums are missing that could mean he had already delivered them,' said Harry.

'Going by the older manifests in his book, it looks like he marked off deliveries when he made them. He hasn't marked off anything on the manifest for this load,' said the sergeant. He placed a brown covered book on the table. 'The manifests are in here.' He opened the book and turned it so that the others could see the list of items in Kieran's neat handwriting. 'He's got customer names but there are no addresses in this book. I guess if he has been doing this for years he'd know where the regular customers live by now.'

'Is the white river oil a regular delivery?' asked Carl.

'Looks like he was making two or three trips a week. The white river oil appears to be a regular item on his Saturday run. Always for the same customer,' said the sergeant.

'Anything else in that folder, Sergeant?' asked Carl.

'It looks like we have the keys to the shack, the van and another house. They were still in the victim's pocket.'

'That's probably his house in the city. Get a team to go over his house and find out where he parked his van, when you get back to the city. I'd like a full chemical analysis of anything you find on the floor of that van, and Sergeant, make sure the pathologist does a full blood analysis before he releases the body to the family.'

'Anything else, Inspector?' The sergeant looked at each inspector in turn.

When both inspectors indicated they had no further questions for him, the sergeant left to arrange for the van to be transported back to the forensics laboratory in the city.

'Looks like your search party might be a waste of time, Bill,' said Carl.

'Maybe, but we still need to cover the possibility that he was dumped somewhere nearby.'

Inspector Norris looked at his watch. 'I need to brief the search party.'

'What do you think, Harry?' asked Carl, after Inspector Norris had left the room.

'He's either had a bust up with BB that led to a fight or he's been robbed and got killed trying to stop them.'

Carl looked at the photographs of the body Forensics had taken. 'I'd say someone hit him pretty hard, going by this bruise. My guess is he got hit in the guts and then kneed in the face, before he fell back and struck his head on the van.'

'That would suggest someone wanted to bash him but not necessarily kill him. It's possible his death was accidental.'

'If his death was an accident, why didn't they report it? Why'd they take the boy?' asked Carl.

'There's got to be something else going on here, Boss. What the hell is white river oil? I've never heard of it. And why describe a customer as BB? That's got to be code for something else.'

'Given Kieran Moore's background, despite his clean sheet for the last twenty odd years, I wonder if he's been playing with his old friends right under our noses.'

'You think he might be running drugs?'

'We've busted a few methamphetamine labs up here over the years. If I remember correctly, some of the ingredients come in liquid form. Might be some interesting results when Forensics do their chemical analysis.'

Inspector Norris came back into the room.

'I'm about to leave with the search party. We'll do a sweep of the area around the shack and along both sides of the access road. What are you planning, Carl?'

'I want to speak to some of the customers listed in this book. We'll start with the phone book while you're out with the search party. And, I'd better call Rankin, before he starts pestering us.'

Inspector Norris left them to join the search party heading out to Sally Arthur's shack.

'Harry, go and have a chat with the duty constable. See if he knows where any of Kieran's customers live.'

Before Carl could do anything else his mobile phone rang.

'Inspector West?'

'Yes, this is Inspector West.'

'Inspector, it's Sally Arthur. I've just heard about Kieran on the radio. They said to call you.'

'Thanks for calling, Sally. Where are you calling from?'

'I'm with May, May Butterfield. We're collaborating on a large canvas, so I'm staying at her place.'

'Where's that?'

'Inspector, are you in the Riverland or the city?'

'I'm in the Riverland, at the police station.'

'Might be easier if we come to you. We'll be there in about an hour.'

'Okay, I'll be waiting for you.'

After the call ended, Carl called Bill Norris to let him know that he could call off the search for Sally Arthur.

While Carl was waiting for Sally Arthur, Chief Inspector Rankin called for a personal update.

'Everything points to the boy being alive when he left the scene, Chief. Appears the killers took him with them. Looks like they also took three drums of something described as white river oil from Kieran's cargo. I have two sets of Rossi boot prints and a clear tyre tread pattern, which Forensics reckons is a match for a Goodyear G26.'

'I've seen the preliminary report, Carl. Got robbery gone wrong written all over it. Can only assume what was in those drums was either valuable or illegal or both. And, you realise, Carl, with those timings they would have spirited the boy away before anybody was aware he was missing. We'll need a lucky break to find him if he's still alive.'

'You'd think they would have killed him on the spot, if they were going to kill him to shut him up, Chief.'

'Hope you're right there.'

'Chief, do the initials BB ring any bells for you in relation to Kieran Moore?'

'Means nothing to me, Carl. By the way, let Bill Norris look for the boy. It's his backyard. I want you on the murder. Is that understood?'

'Yes, Chief. That's the way we're playing it. Bill's out with the search party. I'm waiting to interview Sally Arthur, the woman Kieran stays with up here. She's just this minute called to say she's coming to see me.'

'Let me know what turns up. The media are already starting to bug me for details. I'll let you know if Forensics find anything when they go over Kieran's place.'

'Thanks, Chief. I'll be in touch.'

Carl wondered what kind of Pandora's box Kieran Moore had accidentally opened for them, when he'd decided to take Toby away for the weekend.

Carl looked at the plump, grey-haired woman sitting across the table from him and Harry in the interview room. She had to be close to sixty. He could feel the fear emanating from her and her companion, a tall, skinny blond woman of a similar age, who looked like she could use a good feed.

The plump woman had introduced herself as Sally Arthur, and her skinny friend as May Butterfield.

'I'm not sure where to start, Inspector,' Sally began, when Carl asked her what she wanted to tell him.

The two women exchanged nervous glances.

'We think Kieran's been murdered and we're scared we might be too,' said May.

Harry opened his notebook to take notes the old fashion way, with a pen.

'Why would someone want to kill you?'

'Because they might think we know what's been going on,' said Sally.

'And, do you?'

'Yes,' they said together.

'Would it be okay if we recorded this conversation?' asked Carl.

The two women exchanged glances again. 'That would probably be a good idea, Inspector. We might not be able to tell you again,' said Sally.

Harry put down his pen and switched on the recorder.

'This is a recording of a conversation between Inspector West, Ms Sally Arthur and Ms May Butterfield made by Detective Harry Fuller.'

'Who's going to start?' asked Carl.

Sally waved her hand. 'I'll start. This story starts a long time ago. There used to be three of us. May, me and Martha. We grew up here. We went to school together. We all went down to the city and studied art. We got mixed up with the party crowd and one thing led to another. We got into drugs, grass mainly. It was good for the art,' she smiled apologetically before continuing.

'One of the guys supplying the stuff was Kieran's son, Sean. He was doing landscape design by day and screwing every girl on campus at night. If you didn't have enough cash for the weed or one of his exciting little pills, he'd give you discount for sex. That all stopped when that Louise tart got her claws into him. After that we had to pay or there was no deal.'

'We thought that Louise had gotten him out of the drugs. It wasn't long after he met her that we had to start dealing with Kieran, direct. I was shit scared of him when I first met him,' said May.

'Me too,' said Carl.

'It was all bluff,' said Sally. 'You know he went to prison to protect Sean, don't you?'

'I wasn't aware of that,' said Carl. 'That all happened before I joined the force, but my boss might have suspected something. Kieran was his first big case.' Carl waited for one of them to continue. He'd ask questions if he needed to prompt them.

'Not long after Kieran was arrested, something else happened. May here fell in love with a smart-arse chemical engineering graduate with a lust for money. Bob Butterfield.'

'We got married. I got pregnant and he got busted for embezzlement,' added May.

'He met Kieran inside,' said Sally.

'They got out around the same time and came up here. We were both back here by then. I was living with my parents. Sally was leading the good life screwing all the young teachers in the district and selling her paintings to the tourists.'

Both the women laughed.

'Yeah, those were the days,' said Sally.

'Kieran was a grandfather by then, but that bitch Louise wouldn't let him near her precious little Terry. Said he was a bad influence and kept reminding him what he had done to Sean. Anyway, Kieran hooked with Martha. You would have liked Martha,' said May.

'Would have?' asked Carl.

'She died a little over six months ago. Breast cancer,' said Sally.

'Anyway, by the time they arrived here after serving their time, I had a five-year old, Brian. He's the manager of Riverland Motors,' said May.

The tone of her voice let Carl know she was proud of her boy.

'The only jobs they could get were things like fruit picking and day labouring. There wasn't much money in that. I was doing some part-time teaching at the primary school but it wasn't enough. We were struggling. Anyway, Kieran had connections and Bob had the know-how, so they set up a meth lab in one of the sheds on the other side of the orchard and started their little business. Then, when Martha's mother passed away around fifteen years ago, they moved the lab to her place. It's still there, or at least it was until this morning.'

'Want to tell me about that?'

May looked at Sally. 'You tell him.'

'May and Bob split up about ten years ago. Bob's been depressed for years. I don't think he ever really got over being in prison and getting himself mixed up with Kieran's friends. We suspect he's using the stuff he makes. Anyway, after we heard the news about Kieran, we went over to see if he was alright, before we called you this morning. He's not there and all the equipment he used is gone. We're worried they might have killed him too.'

'Who is they?' asked Carl.

'Inspector, that's the part of the puzzle we can't give you. Kieran never told us. He always referred to his associate in the city as 'the man',' replied Sally.

'What do you know about Kieran's courier business?' asked Carl.

'That started when Kieran and Martha moved down to the city. They had to have some way of moving their stuff between here and there. A few of us have been using Kieran to get our art supplies and things. He's cheaper than the other couriers and quicker than the post. Even my son uses him when he needs parts from smaller suppliers in the city,' said May.

Carl looked directly at Sally Arthur. 'Why was he at your place?'

'He used my place as his drop off and delivery point, and they stayed with me overnight most times they came.'

'They?'

'Yes, Martha used to come with him sometimes. She was our agent in the city, for our paintings.'

'How often has Kieran been coming up over the last few months?'

'Two, sometimes three times a week. Sometimes he didn't even have any stuff to deliver. He was very lonely after Martha died. He used to come up just to talk.'

'Did you know he was bringing Toby with him this time?'

'Yes, he called me on Wednesday night. That's why there's plenty of food in the place. I had already arranged to work with May on Saturday. We're having an exhibition at the Resort Hotel in three weeks.'

'Did he tell you that Toby's parents didn't know he was bringing Toby?'

'Yes. He told me it would probably be on the radio. He just wanted to shock them into thinking about the kid instead of themselves. He'd had a rough time as a kid himself. He loved that little boy. I hope they haven't hurt him.'

They sat in silence, all thinking of that little boy and hoping he hadn't been hurt.

'Where exactly is this place that Bob was using as a lab?'

'It's a bit hard to tell someone who isn't a local, Inspector. Got a piece of paper? I'll draw you a map.'

Harry stopped the recorder, pushed his notebook across the table and gave Sally his pen. Sally picked up the pen and drew the map.

When she finished, Sally asked, 'Inspector, can you protect us?'

'Do you mind spending a few nights in the lock up? We can hold you for forty-eight hours without charge, and you've told me enough to charge you with something if I need to.'

'Can I call Brian to move my car off the street?' asked May.

'Of course. Do you need a telephone or do you have a mobile?'

'I have a mobile in my bag.'

'Harry, can you take Ms Butterfield into the next room so she can call her son.'

'Are we in trouble, Inspector?' asked Sally, as May left with Harry.

'For the time being, I'm prepared to consider you as informants that require protection. I don't get to decide who gets prosecuted, Ms Arthur, but I do get to make a recommendation. Besides, my job is to find out who killed Kieran and who's got Toby. What you've told me has put Kieran's death into a context that may have taken me a lot longer to figure out on my own. Do you need to call anyone?'

'The only person I care about is dead, Inspector. Kieran may be a criminal in your eyes but he was a good friend to me.'

'I understand what you're saying. No-one is all bad.' Carl stood up. 'Shall we go and arrange your protective custody?'

After securing Sally and May in the police lock-up, Carl and Harry discussed Sally's map with the duty constable, who provided them with a map of the region and a set of instructions for getting to the place Sally Arthur had marked on her map. It took them almost an hour to navigate through the maze of orchards and vineyards that hid the house from the world.

The orchard around the house had been decimated in the last drought, when water restrictions had made life extremely difficult for irrigators. Most of the citrus trees were dead, though the handful in the backyard of the house, which had been severely pruned back, were showing signs of life after the recent rain. The house itself had seen better times. The iron roof was heavily rusted. The floorboards of the front veranda were cracked and buckled. It looked like no-one had used the front entrance to the house in years.

Carl and Harry walked around to the back of the house. The door was open.

'Hello! Police! Anybody home?' called Harry.

The only reply was the sound of a crow cawing from a tree next to the sheds, across the yard from the house.

They drew their pistols and entered the back door into a dimly lit enclosed veranda. There were two doors leading into the house. Harry opened the one off to the right to reveal a toilet. Someone had obviously been home in the not too distant past, as the small room was spotlessly clean. Carl opened the door that led into the house.

'Police! Anybody there?' he called. When there was no reply he advanced into the gloom of the corridor, pistol in hand.

Harry found a light switch and flicked it on. They stood still for a few moments to allow their eyes to adjust to the light. They took it in turns going into the rooms that led off the corridor. It was a small house: two bedrooms, a sitting room, a kitchen, a bathroom and a laundry. If this was where Bob Butterfield lived, it told them he was meticulously clean. The place had the sterility of a medical clinic.

Carl pulled a pair of rubber gloves out of his pocket, and slipped them on before opening the wardrobe in the front bedroom. It was empty, even though the bed was made up. There was no wardrobe in the second bedroom, where the bed was covered with a plastic sheet.

The kitchen cupboards appeared to hold a full set of utensils, cups and plates but there was no food in the fridge.

They went over to the sheds. There were two of them. The smaller one, closest to the house was an earthen floored garage. It was empty, apart from a few oil cans standing along one side just inside the small side door. The second shed had a polished concrete floor, a ventilator and several white topped benches.

'Boss, this room has air-conditioning.'

'See those marks on the floor there, Harry? This place has been scrubbed clean but I guess there are some stains you can't wash out, especially if you have been using the place for years. Let's have a look outside. There must be a rubbish dump here somewhere.'

They went outside and split up. Harry searched the area around the sheds while Carl looked around the orchard.

Carl was just about to give up when he noticed a depression in the dry earth between the trees and the overgrown fence separating the orchard from the yard. The depression was about the right size for a grave. He went to find Harry, to see if he had located a rubbish dump, and found him standing next to another patch of disturbed earth.

'Looks like they buried it, Boss.'

'Think they might have buried a few things, Harry. I found what could be a grave over in the orchard.' Carl turned and pointed back towards the rows of dead trees.

Harry watched as Carl took out his mobile phone and checked for a signal.

'Did you see a telephone in the house, Harry?'

Harry wasn't surprised. After all, they were in the middle of nowhere. 'In the kitchen; on the wall.'

'See what else you can find. I'm going to make a call.'

Carl walked over to the house, put his gloves back on, and went into the kitchen. The telephone was attached to the wall above the table. He picked it up and put it to his ear. There was a dial tone. He checked the number in his mobile and called the station. He asked the duty constable to find out when either of the women in the lock-up had last seen or spoken to Bob Butterfield.

Carl looked at the kitchen while he waited, and wondered if Bob Butterfield really was paranoid about cleanliness or whether someone had sterilised the place to remove all trace of their presence. The place was too clean. Even his cleaner didn't leave his kitchen this clean. It was highly unlikely a man living on his own, and subject to bouts of depression, would keep his house this clean.

After about five minutes, the constable came back on the line and told him the women said they hadn't actually seen Bob or talked to him for months. Apparently, he didn't answer the telephone. He added that Sally Arthur had said that, according to Kieran, Bob was training up some young blokes to take over the operation.

Carl thanked the constable and placed a call to Chief Inspector Rankin. When the chief came on the line Carl explained where he was and why he was there.

'Chief, you'd better send Forensics back. This place has been wiped clean and I suspect its former resident might be buried in the orchard. And, Chief, if what these women have told me is true, you'd better have someone pick up Sean Moore. Who knows how deep this goes in that family?'

The chief said he'd make the arrangements and rang off.

Carl called Bill Norris and updated him on the situation. Bill said he'd send someone out to secure the place, and asked Carl to wait until they arrived.

Carl and Harry sat in the car while they waited.

'We've got some interesting dots here, Harry. What do you make of them?'

'Don't know about your dots, Boss. What I want to know is, if these guys have been doing this for around twenty years, and Chief Inspector Rankin has been keeping some sort of watching brief on Kieran all that time, how come he didn't know about this little operation?'

'Good question, Harry. The chief obviously knows some-thing, otherwise we'd still be home reading the paper or what-ever, and Bill Norris would be trying to figure this out. Chief Inspector Rankin is a big game hunter, Harry. These guys were never his target.'

While they were going over their observations, and the infor-mation they had received from the women, to see if they could join their dots into a coherent pattern, two young constables arrived in a patrol car to secure the scene for Forensics.

On their way back to the station, Carl's mobile beeped to let him know he was back in range and had a message. He checked his voice mail.

'Seems nobody knows where Sean Moore is.'

When they got back to town they paid a visit to Brian Butter-field, who told them he hadn't seen his father for years. The old man was anti-social according to his son, who laughed at the idea that his father kept a spotlessly clean house.

'The last time I was out there, and mind you that was years ago, his house looked like a rubbish tip.'

'Were you aware of what he was doing out there?' asked Carl.

'Nothing, as far as I know, not since the drought anyway. It wiped out his orchard. Before that he was supplying oranges to the Co-op.'

'The drought ended a couple of years ago. How's he been supporting himself since then?'

'I think you'll find he's been on social security since the drought wiped out his orchard. The government put in some sort of package for guys like him who lost their trees.'

'Your mother told us your father was running some sort of drugs lab,' said Carl. 'Know anything about that?'

'News to me, Inspector.'

'What was your arrangement with Kieran Moore?'

'A lot of people up here drive older model cars, Inspector.

Sometimes I need to get spare parts from wreckers or recyclers. Kieran would go around and look for parts and bring them up when I couldn't get them from my regular suppliers.'

'How did you come to that arrangement?'

'Kieran's been bringing stuff up for Mum and her artist friends ever since I was a boy. He offered to do it one day, when I was complaining about how hard it was to get parts for some older cars. He had plenty of time on his hands after he lost his contract with River Transport a few years ago. Said it gave him something to do. He wasn't ready to retire.'

'Your mother and her friend think they are in some sort of danger because of their links to Kieran Moore and your father, and what they know about their drug running activities. Do you think you're in any danger, Mr Butterfield?' asked Carl.

'All this drug stuff is news to me, Inspector. I don't know any more than what you've told me.'

'Did you know that your father had been in prison around the time you were born?'

'Yes, I knew that, Inspector. That's one reason why I sided with my mother when they split up. Besides, he always called me a mummy's boy. He isn't a very nice person to be around. I'm surprised my mother ever got together with him in the first place.'

'Thank you for your time, Mr Butterfield.'

'Is my mother in trouble? Will she need a lawyer?'

'At this point, let's just say I have your mother and her friend in protective custody.'

Carl shook hands with Brian Butterfield and he and Harry returned to the station, where Bill Norris was waiting for them.

'Any sign of the boy?' Carl asked after he had briefed Bill on what he'd found out over the course of the morning.

'We have a possible sighting. A call from a woman saying she saw a new looking, grey van come out of the road that leads down to Sally Arthur's place, and turn onto the highway and head in the direction of the city, around ten o'clock yesterday morning, with a boy sitting between two men in the front.'

'That's the best news I've heard all day,' said Harry.

Inspector Norris looked at him as if he was on drugs.

'It means Toby was alive when they left the scene, Inspector.'

'I hope you're right, Harry.'

'Did your witness manage to see what sort of van it was,' asked Carl.

'We had to show her some photos, but she thinks it's one of those new Mercedes vans.'

'That could explain the new tyre tracks Forensics picked up,' said Harry.

'Unfortunately, she didn't get the number. However, I wouldn't think there'd be too many of those around here. I've got one of my people calling all the service stations between here and the city to see if we get lucky with CCTV. They might have called in to get petrol somewhere, if they've gone all the way back to the city.'

'That's a big if, Bill. There are plenty of places between here and the city they could have gone to ground,' said Carl.

'We're still looking locally, Carl. Hopefully, once we get the description of the van out we'll get lucky.'

Carl decided to see if he could spend some time with Nina, while they were waiting for Forensics to return and examine the farm where Bob Butterfield had supposedly operated the meth-amphetamine laboratory. He hadn't seen her since Friday. It seemed like ages ago to Carl. He wasn't sure whether that was a good sign or not, but he couldn't resist the desire to be with her. After all, she was only up the road and what else was he going to do while they waited? Every police officer in the state was on the lookout for Toby, and he'd be heading back to the city after Forensics had examined the farm. Nina wouldn't be back in the city until sometime next Sunday, a week away. Who knew what would be happening in a week's time? His mind was made up; better to see her now while he could.

He called her and agreed to dinner at her parent's place. She offered to come and get him and drive him back. That sounded like an offer he couldn't refuse, even if he had to meet her parents. So he didn't. When he told Harry he'd have to eat alone that night, Harry gave him one of those knowing smiles and wished him luck with his new 'in-laws'. Carl admitted to himself that he'd have to meet them sometime, if he was going to continue the relationship, and continuing was feeling like what he wanted to do.

Nina arrived just after five pm and they spent the half hour of the drive back to her parents' discussing the case, as if she was still part of the team.

'So, I was right about the chief wanting you to focus on the murder?' she said, after he had briefed her.

'I have a feeling this is about more than the murder of Kieran Moore,' Carl said. 'I think the chief is after whoever is co-ordinating this operation. He's been keeping tabs on Kieran for years. He told me once that he thought Kieran had taken the fall to protect a lot of people, some big, some small.'

'Didn't you say that one of the women said he's taken the fall to protect his son?'

'Rankin thinks he took the fall to protect the whole operation, from top to bottom. If you ever get a chance to read the case notes, you'll see Kieran pleaded guilty to all the charges and wouldn't answer any questions.'

'So, what he told the women could be right, just not the whole truth,' said Nina.

'Let's talk about something else. I need to think about something pleasant before I meet your parents, otherwise I'll be a grump. Tell me what you've been doing while I've been playing policeman?'

'Taking it easy, and telling my mother all about you. She doesn't want me making the same mistake I made last time, so I've been telling her what a wonderful, considerate man you are. She's so excited you're coming to dinner. She's been dying to meet you ever since I told her about you.'

'And when was that?'

'About three months ago, when I realised I was more in love than in lust with you.' Nina flashed him a smile in the fading light of the winter afternoon.

Carl thought how beautiful she looked in her jeans and body hugging sweater, and how relaxed he felt being with her in the car. She was a more relaxed driver than Harry, and smelt a lot better too. Harry's cheap aftershave was no match for the expensive perfume Nina had splashed on herself before getting in the car.

'I think I've been in love with you ever since you sat down in my office the first day you joined the team.'

'You hid that well, for a while.'

He could see the grin spreading over her face even though she kept her eyes on the road.

'Obviously not well enough, given what the chief had to say on Friday. Who do you think tipped him off?'

'Maybe he just put two and two together. You've been a lot more pleasant to be around since I joined the team, according to Harry, and if Harry noticed, don't you think some of the others might have noticed as well?'

'I'm sure Harry wouldn't have said anything. I'd trust him with my life. In fact, I have on several occasions.'

'Who are you going to replace? Me or Harry? You know he's ready for sergeant.'

Nina turned into a long, tree lined driveway and drove down to a cottage, surrounded by an extensive garden, by the river.

'Who's the gardener?' asked Carl.

'Dad. He had a plant nursery in town before he retired. Now he's growing things to put on the table and flowers for a local florist. Keeps him busy and out of the house, and that keeps Mum happy.'

'What's your mother do to pass the time?'

'You'll see when we go inside.'

The elderly border collie, sleeping on the veranda of the cottage, opened its eyes and briefly looked up at the sound of the car doors closing.

'Active watch dog, I see.'

'Don't let him fool you.'

At the sound of Nina's voice, the dog got up slowly, stretched and ambled over to give Carl the sniff test. Carl stood still as the old dog sniffed his hands and then around his crotch. Satisfied he wasn't a threat, the dog let Carl scratch his ears, and then walked back to his spot on the veranda and resumed his snooze.

'Bet you all sleep peacefully with him guarding the door.'

Nina walked around beside him, placed an arm around his waist and lent into Carl's side. 'We don't need a guard dog out here. This isn't the city. We actually know who the neighbours are and spend time with them. We only have the dog to check out city slickers like you, and fortunately you passed the test, otherwise Pedro here would have torn you to threads.'

She tickled him on the belly with her free hand and then ran off around the side of the house. Carl followed her at a leisurely pace around to the garden at the back of the house, where a man in his early sixties was firing up a barbecue. The man turned when he heard the crunch of Carl's boots on the gravel path.

'Hi, I'm Don. I see you got Pedro's approval,' said the man, putting down his tools and offering Carl his hand.

Carl shook the offered hand. 'Carl. Pleased to meet you, Don. Nice quiet spot you have here.'

'We like it. Can I offer you a red?'

'Don't see why not. I'm not driving.'

'Come inside and meet Alice. She won't forgive me if I keep you outside talking and, besides, it's a lot warmer inside.'

'I've noticed it gets pretty cold up here at night.'

Don led Carl in through the backdoor. The coloured fabrics on the walls and the chairs caught Carl's attention. Nina was right. He only had to open his eyes to see that Alice spent her time quilting. He realised he should have known, as a memory of the colourful quilt on Nina's bed and the cushions on the sofa in her apartment, popped into his mind.

'Hello, Carl. Finally, we get to see this famous policeman that has arrested our Nina,' said Alice, as Carl entered her kitchen.

There was no opportunity for handshaking. Alice stepped up and hugged him. 'Welcome.'

'Thank you, Alice.'

Carl was a little overwhelmed. He hadn't expected Alice to embrace him. When she released him, he was looking into the smiling face of a Nina with grey hair and a few extra wrinkles. Alice had the same sparkling smile and mischievous eyes that he found so captivating in Nina. A wave of relief swept over him. He hadn't realised how nervous he had been about meeting them, and making a good impression, until he felt the tension fading away. He could see Nina's beaming smile across the table, and feel the love in the room. For the first time in a long time, he felt safe enough to relax. These people felt like family, and Carl hadn't been with family for a long time.

Don got Carl a glass of red and went out to cook the meat on the barbecue. Alice ushered Carl and Nina into the sitting room, so she could finish preparing the meal while the meat was cooking.

'Looks like you've made a good first impression,' said Nina, as she guided him onto the sofa and sat down next to him.

'Is that with your parents or the dog?' Carl placed his glass on the side table next to the sofa.

'You're a lucky man, Carl West. You've charmed them all.'

'Well, I'd better be on my best behaviour, then.' He took a sip of the wine and replaced the glass on the side table.

'Just be yourself, sweetheart. That's who they want to meet. Put Inspector West away for tomorrow.' She leant over and kissed him.

Carl relaxed back into the sofa. 'It's so good to just sit and feel loved.'

Nina snuggled up to him. 'I told you that you'd like them.'

'I never doubted that for a moment. It was whether they'd like me that I was worried about.'

'I like you. Why wouldn't they like you?' Nina looked at him with large dreamy eyes.

Carl looked at his hands. 'It's not every day a girl brings home the guy she wants to settle down with. It's a big test all around. What if your parents see things in me that you don't? You know how they say love is blind.'

'Think we've both done the love is blind bit, don't you? I know I certainly have. It's eyes wide open this time lover boy, and you still need to pass the final test.'

'What test is that?'

'You still need to convince me you're committed to us. I know commitment is scary, but I want to know you're in for the long haul. I want more from you than the memory of an exciting affair.'

Carl wrapped his arm around her. 'I've been thinking about what you said about me becoming a father. Do you think I'll make a good one?'

'Sometimes, when I watch you with Harry, I think you're

already a great father. My first inspector was nothing like that with me.'

'I guess I'm nearly old enough to be Harry's father, but he's got one of his own that did a pretty good job before Harry came my way. Have you met Harry's dad?'

'Yes. The girls in the operations room reckon he runs a pretty tight ship. I hear he's very proud of his son the detective.'

'I know I'm good with adults but do you think I'll be any good with little kids?'

'I think if you want to be a father that makes all the difference. Why are you so worried about it? I'm sure you'll be just fine.'

Carl looked across the room at the quilt on the wall, a Chinese landscape scene stitched onto a turquoise background. It looked peaceful, but peaceful was far from the memory that had surfaced with that question.

'It all comes down to father experience. I don't have any. My father died before I was born. I never knew what it was like to have a father of my own.'

'But you had your grandfather, didn't you? Didn't you tell me you lived with your grandparents?'

'That was after my mother got sick and couldn't work. I was a teenager by then.'

'You'll have me to help you.' She gently pinched his cheek.

'Well, if you're as good at helping me with parenting as you are with solving crimes, we should make great parents.'

'Come and get it!' The sound of Don's voice from within the kitchen announced dinner was ready.

Carl picked up his glass and they went in to join Don and Alice for a meal of barbecued meats, roast vegetables and garden salad.

'Tell us a bit about yourself, Carl. We'd like to know just who

PETER MULRANEY

Nina is inviting into our family circle,' said Alice, as she passed
Carl the garden salad.

'Where would you like me to start?'

'Tell us about your family. What do your parents do? Do you
have any brothers or sisters?'

There was a pause while Carl chewed on a mouthful of meat.

'I never knew my father. He was killed in Vietnam six
months before I was born.'

'National Service?' asked Don. 'I was lucky, my number
never came up.'

'No, Regular Army. He was on his second tour. Apparently,
my mother got pregnant on his last leave before he went over. She
told me they had been trying to get pregnant for years. We don't
even know if he ever knew.'

'That must have been awful for your mother,' said Alice.
'How did she cope?'

'We seemed to get by. She got a war widows pension, and
some money for me as well I think, and when I started school she
got part-time work in a department store. We lived in a little flat
right in the middle of the city, so we didn't need a car. I guess
things were safer back then. I used to walk to and from school
and all around the city.'

'Is that how you got all that local knowledge?' asked Nina.

'Now you know my secret. Apart from walking around and
talking to shop owners, all the kids I went to school with lived in
the city as well. It was like one big happy family, especially in the
block of flats where we lived.'

'Your mother never remarried?' asked Alice.

'No.' Carl shook his head and winked at Nina, sitting across
the table from him.

There was a pause in the conversation as they focussed on
eating the meal before it went cold.

'I enjoyed that,' said Carl putting down his fork and knife.

'Would you like some more? No need to be shy.'

'No thank you, I think I've had enough. If I have any more I'll have to spend extra time working it off.'

'What made you join the Police Force?' asked Don.

'We can blame my grandfather for that. My mother had a stroke when I was thirteen. She was paralysed down one side. We went to live with her parents after that. My grandfather was a policeman, a detective actually. He took a real interest in me. He didn't write me off as a mummy's boy just because I didn't have a father.'

'I take it others did,' said Don.

'It wasn't much fun being the only boy whose mother came out to watch him play, especially when all the other boys had their dads there. Anyway, when we moved in with my grandparents, things changed. My grandfather became like a father to me. He was the one that made sure I did my homework and took an interest in my education. He'd come out and watch me play football or cricket and show me how to do things. I wanted to be like him.'

'Not like Nina here,' said Don. 'I wanted her to come into the business with me. She's really good with plants, but once she'd gone away to university I lost her. She told me there were lots of things she wanted to do and none of them involved plants. I still don't understand why she decided to join you lot.'

'Some of us just like to put things right, I guess.'

Alice got up and packed up the plates. 'Anybody for coffee and cake?'

'I'll help you, Mum,' said Nina, getting up and clearing away the rest of the dishes. 'I'm sure Carl will have some of your carrot cake and a cup of coffee.'

'Did you go to uni, Carl, or join straight from school?' asked Alice.

'I joined through the graduate program. My grandfather said

that if I wanted to make a career of it, it would be best to get a degree first. He thought it would open a few doors that hadn't opened for him.'

'What did you study? I didn't know they had any courses for policemen,' said Alice.

'They might have now but they didn't back then. I majored in history and psychology. History was my favourite subject at school. I really liked reading about all the different things people had done over the ages. I did the psychology because I was interested in why people did things.'

'I'd have thought law or something like that would be more useful,' said Don.

'Lots of officers go on to study law. I wasn't interested in what the law says. My interest is in why it exists and why people behave the way that they do.'

Alice put a generous slice of carrot cake on the table in front of Carl. If aroma was anything to go by, Carl decided he would be enjoying the cake. Nina served the coffees and they were all sitting around the table again.

'This sure tastes good, Alice. I hope Nina has the recipe for this one,' said Carl.

He felt Nina kick him under the table. Cooking was not one of her finer points.

Alice shook her head. 'I feel like such a failure. She picked up so many skills from her father, but not from me.'

'She seems to have picked up your flair for interior decorating. Her apartment has the same homey feel as this house.'

Alice laughed. 'I hope you're better at your job than working out the obvious.'

Carl looked at Nina, lost.

'Mum did my apartment. I couldn't make anything inside look that nice. It takes a real effort to keep it looking like it does. The only thing I don't have a problem with is plants.'

A picture of the forest of pot plants in Nina's courtyard popped into Carl's awareness. He couldn't keep anything green alive. He either drowned them or they died from lack of water.

Carl took a sip of coffee. 'It's not the first time I've been fooled by a pretty face, Alice.'

'He's hopeless around beautiful women,' said Nina. 'That's why he's had to have female sergeants, like me.'

Carl shrugged his shoulders and watched as Don and Alice shook their heads.

'How do you put up with her?' asked Don.

'She's the best thing that's happened to me in a long time.' Carl looked directly at Nina. 'I'd put my life on the line for Nina. I think that's why the chief inspector transferred her out of my team.' Carl looked at Don. 'I think the question should be how does she put up with me?'

Alice's face took on a concerned look. 'Are you two serious about becoming a couple? I understand it can't be easy for either of you. It's always a risk starting again.'

'We've got something in common that I don't think either of us had the first time round,' said Carl. 'We know what it means to be a police officer. It's not easy being married to someone who works irregular hours and deals with some of the more unpleasant aspects of life. We've been through some pretty horrible things together, and they've made the other times even more precious. I think we have something to build on, don't you, Nina?'

Nina reached across the table and held his hands. 'I don't think I could have said it any better than that.' She squeezed his hands.

'And how do you feel about becoming a father,' asked Alice.

Obviously, Nina had told her mother she wanted to have children in the not too distant future.

'That's the bit that scares me. I have no experience with little kids or of having a father as a little boy. I'm not sure I'll know what to do.'

'Just think back to how your grandfather treated you. That sounded like a good model to follow to me,' said Don. 'Is he still alive?'

'No. They're all gone. Mum died when I was sixteen and my grandfather died a few years after he retired. Lung cancer. Smoking was the one thing about him he told me not to emulate. My grandmother died a couple of years ago. At least she died of old age.'

'Do you have any contact with your father's side of the family?' asked Alice.

'Yes. They have a farm in the mid-north. I used to spend school holidays there when I was a boy. Think the last time I stayed there was when I was at uni. My cousin runs the farm these days. I catch up with him and his kids when they come down to the city. They're mad Crows' supporters, so I usually see them when they come down for home games. They're always trying to get me to come up for Christmas.'

'Do you ever go?' asked Alice.

'Christmas is usually a busy time for us. I don't think I've had a Christmas off ever,' said Carl.

'I see what you mean about being married to a policeman,' said Alice. 'You sure you want to go ahead with this, Nina?'

'He's exaggerating, Mum. We have rosters and we are entitled to holidays. Some people are just workaholics and they need a little coaxing to get them out of the office.'

'What are you hiding from, Carl? I've heard being a workaholic is about not wanting to face issues in your personal life,' said Alice.

It occurred to Carl that Nina had learnt a few things from her mother, after all.

'Someone else in this room asked me that question. Perhaps if she hadn't, I wouldn't be sitting here with you now.'

'You don't have to tell me. That slipped out before I realised what I was saying. I'm sorry if I've upset you,' said Alice.

'That's okay, Alice. I've come to understand that people ask those questions out of love.' He looked at Nina 'I've certainly learnt a lot about myself since meeting your daughter, and I've started having some weekends off. I even took this weekend off.'

They all laughed.

'Better luck next weekend, sweetheart. Guess I'd better be taking you back to the office. Harry will be starting to get worried,' said Nina.

Pedro was asleep on the front porch and did not stir from whatever old dogs dream about, when they went out to the car. Don and Alice stood in the semi-circle of light spreading out from the front door and waved as Nina drove Carl into the night.

'What did you think of them?' asked Nina.

'Seem like a lovely couple to me,' said Carl. 'I felt welcomed, even though it was a bit strange being the one interrogated for a change.'

'I think they like you.'

He couldn't see her face but he heard the relaxed tone in her voice.

'That's good.'

Nina dropped him at the hotel and said she'd call in to see him on Sunday when she got back to the city. He had to be satisfied with a kiss.

Forensics arrived at the Butterfield farm mid-morning. Carl and Harry were there to meet them. Carl pointed out the depression on the edge of the orchard and the disturbed ground behind the shed, which had served as the laboratory.

'Someone has gone to a lot of trouble to clean this place up, Inspector. This has got to be the cleanest farm shed I've ever seen,' said the sergeant leading the forensic team.

'Wait until you see inside the house,' said Carl.

The sergeant cocked his eyebrow.

'Spotless,' said Carl.

'What are your priorities, Inspector?'

'I want to know what or who is in that hole in the orchard. I suspect you'll find a body.' Carl pointed to the shed. 'We've been told this was a meth lab. Can you confirm that? And I want to know if there is anything here we can use to identify whoever did the clean up job?'

'Who do you think might be in the hole?'

'Someone called Bob Butterfield. He was running the meth lab.'

'Who's been here, apart from the duty patrol, that you know of, Inspector?'

'Two women I currently have in protective custody, Harry and me.'

Carl and Harry went to confer with the local constables, who had just come back from talking with the neighbours. The forensic team erected a tent over the depression in the orchard and started digging.

'Anything interesting?' asked Carl, as he and Harry leant up against the patrol car the two constables had arrived in.

'We spoke to Mr Redden, the old man in the house at the top of the road that leads down here, Inspector. Told us he hadn't seen Butterfield for a couple of weeks. Reckons Butterfied wasn't very friendly, but says he used to see him driving in and out and wandering about the place,' said the senior constable.

'Did he say when he had seen him last?' asked Carl.

The senior constable opened his notebook.

'I asked him that. The best he could recall was that it was a couple of weekends ago. Said Butterfield came home with a couple of young guys in a grey van. He thought Butterfield's ancient Land Rover must have finally died on him, and the young guys had given him a lift. Said they were strangers to him, and he was surprised they'd stayed here until Saturday morning. Apparently having visitors was a rare event for Mr Butterfield, Inspector.'

The senior constable looked up. 'He said they drove out around nine o'clock on Saturday morning and didn't come back. Told us the only other people he's seen here since then, apart from us, were a couple of women in a blue car yesterday morning. Said they didn't stay long.'

'Did you get any details on the young guys or the van?' asked Carl.

'The old man said the van looked new. He thought it was a Mercedes,' said the young constable. 'We showed him the picture Inspector Norris gave us this morning. Said it was like the one in the picture.'

The senior constable looked at his young offsider, who got the message that he had stepped over some invisible line he'd forgotten about.

A look of annoyance crossed Carl's face. He wasn't impressed by officious pricks that hogged all the limelight. He smiled at the young constable and turned his attention back to the senior.

'Mr Redden said one was a giant and the other one was a tall, skinny guy. Reckoned they reminded him of Laurel and Hardy.'

'How old's this Mr Redden?' asked Carl.

'Be in his seventies, Inspector.'

That would explain the Laurel and Hardy comparison, thought Carl. 'Did he see anything going on down here out of the ordinary?'

'When I asked him that, Inspector, he started laughing. When I asked him why he was laughing, he said Butterfield lived in a pigsty. The place was a mess. There was rubbish everywhere. Well, apparently, those two young guys cleaned the place up and had a big bon-fire a couple of days ago.'

'Guess that means the hole behind the shed's going to be full of ash and burnt pieces of equipment,' said Carl.

'Inspector!'

Carl turned. One of the officers from Forensics was walking towards them from the tent in the orchard.

'Better call the pathologist's office, Inspector. You've got a body.'

'Harry, get hold of Mike's office, and get him up here.'

Carl went over to the Forensics van and suited up, so that he wouldn't contaminate the scene. Then he went into the tent to see who was in the hole. As he entered the tent, he was greeted by the odour of decaying flesh. Thank God it's winter, he thought, as he looked down into the freshly dug hole. He was looking at the body of a man aged around sixty, going by his face.

'Looks like his throat's been cut,' said the sergeant. 'This the guy you're looking for?'

Carl took out the photo May Butterfield had given him. 'Looks like him to me,' he said, showing the picture to the sergeant.

'I'd say that's him,' agreed the sergeant. 'This will take a bit of time, Inspector. Guess it will be a few hours before the pathologist arrives, unless they bring him up in the chopper.'

'I'll have a word with the chief,' said Carl.

Carl walked over to where Harry was conversing with the local officers.

'What did the pathologist's office say, Harry?' said Carl, as he started peeling off his plastic suit.

'Should be here in about an hour. They're flying him up,' said Harry. 'Chopper will land on the golf course.'

'Well, we'd better go for a drive and pick him up. Not much we can do here.' Carl turned to the senior constable. 'Did you manage to talk to any of the other neighbours?'

'That house over there,' the senior constable said, pointing to a red roof through the trees beyond the line of sheds, 'is vacant. Mr Redden told us nobody has lived there for a couple of years. The people in the house back up the road, before you hit the main road, told us they'd seen a grey van on Saturday morning, and that they'd noticed smoke on Thursday. Said they assumed Bob was burning his trees.'

'Might pay to take a look around that place over there while you're waiting, just to make sure it's vacant,' said Carl.

'Okay, Inspector,' said the senior constable. 'I'll update you when you get back.'

'Come on, Harry.'

Carl opened the passenger side door and got into the car, taking out his mobile phone as he did, before remembering there was no signal. 'How'd you get in contact with the pathologist, Harry?'

'Used the radio in the patrol car, Boss. We called the station and they relayed the message.'

'What do you make of this, Harry?'

Harry looked both ways before turning the car onto the main road and driving in the direction of the town.

'The grey van seems to be a common element, seen both here and near the place where Kieran was killed. These murders appear to be connected.'

'Wonder why someone wanted both these guys dead. Sounds like their operation has been going on for years.'

'They were both pretty old, Boss. Maybe whoever they've been supplying is upgrading to a newer model.'

Carl couldn't help but smile at that one. 'People aren't like computers, Harry. You might junk an old computer but you usually retire old workers.'

'Maybe this is how they retire old workers in this industry,' said Harry.

'You'd think guys that had given years of faithful service would get looked after better than that, given the amount of money that flows around drugs. Even our retirement benefits are better than that, Harry.'

CHAPTER 6

WHEN SEAN DIDN'T COME HOME on Saturday night, Louise assumed he was on a bender. She'd never understood the relationship between Sean and his father. If she'd been bought up the way Sean had she would have despised her father. Sean, however, loved Kieran, despite the hardships of his upbringing and his multiple 'mothers'. Louise liked to think she had saved him from a life of debauchery and drugs, even if he didn't know how to be grateful or treat her with respect.

Sean had been such a charismatic rogue when she'd first met him. She'd set herself the goal of winning him for herself, once she'd discovered he was exchanging sex for drugs, and when she had him, she'd used her sexual prowess to wean him off the drugs. Louise understood sexuality and was very comfortable with hers.

If Louise had a fault it lay in her possessiveness, and that possessiveness had come to the fore when Terry had been born. It nearly wrecked their marriage when she had tried to keep Terry away from Kieran. It was only when Martha, sweet lovely Martha, had come onto the scene that she had relented and been surprised at what a gentle, loving person Kieran was now that he was off the drugs.

What she didn't know, however, was that sweet, lovely

Martha, Kieran and Sean had some interests unrelated to kinship. She might have been wise in the ways of sex but Louise was naive in many other aspects of life. She'd never had to work outside the home. Sean always had lots of money, even if he seemed to like throwing it away on the horses. She believed him when he told her how successful his garden design business was, and had agreed that it would be good for Terry to work with his father. She'd even encouraged Terry to study horticulture so they could expand the business.

Terry loved plants but he wasn't good with numbers. He knew how to make things grow and had simply continued into adulthood as Sean's shadow. Terry was so good at fertilising things he'd fertilised that pretty little Sloan girl, he had been sweet on since high school, the first time she let him have sex with her. Now they had Toby, the spitting image of his father to look at, but as clever as his mother when it came to everything else.

Louise blamed Sean for the strain in the relationship between Helen and Terry. Sean was always leading him astray and filling his head with bullshit, and Terry, who adored his father, couldn't see it.

While Terry had been staying with them, after the fight he'd had with Helen, Louise had been filled with regret about having encouraged him to work with Sean. On Friday night, while Sean had been at the trots, Louise had explained to Terry how relationships should work. She hoped he'd listened.

Even though she was not particularly religious, she'd prayed he'd swallow his pride and get back together with Helen, for all their sakes. She'd also prayed that he'd have the courage to make the break he needed to take from Sean, and get out from under his father's shadow.

Then Kieran had stepped in, after being off the scene for months after Martha's death. Toby had opened up to Kieran. The boy was hurting and Kieran could feel it. That was when Kieran had told her the story of his own childhood. It was that story that had allowed Louise to figure out where Toby was.

Now Kieran was dead, murdered according to the police, and Toby was missing for real.

When Sean wasn't home in the morning, Louise's anxiety level went up. Sean rarely stayed out all night. He'd usually be brought home by one of his mates or he'd arrive in a taxi and sleep in the spare room, mostly because he couldn't make it up the stairs, not because it was the considerate thing to do.

She rang Sean's mobile number. The call went through to his voice mail. She left a message asking him to call when he woke up, wherever he was. Then she rang a couple of his regular drinking buddies and was told they hadn't seen Sean at the pub since Friday night.

She rang Terry.

'Terry, any news?'

'Nothing yet.'

'How's Helen?'

'Beside herself. We didn't get much sleep last night.'

'I didn't get much either.' She paused, 'Terry, have you heard from your father?'

The question caught Terry off guard and it was a few moments before he realised the significance of the question.

'Hasn't Dad come home yet?'

'Terry, I rang Henry Newson. He said Sean wasn't at the pub last night.'

'Didn't he say he was going to the pub?'

'That's what he told me.'

'Maybe he changed his mind and went to Kieran's. You know how much Kieran meant to him. Did you ring his mobile?'

'He's not answering. I don't know what to do.'

'Mum, I'll drive over to Kieran's. We need to get out of the house before we drive each other nuts. I'll call you when we get there.'

Louise waited. She knew it would take Terry around twenty minutes to get to Kieran's from his place. To pass the time, she decided to have breakfast, and was sitting down with a cup of coffee when the telephone rang.

'Mum. It's Helen. Terry's calling the police.'

'What's happened?' asked Louise. 'Has something happened to Sean?'

'There's no sign of Sean. We spoke to the man that lives next to the office. He said he heard Sean's truck drive in and out around seven last night but he didn't see Sean. It was dark.'

'Why is Terry calling the police, then?' asked Louise.

'Someone broke into Kieran's and trashed the place.'

'Oh. I suppose you'll have to wait there until the police arrive, won't you.'

'Yes. I'll get Terry to drive us to your place on our way home.'

'That would be good.' Louise took a deep breath. 'I guess Sean will show up when he's ready. '

Louise went back to the kitchen to finish her breakfast and wait.

Terry was expecting a patrol car. He was surprised when Detective Inspector Reid arrived in an unmarked car, accompanied by two officers in a white van. The inspector showed Terry and Helen his badge and explained that the other officers were from Forensics.

'Do you have a key to the front door, Mr Moore?'

'I can open it from the inside, if you like. My key only opens the side door from the shed.'

As Terry had opened the roller door while they were waiting

for the police to arrive, they walked into the shed. The officers from Forensics went inside to examine the interior of the house. The Inspector detained Terry and Helen in the shed.

'Have you been inside?'

'Yes, but we didn't touch anything except for the door, once we saw the mess inside.'

'And if I may ask, Mr Moore, what exactly were you and your wife doing here this morning?'

'Looking for my father. He didn't come home last night. We thought he might be down here. He was pretty close to Grandpa.'

'What were you expecting to find?'

'A man with a hangover,' said Helen. 'We all thought he'd gone on a bender after finding out Kieran was dead.'

'Liked drinking alone, did he?' asked the inspector.

'Not usually. He told Mum he was going to the pub. She called one of his drinking mates this morning. He told her Dad hadn't been at the pub last night. Hadn't been in since Friday night,' said Terry.

'So you figured he might be here?'

Terry nodded.

'One of the neighbours told us he was here last night, around seven. At least, he said he heard Sean's truck drive in and out,' said Helen.

'Which neighbour?'

'Mr Jones, he lives next to the driveway of the office,' said Terry.

'Where's that?' asked the Inspector.

'Come on, we'll show you,' said Terry.

They took the inspector out through the back of the shed, through the gate in the fence, and into the yard of the house behind Kieran's. The inspector found himself standing in a yard full of mounds of earth, mulch and gravel of various sizes and colours. Along the side of the yard opposite the shed was a plant nursery. The shed itself was full of gardening equipment and an assortment of bottles and cans.

'This is our workshop,' said Terry. 'Dad has his office in the house.'

'Do you have a key to the house?'

'Sure. We checked in there, too. Dad's not in there either.'

'That your car?' said the inspector, pointing to the Honda Civic parked in the driveway.

'Yes,' said Helen. 'I wasn't going to let him bring me over here in his dirty old truck.'

The inspector did his best to suppress the smile that wanted to spread across his face.

'What was the name of the neighbour again?'

'Mr Jones. He's about the same age as Grandpa,' said Terry. 'Nice old bloke. Bit on the deaf side.'

'If you'll wait for me here, I'll go over and speak to Mr Jones,' said the Inspector.

'We'll be in the plant nursery over there. I want to show Helen some of my new plants.'

The inspector nodded and walked down the driveway to go next door. Terry took Helen over to see the miniature roses he was growing for one of his customers.

Helen loved being with Terry when he was with his plants. He was a totally different person when he was surrounded by plants. It was like the plants opened a window in his soul and let the light out. She let herself be mesmerised by that light. In that light it always felt like everything was fine, that there was nothing ever to worry about. She placed her hand on his shoulder as he lifted the tiny roses up for her to see.

'Terry, they're beautiful.'

The smile on his face let her know everything there was to know about how proud he was of them. He'd told her how hard they were to cultivate, and how many times he'd tried to get them to grow before he'd worked out their secret. The sound of footsteps on the gravel outside the nursery broke the spell. They walked out to meet the Inspector.

'Want to show me inside?' asked the Inspector. 'My wife is always looking for something different in the garden.'

Terry gave the inspector a tour of his nursery, and his card so the inspector's wife could call him to arrange a visit.

'Any sign of anything amiss in the house?' asked the inspector, as they walked out into the yard.

'Looks the same to me,' said Terry. 'I usually only use the lunch room and the toilet. Dad does all the paperwork. I don't go into his office much, so I wouldn't know if anything was missing from there. Anyway, the house was locked when we got here. It was Grandpa's place that was open. The door into the shed wasn't locked.'

'Is it usually locked when your grandfather isn't home?'

'Yes. Grandpa's pretty particular about security. He always locks up and insists we do the same.'

The inspector's mobile phone rang. He turned away to answer it. Terry and Helen held onto each other while the inspector walked across the yard and then walked back towards them.

'Did your grandfather have a laptop?'

'Yes, he kept one in his office. Used it to Skype Toby. Why do you want to know that?'

'That was the sergeant next door. Said it looked like there had been a laptop in your grandfather's office. Now there's only the power cord. He thought maybe it had been taken.'

'Grandpa might have taken it with him.'

'We can check that out. If he had it with him, it might still be in his van.'

'The other thing the sergeant said was we'd need someone

with intimate knowledge of the contents of the house to work out if anything else was taken.'

'We can't help you much there, I'm afraid. I didn't go in there much. Mostly they came to visit us or he came to see me here in the yard. Dad might know.'

'We could be here for some time dusting for prints and so forth. Can I have the key to your grandfather's house? I'll see that you get a receipt. It would be best if you didn't go in there until after we have finished.'

Terry took the key from his keyring and handed it to Inspector Reid, who slipped it into his pocket and then gave Terry his card.

'Get you father to call me on this number when you see him.'

'Have you heard anything about our son?' asked Helen.

'I don't want to give you false hope, Mrs Moore, but it looks like he was alive when he left the scene, however, we've had no reported sightings of him since.'

'I wish I hadn't slept in,' said Helen.

'Don't blame yourself, Mrs Moore. Trust me, it won't help,' said the inspector. 'You need to support each other, no matter what happens.'

'Thank you, Inspector,' said Helen.

'Mr Moore your grandfather's death is being investigated by Inspector West. I'm sure he'll be in touch when he gets back from up the river.'

Inspector Reid shook hands with them and headed towards the gate in the fence. Terry and Helen got into the Honda and drove to Terry's parents' place, where Louise was waiting for them, alone.

Louise asked Terry and Helen to stay for lunch.

'Where do you think he is?' she asked, as they sat down to eat.

'I've got no idea, Mum. There are no races on today; it's Sunday.'

'Maybe he's got a girlfriend, and he's slept in,' teased Helen.

'Not bloody likely,' laughed Louise. 'I don't think anybody else would put up with him like I do.'

'I know he's not a saint, but he's not that bad, is he?' said Helen.

'There are times when I ask myself why I'm still here,' said Louise. 'He can be very exasperating.'

Helen looked at Terry, as she recalled what he had told her about how Sean treated Louise. Terry shrugged his shoulders.

'It's not like him not to call. He even calls when he's had too much to drink. I'm starting to get worried. I hope he hasn't gone and done something stupid about Kieran being killed.'

'What would he do?' asked Terry. 'We don't even know who killed Grandpa.'

'There are somethings you don't know about your father and your grandfather,' said Louise.

Terry looked at Helen, and then back at his mother. 'What sort of things?'

'Your grandfather getting killed is going to bring up a lot of old stuff. I suspect the police are going to be asking questions trying to work out who killed him.'

'What's that got to do with Dad?'

'Your father used to work for your grandfather before he went to prison.'

'What do you mean work? Didn't you say Grandpa was a Hells Angel or something like that?'

Louise looked at her hands. She wasn't sure she could look them in the eyes as she told them what she needed to say.

'I met Sean at university,' she said. 'To be honest, study wasn't the only thing he was doing. He was the one selling drugs on campus, and the drugs were coming from Kieran. I persuaded him to stop using but I never really knew if he ever stopped working for his father, well not until Kieran went to prison. That scared the shit out of him. He got himself a real job after that.'

'You think Dad's trying to find out if some of the people from back then know about what happened to Grandpa?' asked Terry.

'Some of those people were not nice people. I'd thought we'd never see any of them again when Kieran got out of the drug game after prison. I hope Sean hasn't been silly enough to try and find them again.'

They sat in silence as the realisation dawned that Sean could have gotten himself into serious trouble by asking questions in places he was no longer welcome.

Their moment of reflection was interrupted by the ringing of the telephone. Louise got up and took the call in the hallway, hoping it would be Sean. She came back into the kitchen with a dazed look and sat down.

'What's wrong, Mum?' asked Helen. 'What's happened to Toby?'

When Louise didn't answer, Terry shook her arm to get her attention.

'Who was on the phone, Mum? Was that Dad?'

Louise blinked, and looked at him with a vacant stare. Helen collapsed back into her chair, thinking the worst.

'Mum! What's going on?' The desperation in Terry's voice was palpable.

Louise came back into the kitchen from wherever she had been.

'That was the police. They've just pulled Sean's truck out of the harbour.'

'Did they say anything about Dad?'

'Terry, there's no need to shout at me.'

'Sorry, but I thought we'd lost you.' Terry sat down and waited for her to continue.

Louise looked at him as if he was the one who hadn't been listening. 'The police divers are looking for his body. They think he might have been in the truck when it went in.' Louise placed her hand over her mouth. She didn't know what to think. 'What the hell would he be doing down at the port?' She looked at Terry as if he should know.

'Why would he drive his truck into the water?' said Helen, relieved it wasn't bad news about Toby. 'It doesn't make any sense. He can't even swim.'

'Maybe he parked it on the wharf and the handbrake failed,' suggested Terry.

'He might not have been driving the truck,' said Louise. 'You know what he's like. He hardly ever locks it. Anybody could have taken it and driven it off the wharf. What I want to know is where the hell is he? Why hasn't he called me?'

No-one had answers for those desperate questions. This was turning into a dark weekend for the Moore family. One death, and now two missing persons.

Helen was the first one to start thinking outside the square.

'This is not looking good, Terry. I can't imagine your father staying out all night with Toby missing, and with what's happened to your grandfather. We need to find out what's happening.'

'How are we going to do that?' said Terry.

'We need to talk to the police. I don't think we have the whole picture about what your father and your grandfather might have been up to.'

Louise came out of her daze. 'They weren't up to anything! What makes you think they were up to anything? How dare you suggest they were up to something!'

Helen was surprised at how calm she managed to stay.

'Louise, none of us know what those two have been doing. You told us yourself you didn't know if Sean had ever stopped working for his father. What if Kieran never really stopped working in the drug trade?'

As soon as Helen had called his mother by her name, Terry knew Helen was taking charge. She was a lot smarter than he was, and she knew things about the law and other stuff that were a complete mystery to him. Plants and sport were Terry's domain. He couldn't manage his money without her help. He'd been handing over his wages to her every payday ever since they'd been married. She gave him an allowance, so he couldn't blow it all on the horses when he went to the races with his father.

'Now you're the one talking rubbish, Helen,' scoffed Louise. 'They couldn't hide that from me for more than thirty years.' Louise realised the weakness of her position even as she voiced it. 'Could they?'

'Have either of you ever seen the books for the business?' Helen already knew that Terry hadn't, and even if he had he wouldn't have understood them. She was the one who filled out his tax return. All he did was sign it. Terry couldn't add up to save himself, unless it was a football score. Even Toby complained about Terry's lack of arithmetic skills.

Louise shook her head. 'He's never shown me the books. I don't have a head for business. My job is to look after the house and answer the phone. Nothing else. All I know is there's always money in the bank when I want it, and if I use the credit card, he always clears it for me.'

Helen wanted to punch her, but decided on taking a couple of deep breaths instead.

'So, none of us really know where the money comes from. We've all assumed it comes from the business. What if some of it comes from somewhere else?'

'Some of it comes from the races,' said Terry. 'Dad wins a lot of money at the races.'

'How do you know he isn't just telling you that?' said Helen.

'When we go to the races, he always gives me money to bet for him.'

'You place some of his bets?'

'Yeah, he gives me a bunch of envelopes with a list. I go to the bookies on the list and give them the envelopes and get the tickets. Dad wins a lot of money. I've seen it.'

'How long's that been going on for?' asked Louise.

'Ever since I started working with Dad.'

Terry felt as if he had confessed to a crime. He always did whatever his father asked him to do. Terry loved his father like an only child could. Until the talk with his mother on Friday night, Terry had never seen anything wrong with his father. Even now, he was having trouble believing there was anything to Helen's suggestion, but he knew Helen was clever and saw things he didn't. Terry's devotion to his father was the underlying tension that had fuelled the arguments over the last couple of years; the same arguments which had culminated in their separation. He knew in his heart that he had to side with Helen, regardless of what the voice in his head was saying.

'Sean's been going to the races for as long as I've known him. At first, I didn't know whether he was addicted to drugs or gambling. I got him off the drugs,' said Louise. 'I never got him off the horses.'

By Wednesday, Forensics were able to tell Carl that Bob Butterfield had been dead for at least a week, and that the hole behind the shed contained little else beyond ash, burnt tins and the remains of some incompletely burnt pieces of clothing. Whoever had cleaned the house and the shed had been wearing rubber gloves, however, Forensics had picked up some hairs that at first glance appeared to belong to different people. Further testing would reveal more. They had also determined that the murder appeared to have taken place in the bathroom. The room had been thoroughly scrubbed and still smelt of disinfectant, but there were some things household cleaning products could not erase beyond the reach of Forensics.

Bill Norris' people had confirmed that, apart from the two men seen in the grey van, no-one else had been seen in the vicinity of Bob Butterfield's farm over the last month, except for May and Sally on Sunday morning. Bill's people had also confirmed that two men, one described as being a giant and the other as a bean pole, had filled up a grey van with diesel at a local petrol station early Saturday morning. Unfortunately, the attendant couldn't provide a more informative description, and the station's CCTV cameras had been offline for more than a week, waiting for a technician from the city to arrive and fix whatever the problem was. The only reason the attendant had recalled seeing a grey van at all was the impression the comical scene of the two men of disparate size had created in his mind.

'Not much to go on,' said Bill Norris. 'What have we got besides Laurel and Hardy in a grey Mercedes van?'

'At least we know that van is significant. It was seen at or near both crime scenes.'

'We don't have a registration number.'

'It's a new model. There can't be too many of them around here.'

'Carl, if they were locals we'd know who they were from the descriptions we have. Besides, you can't buy a new Mercedes here, you have to go down to the city.'

'There's hundreds of them down there. They seem to have

become the delivery van of choice since Ford announced they were leaving.'

They looked at each other. It was becoming obvious the solution was not going to be found in the Riverland, unless the killers had gone to ground somewhere in the zone. Both parties involved in the drug operation that Sally and May had disclosed were dead. It looked like someone was closing up shop or re-arranging their operations.

'I'll get the lad from the service station to look through some mugshots. We might get lucky. They could have a record,' said Bill.

'Worth a try, I guess.'

'Anything on the boy?'

'He's disappeared into thin air. Not one sighting, apart from the one we already have.'

'His parents must be beside themselves by now. You've got kids, Bill. How do you think you'd cope if one them was abducted?'

'Would depend on which one they took.'

'Sam still giving you grief?'

'Why do you think I took this posting? Anyway, she's been a lot more co-operative since we moved here. She's made some new friends and she's doing pretty well at school. I hope it holds. I'd hate to lose her to drugs again.'

'That must have been hard, Bill.'

'Yes, when you think you've lost your child it's almost impossible to focus on anything else. If I could have, I would have killed the little prick that introduced her to drugs.'

'Did you ever find out who it was?'

'The fucking boyfriend!'

'Did you turn him in?'

'Fat lot of good it did. Sam hates me for doing it and the little shit only got a two year good behaviour bond.'

Carl's mobile phone rang. He fished it out of his pocket and answered the call.

'DI West.'

'Where are you, Carl?' said Chief Inspector Rankin.

'I'm with Bill Norris, Chief,' said Carl, so that Bill would know who was on the line.

'Get Bill to take charge of the local operation. I need you back here. Sean Moore turned up dead this morning, in a warehouse down by the port. This is starting to look like a planned wipeout of Kieran's operation.'

'This is not sounding good for our missing boy, Chief.'

'I've got Bob Reid organising protection for the boy's parents and Sean's widow. We need to find out who knows what Kieran and Sean were up to. Bob's people are searching Sean's office and house as we speak. At least no-one's done them over like they did to Kieran's place. Come and see me when you get back. If you leave now you should be here in time for lunch. We can go to Lena's.'

Chief Inspector Rankin hung up before Carl could respond.

'Sounds like I have a lunch appointment with the chief.'

'You better get going then. You don't want to keep him waiting.'

'You're right there. I'll just collect Harry and get going.'

'What do you want me to do with those two women?'

'We only had them in for protective custody. I reckon we can let them go home. I think any danger they might have been in has passed. Maybe you can keep an eye on them for the next week or so.'

'You going to press charges?'

'I'll let the public prosecutor make that call when we get this sorted out. I don't have time for that now.'

'Fair enough. Have a safe trip.'

The inspectors shook hands and Carl left Bill's office in search of Harry.

When Carl arrived at Lena's, a small Italian restaurant located a short walk from Police Headquarters and Chief Inspector Rankin's favourite eating place, he found Bob Reid sitting with the chief.

After exchanging greetings, they ordered. Carl ordered the pasta marinara, while Bob and the chief inspector both ordered the wood oven pizza. They restricted their drinking to mineral water and coffee. The chief inspector enjoyed his food but he was a busy man.

While they waited for their food to arrive, the chief asked Bob to bring them up to date.

'There was an invoice from Lennard's Storage Warehouse stuck to the front of the fridge in Kieran's kitchen. I sent Wayne down there this morning to see what he was storing in the place. Wasn't expecting him to find Sean's body with a couple of bullets in it'

'What sort of security do they have at this storage place?' asked Carl.

'There are five entrances into the warehouse, all with CCTV coverage. It's a fairly big place with three levels of storage units. You need an access code to get into the building, and another one to get into your storage unit. They also have a perimeter alarm that alerts their security firm if anyone attempts to get in without using an access code. According to the manager, each user has a unique access code to both the door of their choice and their storage unit.'

'So, when did Sean make his last visit?' asked Carl.

'Saturday night at 6.10 pm, in the company of a woman

wearing bike leathers. She came out again after fifteen minutes carrying a box. He didn't.'

'Do we have a good visual of the woman?' asked the chief inspector.

'She must have been aware of the camera. She didn't look at it directly, kept her head down and used the box to shield her face. Hopefully someone will recognise her from her overall appearance,' said Bob.

'Find anything when you searched Sean's place?' asked Carl.

'Nothing at his house but his office was a different matter. We found a floor safe with ten thousand dollars in cash and a bag of about three hundred ecstasy tablets.'

'You don't sound all that excited about that,' said Carl.

'I have a feeling that it's a plant.'

'What makes you say that, Bob?' asked the chief inspector.

'If you had a wall safe holding that sort of stuff, where would you keep the combination, Chief?'

'In my head or in some encrypted file stored in a different location, I suppose,' replied the chief.

'Not on a post-it note stuck to the inside of the top drawer of your office desk?'

'Little bit obvious.'

'I'm having the note analysed. It didn't look all that old to me. I'm also getting them to compare the handwriting on the note with some samples of Sean's handwriting,' said Bob. 'And, when I was checking the reported break-in at Kieran's, one of the neighbours told me that he had heard Sean's truck drive in and out of the driveway sometime around seven pm. We now know Sean was dead by then, so some-one else had to be driving the truck, and if they had the truck they had the keys to Sean's office. The keys were still in the ignition when we pulled the truck from the harbour.'

The waitress arrived with their meals. They spent the next

ten minutes enjoying their food. When they finished eating, the chief looked at his watch.

'I have an appointment in ten. Carl, I want you to talk to young Terry. We need to know if he is part of Kieran's business or not,' said the chief inspector.

Chief Inspector Rankin left Carl sitting with Bob Reid.

'What did you find out up the river?' asked Bob.

'Some-one's either cleaning up or eliminating the opposition. Whichever it is, they have shut down Kieran's operation. Bob Butterfield, the guy who was making the stuff, was taken out some time last week. Kieran was eliminated on Saturday morning and Sean Saturday evening. Looks like a planned operation to me.'

'They obviously knew where to find everyone,' said Bob. 'How does the kid fit into this?'

'I think he was simply in the wrong place at the wrong time. I'm surprised they didn't kill him,' said Carl.

'Maybe they're planning to use him to put pressure on his parents or at least his father. He worked with Sean.'

They finished their coffees and headed back to the office. Carl wanted to read the Forensics' reports on Sean's murder and the search of his office before interviewing Terry and Helen Moore.

When he'd read the reports, Carl decided he'd conduct the initial interview at the Moore's home, where they'd probably feel more comfortable and more inclined to talk. He took Harry with him. A protective services officer let them into the house when they arrived.

The Moores were waiting in the living room.

'I'm Detective Inspector West and this is Detective Fuller.

We're part of the team looking for your son and trying to work out who killed Sean and Kieran. We got back from the Riverland this morning.'

'Is there any news on Toby?' asked Helen.

'We've had one possible sighting, which I understand my colleague, Inspector Reid, told you about,' said Carl.

'Do you think he could still be alive, Inspector?' asked Terry.

'I don't know, Mr Moore. I hope he is.'

'If you don't have any news on Toby, why are you here?' asked Helen.

'We need to talk about Sean's business interests. I need to work out whether you're in any danger.'

Terry looked at Helen.

'I understand you work for your father, Mr Moore. Is that correct?'

'I work in Dad's gardening business, Inspector. He designs gardens and I grow the plants we use. We do garden maintenance work as well. You know, things like cutting lawns, weeding garden beds and cutting back trees.'

'Do you make a lot of money doing that?'

'I suppose. Dad does all the books. He pays me,' said Terry.

'Terry's an employee, Inspector. He's not very good with numbers. His father did all the quoting and invoicing, and handled all the payments. Terry's really good with plants but he's going to need a lot of help to keep the business going,' said Helen.

'Mr Moore, did your father have any other business interests?' asked Carl.

'I don't know whether you would call it a business, Inspector, but Dad made a lot of money on the horses. He was always betting on the horses. He used to take me with him sometimes.'

'To the betting shop or the track?' asked Carl.

'Dad always went to the track. He'd work out his bets before he went and divide them up into envelopes. Sometimes he'd get me to place the bets when I went with him. That's how I know he won a lot of money. I've collected the winnings.'

'Do you know anything about horses?' asked Harry.

'Every time I placed a bet using my own money on a horse I picked myself I lost. The only time I ever won was when I bet on the same horses Dad bet on. Helen doesn't like me betting on horses. She cut my allowance to stop me losing my money.'

Terry looked down at the floor.

'We've been fighting over this for months, Inspector,' said Helen. 'I suppose you've heard that we have been living in separate houses for the last few weeks. At least Terry has finally come to his senses.' Helen smiled and rubbed Terry's knee.

'What else can you tell me about your father's betting, Mr Moore? Did he always use the same bookies for example?'

Terry spent a few moments thinking about the last time he'd gone to the races with his father.

'I think you might be right. He always used the same bookies at the races.'

'Do you remember their names?'

'No, but if we went to the races, I could pick out their stands.'

Carl placed a photograph, a still shot taken from the CCTV footage of the woman leaving Lennard's Storage Warehouse, on the coffee table.

'Do either of you recognise this woman?'

Terry and Helen looked at the photograph. Helen shook her head. Terry looked at the photograph for a long time. He picked it up and looked at it from different angles.

'I can't be sure because you can't see her face but this looks like the motorcycle courier that brings stuff to Grandpa's. Sometimes she drops things off with us when Grandpa's not home. Her name's Clare. Why do you want to know?'

'This photograph was taken at Lennard's Storage Warehouse.

We think this is the woman that shot Sean. She was photographed going in with him.'

'Clare?' Terry shook his head.

'You don't think Clare is a killer, Mr Moore?' asked Carl.

'I've only met her a few times but she seemed nice enough to me. She'd always flirt with Dad and give me a big wink when he wasn't looking.'

'Do you know who she works for? Which courier company?' asked Harry.

Terry pictured Clare riding in on her motorbike.

'She rides a big Suzuki. I don't recall seeing any courier company name. She always wore black and her bike is black. Sometimes Dad would give her a package Grandpa had left for her.'

Carl waited until he was sure Harry had noted that bit of information.

'Do you know the combination to your father's safe, Mr Moore?' asked Carl

Terry looked at Helen and then back at Inspector West. 'What safe?'

'The one in the floor of his office,' said Carl.

'News to me, Inspector. I hardly ever go into Dad's office. I spend most of my time looking after our clients' gardens or in the nursery getting plants ready.'

'Do you know what ecstasy is, Mr Moore?' asked Carl.

'Not really. I've heard it mentioned on the news. It's some sort of drug kids take at parties, isn't it?'

'Have you ever taken it?'

'No. I don't do drugs. Mum would kill me. She's so anti-drugs she wouldn't let Grandpa near me when I was little.'

'As you've no doubt noticed, we've put a guard on your house. There's one at your mother's as well.'

'Are we really in danger, Inspector?' asked Terry.

'I don't know, to be honest, but it appears anyone connected to your grandfather's drug operation has been murdered in the last week or so,' said Carl. 'Were you involved?'

'Drug operation? What drug operation?'

The look on Terry's face suggested to Carl that he had no idea what they were talking about.

'Apparently, your grandfather, and a man named Bob Butterfield, who your grandfather met while he was in prison, have been making ecstasy tablets in a lab in the Riverland, for more than twenty years. Your grandfather was taking up the raw ingredients and bringing back the finished product. Seems his courier business was a cover. We think your father was also involved because we found ten thousand dollars in cash, and a pile of ecstasy tablets, in his safe. If you're involved, I'd say your life is in danger. It looks like someone has decided to shut down the whole operation and make sure we knew your father was involved.'

'You'd better talk to Mum, Inspector. She knew Dad was involved with Grandpa in the drug trade before Grandpa went to prison. That all happened before I was born. She told us the other day that she thought Dad had learnt his lesson.'

Terry looked at Helen and shrugged his shoulders.

'Terry's not good at keeping secrets, Inspector. I doubt very much that either Kieran or Sean would have trusted him with that information, if what you have told us is true. I think Terry may have unwittingly been duped into taking part in Sean's money laundering activities. You might want to talk to the bookies he placed his bets with, if Terry can identify any of them for you,' said Helen.

Carl looked at her. He hadn't gone down that pathway himself yet. This was one smart lady. He wondered what she was doing with a guy like Terry.

'Which race track did you go to with your Dad?'

'Mostly we went to The Brook.'

'We've missed the mid-week meeting, so I'll see if we can arrange a trip down there on Saturday.'

'Sure,' said Terry.

Carl stood up, his signal to Harry that they were leaving.

'We'll be in touch.'

'Are we allowed to leave the house?' asked Helen.

'As long as you take one of the protective services officers with you. Otherwise, I think you're safest here,' said Carl. 'I know it won't be easy but it might be best if you stay put for the next few days.'

HELEN WAITED until the two policemen had gone. She was unsettled by what the inspector had told them about Sean and Kieran.

'Are you telling me the truth, Terry?'

Terry looked at her. She could see a scared little boy looking back at her, and wondered whether it was her he was afraid of or the implication that he might be in danger.

'Honey, if either of them were doing this drug stuff, it's news to me. Dad didn't say anything about it to me. I swear, I didn't know anything about it until they told us just then.'

Helen was inclined to believe him but was still angry that he hadn't suspected anything, especially about all the money going to and from the races.

'Where did you think all that money came from?'

Her exasperation, with his blindness towards anything associated with his father, came through a little more forcibly than she had planned. Terry started fidgeting and looked down at the floor.

'I thought it was from his winnings. Dad's been betting on horses for as long as I can remember. Even Mum used to brag about him winning all the time when I was a kid.'

Helen decided she could probably believe him but was left with a lingering fear.

'What if this person that's killed them thinks you're involved? What if that's the real reason they've got Toby?'

Terry sensed the fear in Helen and moved to wrap his arm around her, not that he felt any stronger or less afraid than she did. He just knew she needed to be comforted.

'How would they have known that Grandpa was going to have Toby with him?'

Helen looked through the front window, across the lawn, to where the protective services car was parked in front of the house.

'What if taking Toby with him was part of some plan Kieran had that went wrong?'

'Grandpa loved Toby. He wouldn't have taken him somewhere dangerous if he had known.'

'Fat difference it made.'

They both knew that was an accurate assessment. Kieran was dead and Toby was still missing, presumed abducted but, in all likelihood, probably also dead.

'What are we going to do?' asked Terry.

It took Helen a few minutes to answer. She didn't want to think the worst, she so desperately wanted Toby to come home safe and sound, but the realist within her head was telling her she needed to start getting used to the idea of her life continuing without him. She looked at the man she loved, he was trying so hard to be supportive, and told the realist to shut up.

'My mother was right. Your family is nothing but trouble and heartache.'

Terry turned and looked at her. She was smiling at him.

'That doesn't mean I don't love you, though. It was you I wanted to be with, not the rest of your family.'

'I'm really sorry, honey. I had no idea any of this stuff was going on. Guess I trusted Dad way too much.'

'Yes. I was starting to despair that you would ever grow up and move out from under his shadow. Still, I didn't want it to happen like this. I thought that maybe I could get you to find another job.'

Terry wondered if he would have to find another job in any case, since he knew so little about running the business.

'I wonder how much of a business there is. Will there be enough work there for me to earn decent money?'

Helen almost laughed out loud but managed to contain herself.

'You think you could run the business on your own? You can't even add up.'

'Might have to get you or Mum to help me.'

Helen thought that might work but she also knew there was no way she would be giving up her own job. At least that gave them a steady income. She was still intent on completing her law studies and becoming a lawyer. Louise had helped Sean when he had started the business. Perhaps she could help Terry resurrect it after this had all died down.

'Louise might be able to help you with the business. After all, she helped your Dad set it up. I wonder what she is going to do now that Sean is gone. How is she going to survive?'

Terry knew the burden would pass to him. He'd have to make enough money for both of them. He couldn't leave his mother with nothing.

A thought popped into Helen's head from one of the assignments she had completed earlier in the year.

'She could lose everything if the police can show that it was bought with the proceeds of crime.'

'Does that mean we could be in trouble as well?'

'What do you mean? You just told me you weren't involved.'

'But what if Dad was paying me with drug money?'

'We'll need to have a good look at the books. After all, you have been working for the business, growing plants and doing gardens. I think you'll be in the clear as long as what you've told me is the truth. If I find out you've lied to me, Terry, it will be over for us.'

'I haven't lied to you, ever.'

She tousled his hair. 'That's only because you couldn't tell a lie to save yourself.'

They embraced and held each other.

'I wish Toby was here,' said Helen

'What are we going to do if he doesn't come home?'

'Let's not go there, Terry. We have to hold on to the hope that he will come home, right up until when there is no more room for that hope.'

Mary Sloan hadn't been able to sleep since hearing the news that Kieran was dead and Toby was missing. Her doctor had prescribed anti-depressants. They didn't appear to be doing her any good. When Kevin told her that Sean had been killed, her anxiety level hit a new high.

It wasn't about Toby anymore. Now it was about her only child being caught up in that dreadful family, and being in danger because she insisted on staying with that idiot she had chosen to marry.

If she'd had the strength, and access to the means, Mary would have killed Terry herself. Fortunately for Terry, all Mary could do was lie down and feel sorry for herself.

Kevin had just about given up on Mary. He couldn't cope with what he saw as her self-indulgent suffering. Kevin had no appreciation or understanding of her struggles with the hot flushes, mood swings and irritability of approaching menopause, or of her depression over the lack of recognition she felt in her workplace and her feelings of envy about the success of her sister.

Things had always gone well for him, even if not always to plan. He was enjoying an upswing in his real estate career, now that the property market was picking up, and was building a sizeable portfolio of properties and shares with his earnings. And, while Mary had lost interest in sex, he had discovered the pleasures of a hot physical affair with Louise. Where Mary hated Terry, Kevin was grateful to him for the introduction to his libidinous mother.

Every time he tried to talk to Mary she didn't want to listen to his soothing words. When he tried to reason with her, to hold onto the hope that Toby would come home or to explain that there was no way any criminal in his right mind would take Terry into his confidence, she only screamed at him, telling him he was an imbecile and totally insensitive, and that he didn't love their daughter if he wouldn't go and bring her home where they could keep her safe.

Following her latest outburst, Kevin chose to go to the office. Not because he wanted to work but to get some relief. Something else he could do from the office was call Louise to see how she was coping.

Louise told him she was more upset about Toby being missing than Sean being dead. She was pissed off with Sean for having lied to her about not doing drugs anymore with his father. Kevin got the strong impression that she would not be forgiving Sean anytime soon.

When she had finished telling him what the police had told her, she let him know there was a protective services officer staying with her in case she was a target.

Kevin felt another wave of frustration. To distract himself, he asked Louise what arrangements she was making for the funerals.

She asked him to come by and help her sort it out, as she had no idea how she was going to do that. Kevin liked to be useful, especially when it came to Louise, and the idea of spending some time with a rational woman for a change appealed to him, even if it meant he'd be spending time with Lousie without screwing her or rubbing his hands over her naked body.

He arranged to drop by on his way home.

Louise had afternoon tea ready when Kevin arrived. As they ate cake and enjoyed coffee together, Kevin explained what she would need to do to arrange the funerals. He gave her the number of one of his associates, a funeral director, that he thought had done a good job of his father's funeral.

'I suggest you give Ron a call and start the ball rolling so that things can be put in place as soon as the police are ready to release the bodies.'

'When do you think that will happen?'

'Probably in the next couple of days. Can't imagine them wanting to hold the bodies much longer than that. Sounds like they pretty much know how they were killed. Now it will be a question of who did it. Can't be all that difficult to gather the evidence once you have the body.'

'Hope you're right. Guess I should get Terry involved in this as well. There's no-one else really. How much do you think it will cost?'

'Depends how flash you want to be.'

'I'd bury the bastard in a hole in the backyard if I could.'

'I think there might be a law against that, Louise, but there's always the pinewood box option, and I read the other day that they now have a cardboard coffin that speeds up the cremation process.'

'Might use that then. That way they can start the burning in hell bit as soon as possible,' said Louise. 'Would you like another coffee?'

'You don't sound like the grieving widow to me. Not happy with the turn of events?'

Louise smiled and looked over to where the protective services officer was reading the paper in the living room.

'If I'd known Sean and his father were dealing in drugs, I would have left him. I made Sean promise me that he would never do that again, when Kieran went to prison. He gave me his word. That's when we started the gardening business. He did all the hard work. I answered the telephone and did the books until Terry was born. By then, Sean had it all under control. He even had a couple of employees, right up until Terry joined the business.'

'So, you had no idea?'

'I thought the money was coming from the business or his winnings at the races. He was always winning at the races. Claimed he had a head for numbers and horses.'

'Too bad he didn't pass those skills on to Terry,' said Kevin.

'He tried. But now it appears that it was all bullshit. The police are saying that Sean was using the races to launder money. They're trying to identify the bookies he used. That Inspector West reckons they were all in it together.'

'The police told you that?'

'Not exactly, but that's what Helen said. She a pretty smart girl that daughter of yours.'

'Looks like Kieran got what he wanted,' said Kevin.

'What do you mean?'

'Terry and Helen are back together. Mind you, Mary's not very happy about that. Terry is still blacklisted as far as she is concerned.'

'Mary doesn't seem too happy about anything at the moment. How is she coping with the latest news?'

'I wouldn't be surprised to find her with her head in the oven when I get home.'

'That bad. You'd better go and check on her. I don't want that on my conscience as well. It's bad enough knowing I helped Kieran get to Toby.'

'Don't blame yourself for that.'

'God, I hope that boy turns up safe and sound.'

'Me too.'

Kevin finished his afternoon tea and set out for home, dreading what he might find there. Finding Mary with her head in the oven was one possibility but the more likely outcome was encountering a very angry woman intent on making his life hell, to match her own.

Mary hated it when everybody else seemed to be okay and she wasn't.

CHAPTER 8

Malcolm turned the van onto the highway and headed in the direction of the city. George played a game on his iPhone. Toby stared ahead. He was pretty sure they had killed Kieran and wondered why they were taking him with them.

He looked at Malcolm out of the corner of his eye. Malcolm was concentrating on the road. He took a quick look at George and noticed how small the iPhone looked in his big hands.

'Where are we going?' Toby asked.

'Relax, kid. We're taking you home,' said Malcolm, without clarifying that he meant his home and not Toby's.

Some holiday, thought Toby. Six hours in a van. Three going to the Riverland and then another three going straight back to the city.

Malcolm turned on the radio and they listened to a program discussing the design of the modern city on Radio National. When the program ended, the news came on. The headline story was about Toby, who had been reported missing by his parents and was suspected of having run away from home. The police were asking for assistance from the public to locate him.

George poked Toby in the side.

'That you?'

'Yeah.'

'You told us you were on a holiday with your grandfather. You're a naughty boy, aren't you?'

'I was on a holiday with Grandpa Kieran. It's just that we didn't tell my mum I was going,' said Toby.

'Why's that?' said Malcolm.

Toby didn't say anything.

'Come on, Toby. You can tell us,' said George.

'My parents have been fighting. I wanted them to stop and get back together. Grandpa Kieran said running away for the weekend would get them back together, because they'd be so worried about me they'd stop fighting each other.'

'I suppose that would work. I reckon we can help you with that,' said Malcolm.

'What do you mean?'

'They'll be really worried when they find out that your grandfather is dead and you've disappeared, don't you think?'

Toby thought about that for a while.

'Why did you kill Grandpa Kieran?'

'Best you don't know, Toby. Let's just say that your grandfather was not a very nice person. He might have been a loving grandfather to you but what he was doing to other people was not very nice,' said Malcolm.

'He was my great-grandfather, actually.'

'Is that so?'

'You're not really taking me home are you?'

'Not straight away. At least your parents will be so worried about you they won't have time to fight over anything else, will they?' said Malcolm with a smirk.

Toby thought of all the gangster movies he had watched with his father. In those movies the killers didn't leave any witnesses, and they only kidnapped people when they could get something in exchange for letting them go. He wondered what they might want in exchange for him.

With the rocking of the van as it sped along the highway, it wasn't long before Toby was asleep, again.

Toby woke up when George gave him a gentle shake.

'Wake up, sleepy-head. We're home.'

Toby looked around. The van was parked in the driveway of a suburban house that looked a lot like the house his mother's parents lived in, and it had the same sort of landscaped garden in the front yard. Toby wondered if it had been designed by Grandpa Sean.

George grabbed Toby by the arm, shepherded him into the house through the front door and took him into the kitchen, where a tall woman about the same age as his mother was making lunch.

'Who's this?' the woman said, as they entered the kitchen.

'Toby, say hello to Clare.'

Clare glared at George.

'What's he doing here?'

'He was with the old man. What were we supposed to do with him?'

'I'll talk to you later,' said Clare. 'You hungry, Toby?'

Toby nodded his head.

'Sit down. I'll make you a sandwich. You like salad?'

'Yes, thank you,' said Toby, finally finding his voice and feeling a little more relaxed in her presence.

After lunch, Clare took Toby on a tour of the house to show him how to find the bathroom and the toilet. Then she took him into a room with a television and turned it on for him.

'I hope you're a smart kid, Toby.'

Toby looked at her with interest.

'What do you want me to do?' he asked.

'I want you to stay here and watch TV. You can use the toilet if you need to or get yourself something to eat from the kitchen. There are drinks in the fridge. Think you can do that for me?'

Toby nodded his head and sat down in front of the TV.

'Don't make any noise or do anything silly, otherwise I'll let George hit you, and you don't want that to happen, do you?'

'No,' said Toby, remembering the size of George's hands.

Clare handed him the remote.

Clare stood in the backyard, where the others wouldn't hear her, and called Steve.

'What's up, babe?'

'We have an unexpected package, something the boys brought back from their trip,' said Clare.

'Anything of value?'

'Depends on your point of view. I think you should come and take a look.'

'What's in this package?'

'Listen to the news. They're talking about it on the radio. When you decide what you want to do about it, you know where I'll be,' said Clare.

'Okay. I'll call you when your boyfriend is ready for you,' said Steve. He ended the call.

Clare went back into the house to wait for Steve to either show up or call back. She knew he wouldn't be happy that Malcolm and George had brought Toby back with them. The whole point of the exercise was to eliminate Kieran's operation, and the Moore side would be gone once she had taken care of Sean. Toby would be just another complication she would have to eliminate if Steve had no use for him. Pity, she thought, he was a cute kid.

She wondered what she could do with Toby while they were taking care of Sean, and decided she would have to tie him up so that he couldn't do anything foolish while he was waiting alone in the house, unless Steve had decided his fate before then.

Around five pm Steve called Clare.

'Your boyfriend is at the office. Time to go. Tell Malcolm I'll pick him up at five thirty so George can look after the package.'

Obviously, Steve had worked out what the package was. Clare told George and Malcolm the new arrangements, changed into her motorcycle gear and left for her meeting with Sean, on her black Suzuki GSX-R1000.

George and Toby were eating pizza and talking football when Clare got back. George, a Power supporter, was ribbing Toby about the Crows going down to the Power in the game they had watched that afternoon.

'See you two have become mates,' said Clare as she entered the kitchen. 'Any pizza left? Or do I have to order in?'

'In the oven,' said George.

'Thanks, be back in a minute.'

Clare went to her room and changed out of her leathers. She checked the safety catch before putting her loaded pistol back into the box under the bed. She locked the box and viewed her reflection in the mirror. She was tall and slim, with a body toned by daily workouts in the gym she had set up in the garage, where she kept her motorbike and several other weapons.

Assassin was a long way from being an army sniper but, as she continually asked herself, what else could she do with her specialist skills. The taxpayers had invested a fortune in her training. Shame to let all that training go to waste was how Steve saw it.

In Clare's mind, once you had killed men, women and children for your country, it wasn't much of a transition to doing it for some other cause; and the money was much better working for Steve than what it had been working for the government.

Clare went out to join George and Toby in the kitchen. George was getting her pizza out of the oven as she entered.

'Is Malcolm coming back?' asked Toby.

Malcolm gave Toby the creeps. Initially, he had been afraid of George, based on his imposing presence. George was the biggest man Toby had ever seen. He was even bigger than Grandpa Kieran. But after spending the afternoon watching football with George, Toby had decided that he was okay. Malcolm, on the other hand, was not so friendly, now that they had rejoined civilisation. Toby had the feeling that he couldn't trust Malcolm.

'Missing him, are you?' said Clare.

'No, just wondering.'

'He'll be back soon enough,' said Clare.

Toby felt comfortable with Clare, so he asked her, 'What's going to happen to me?' He knew there was no point in asking when they were going to take him home.

Clare looked at him. He was the cutest little boy she'd ever met and he was trying so hard to be brave. He was obviously bright enough to realise the pickle he was in. He was looking at her with those imploring eyes only an innocent child possessed. Despite herself, she could feel him reaching out to her and she wanted to cuddle him and say that it would be all right.

If she had to kill him, she would never forgive George and Malcolm for bringing him home. Obviously, they didn't have the stomach for doing what they knew should have been done. It would fall to her now, if Steve had no use for the boy.

'We'll have to wait and see what the man says.'

'What does that mean?'

'Means it's not up to me,' said Clare. 'By rights you shouldn't be here.' She glared at George. 'These clowns should have left you in the Riverland.'

Toby looked at George. He didn't look much like a clown to him and he suspected, even though he hadn't seen any of the action, that George had hit Kieran hard enough to kill him. He looked up at Clare. She wasn't pretty like his mother but she had something about her that he liked, even if he couldn't name it.

'You mean they should have killed me like they did Grandpa Kieran, don't you?'

'You watch too much TV. I meant they should have left you there for someone else to find you, that's all.'

Toby's eyes told her he didn't believe her either.

Clare picked up her pizza and went into the TV room.

'Now you're in big trouble, mate. You've upset her,' said George. 'Want some more coke?'

Toby pushed his glass towards George.

'Thanks for not killing me, George.'

'I don't kill kids, Toby. What sort of a man kills little kids that haven't done anything wrong? Nah. You're safe with me.'

It's not you I'm worried about, thought Toby, as he sipped the coke George had poured into his glass.

Toby was asleep in the bed in Clare's room when Malcolm and Steve arrived. Clare had shut and locked the door to her room so there was no chance of Toby seeing Steve.

They sat in the living room, Steve in the armchair, Malcolm and George on the couch, and Clare on the floor.

Steve was feeling pleased with himself. Things had gone to

plan. He'd rubbed out the main players in the little, insecure operation he had inherited from his father, which had been threatening to undo his plans for selling the business. He'd even been able to track down the bookies involved in Sean Moore's money laundering operation, for Clare to eliminate, and nobody had even noticed they were gone. Steve figured it would take the police some time, and considerable luck, to find those bodies, as it would be a long time before the foundations of the new hospital were dug up.

His plan called for Kieran's and Sean's bodies being found, and making it appear as though they were the main players. He'd arranged for Malcolm to plant enough ecstasy tablets in Sean's safe to make it look as though that's where they ended up, until Sean sold them.

They had a good laugh when Malcolm told them there was a bag of cash in Sean's safe. Steve thought that would help fool the police into believing what he wanted them to believe.

There was only one little problem to resolve: the kid.

'Where's the kid?' Steve asked Clare.

'Asleep. I've locked him in my room so he can't get a look at you,' answered Clare.

Steve turned to Malcolm and George.

'Why the fuck did you bring the kid here?'

'Because he's a kid. I don't do kids,' said George.

Christ, thought Steve, I'm paying these morons to kill people, and they don't do kids.

'And, what's your story?' Steve asked Malcolm.

'We couldn't just leave him there. We don't know how much he's seen,' said Malcolm.

'Well, he's seen fucking plenty now, hasn't he?'

'He's still just a kid,' said George.

'That might be true, George, but that kid can describe you, Malcolm, and Clare to the police. Have you thought about that?'

Silence.

George looked at Malcolm and then down at his hands.

'You want us to bump off the kid, then?' asked Malcolm.

'Do you have any other ideas about what you could do with him?'

'Can't we sell him to one of those child porno groups?' asked George. 'At least that way we don't have to kill him.'

'Do you have any idea what happens to those kids?' asked Clare. 'I'd rather shoot him than hand him over to those sickos. At least he won't suffer if I put a bullet in his head.'

'And, let's keep in mind that the police are looking for this kid as well,' said Steve.

'What about the kid's father? Sean's son,' said Clare. 'I've seen him a few times at Sean's workshop.'

'The idiot son. Sean only kept him around to keep him out of trouble. He's of no use to me and of no concern either. He wouldn't know if his arse was on fire. He's going to be very surprised by what the police find in Sean's safe. They'll probably arrest him and charge him with being an accomplice. That suits me fine.'

'What about Sean's missus?' asked Malcolm.

'Sean told me years ago that he had her convinced he was a genius with the horses. I don't think we need to worry about her. Besides, a little birdie told me she has a new love interest, so she'll probably be glad we've removed Sean from the scene.' Steve laughed and then stood up. He beckoned for Clare to follow him out into the hallway and led her down to the front door.

'If you want your final payment, get rid of the kid. And tell those morons to sterilise that van tonight after they've parked Sean's truck in the harbour. I'll send them over a replacement tomorrow; a nice white one to go with their level of courage.'

Clare watched Steve let himself out and walk into the night. Then she went back into the living room and passed on his message to George and Malcolm. She didn't mention anything about the colour of the new van or why Steve had chosen it.

When they had gone, Clare went into her room and sat on the bed next to Toby. George and Malcolm would be gone for several hours, so she'd have plenty of time to get rid of the kid before they came back. She watched Toby sleeping. It would be so easy to suffocate him. That thought made her wonder what she was doing working for a bastard like Steve. It was one thing eliminating idiots that had been pedalling drugs but George was right. Toby was just a kid.

Clare made a decision. She pulled a backpack from the wardrobe and stuffed her clothes into it. She didn't have much at the house, apart from what she was wearing, and her leathers. One thing the army had taught her was how to travel light. She dressed in her leathers and got her pistol box from under the bed. By the time she was ready she had made enough noise to wake Toby.

When he stirred, Clare turned on the overhead light. Toby blinked.

'What's going on?'

'Get up and go to the toilet. Then get dressed. Make sure you put your parka on. We're leaving.'

She had spoken firmly, like his mother, so Toby did as he was told. When he was dressed, Clare grabbed her back pack and took him out the backdoor to the garage.

'Stand over there while I finish getting ready.'

Toby stood by the gym equipment and watched as Clare loaded several boxes into one of the panniers on her motorbike. It was the biggest motorbike he'd ever seen. Finally, Clare stuffed her backpack into the other pannier and called him over to the bike.

'Been on a motorbike before?'

'No.'

'You need to hang onto me really tight and lean when I lean, okay?'

Toby was frightened but he said, 'Okay.'

'Here, put this on.' Clare handed him her spare helmet. It was too big for him but she didn't want to attract unnecessary attention by riding around with a child without a helmet. She did it up as tight as she could and flipped down the visor. Then she put on her own helmet.

Clare used the remote to open the garage door. She mounted the bike and helped Toby climb up onto the pillion seat behind her, and made sure he had a firm grip around her body. Then she hit the ignition.

The bike burst into life. Clare turned on the head lights, and then they were off into the night, with a roar.

Toby was scared and excited at the same time. The world flashed by in a blur, as Clare deftly handled the big bike through dark back streets and then through the traffic on the highway that led up into the hills. Toby let himself move with her body as she leant from side to side.

Finally, after a ride Toby would never forget, Clare turned off the highway and headed down a series of dirt roads that eventually took them to a cottage, hidden by a ring of trees, alongside a stream of bubbling water. Not that Toby would be able to hear that sound for a while yet. All he could hear, even after taking off the helmet, was the roar of the bike.

Clare took off her helmet and smiled at him in the moonlight.

'That was wild,' said Toby.

'Glad you liked it. Come on, let's go inside.'

Clare helped him down from the bike. Toby looked at the small dark house. It looked like no-one was home.

'Where are we?'

'Somewhere safe, my little man, somewhere safe.'

CHAPTER 9

THE INCIDENT ROOM desk sergeant came into Carl's office.

'You might be interested in this, Inspector,' he said, handing over a piece of paper from the folder he was holding. 'Came in last night after you had gone home. I remembered Harry saying you were going to check out some bookies on Saturday in connection to the Moore case. This guy is a bookie.'

Carl looked at the Missing Person report. One Michael Murphy, aged sixty, had been reported missing by his son.

'What's the son's story?'

'Reckons that his father hadn't answered his phone for a few days. Thought he'd better check on him. Found the place open but no sign of his father,' said the sergeant.

'Do we have a picture?'

The sergeant took an A4 print of a photograph out of the folder he was holding.

'Call the son and tell him we'll check the house for any clues as to what's happened to his father. Ask him to stay out of the house, and send a patrol to secure the place and get the key. If this is one of our bookies, we'll need Forensics.'

'Okay, Inspector.'

Carl took the photograph and walked into the Incident Room.

'Harry, get your coat. We need to talk to Terry Moore.'

———————

Terry and Helen were eating breakfast when Carl and Harry arrived.

'Sorry to disturb you,' said Carl, 'but do you recognise this man?'

Carl placed the photograph of Michael Murphy on the table.

Helen shook her head but Terry looked at the photograph and said, 'Yes. He's one of the bookies Dad placed bets with at The Brook.'

'Do you remember how many others there were?' asked Carl.

'I've been thinking about that since the other day. There was this guy and two others, about the same age.'

'I'm starting to think someone is rubbing out your grandfather's entire operation. This is Michael Murphy. He's been reported missing by his son. I suspect we're going to find the same story when we identify the other two.'

'I don't know any of the names, Inspector, I only remember that they all stood in the same corner of the betting yard,' said Terry.

'That might be enough now that we have the name of one of them.' Carl collected the photograph and prepared to leave.

'Any news on Toby?' asked Helen.

'I'm sorry, Mrs Moore. Nothing new since we last talked.'

Helen sank back into her chair and held her head in her hands, as Terry showed Carl and Harry to the door.

Carl chatted with the protective services officers, who were changing shifts, before he climbed into the car with Harry.

'They seen anything?'

'All quiet on this front. Maybe Terry's telling us the truth.'

Carl put a call through to the desk sergeant and asked him to get Forensics to send a team to check out Michael Murphy's house.

'Tell them I suspect he didn't leave willingly.'

'Where do you want to go, Boss?'

'The Brook. I want to talk to the administrator of the race course to see if we can identify Michael Murphy's mates.'

It took them around forty minutes to drive across town to the race track, and a further fifteen minutes to locate the administrator's office within the labyrinth of offices under the grandstand.

Once they had explained their mission, it only took the administrator a couple of minutes to come up with two names.

'Charlie Boyle and Chris Morris. They're in partnership with this Michael Murphy. They've been on the books for years. Way before I started.'

'Do you have addresses for them?'

'Sure.'

The administrator printed out the details he was reading on his screen and handed it to Carl.

Carl handed the paper to Harry. 'Give them a call, Harry. Let's see if they answer.'

While Harry was calling the bookies, Carl asked the administrator whether there was any CCTV coverage of activity in the betting yard.

'Not yet, I'm afraid, Inspector. They're in the master plan but we haven't been able to fund them to date.'

'Thanks for your help.'

Carl shook hands with the administrator and went in search of Harry, who had stepped out of the office. He found him waiting in the corridor outside the door.

'No luck, Boss. No answer on either number. I've got patrols going to both addresses.'

'Good work, Harry. Let's head back to the office. While we're waiting to see what Forensics come up with, I think we'd better organise a team to talk to all the neighbours.'

As they were driving back to the office, Carl's mobile phone rang.

'Where are you, Carl?' said Chief Inspector Rankin.

'Just leaving The Brook, Chief. Should be back in the office in twenty.'

'You driving?'

'No, Harry.'

Carl wondered why the chief wanted to know if he was driving. They had hands-free kits for talking on their mobile phones when they were driving.

'Carl, there's been an accident. Nina's been cleaned up by some idiot in a truck. Forget what you're doing. Get over to City Hospital. The helicopter has just landed.'

'Is she badly hurt?'

Carl knew that was a silly question as soon as he'd asked it. They wouldn't have flown her down in the helicopter if it wasn't serious.

'There were two fatalities, Carl. Her parents I believe,' said the chief. 'They're not sure she'll make it.'

Carl didn't know what to say.

'You still there, Carl?'

Harry took a look at Carl and pulled over. Carl handed him the phone, opened the door and left his breakfast in the gutter.

'It's Harry, Chief. What's happening?'

Harry listened as Chief Inspector Rankin told him about the accident and directed him to take Carl to City Hospital.

'Call Inspector Reid when you have a moment and bring him up to date on the case. This is not going to be easy, Harry. I think you'd better stay with Carl until you know the state of play. Is that understood?'

'Yes, Chief. I understand.'

Chief Inspector Rankin broke the connection.

Harry waited for Carl to clean himself up. He'd seen Carl in a lot of sticky situations. They'd witnessed the aftermath of some messy murders. They had both lost colleagues on the job, but he'd never seen Carl throw up before.

When Carl shut the door, Harry handed him the water bottle from the console between their seats.

'You okay, Boss?'

Carl shook his head.

'Fuck, Harry. I've only just found her. I don't know what I'll do if I lose her like this. Come on, let's go.'

'I'm sorry, Inspector, we can only release patient details to next of kin,' said the nurse at the reception desk of the intensive care ward.

'I'm the closest she has to next of kin,' said Carl.

The nurse raised an eyebrow. Harry sensed that Carl was about to hit her, so he stepped up next to him at the counter.

'He's not just her boss, he's the boyfriend. If you can't tell us what's going on, find someone who can.'

Harry flashed her a smile. The nurse melted.

'I'll ask Doctor Tran to speak to you when he comes out. You can wait over there.'

'Thank you,' said Harry.

He took Carl by the arm and led him over to the waiting area.

'Thanks, Harry,' said Carl, as they sat down.

'I'm sure you'll return the favour someday, Boss. Do you want a coffee?'

'That sounds like a good idea'.

Harry went to the cafeteria and bought two coffees, which were long gone by the time Dr Tran came out to speak to them.

'She's stable for now, Inspector, but she's not out of the woods by a long shot yet. She's suffered multiple fractures and a punctured lung. She's also got severe bruising to her face and upper body,' said Dr Tran, moving his hand across his chest, 'from the seat restraint. She's also taken a pretty solid blow to the head. We won't know if there is any permanent damage until she regains consciousness.'

'Any idea when that might be?' asked Carl.

'Hard to say,' said Doctor Tran. 'Is there any other next of kin we should be informing?'

'I understand her parents were killed in the accident,' said Carl. 'So for now, until we can track down any other relatives, it's me.'

'You realise she's probably not aware that her parents are dead.'

'I'll worry about that when she regains consciousness, Doctor. We've all had some experience breaking that news to people,' said Carl.

'Yes, I'm sure you have, Inspector. Look, I don't think there is much point in you hanging around here. If you give me a contact number, I'll make sure they call you as soon as she comes round.'

Carl handed him his card. Doctor Tran took it and then spoke to the ward sister to ensure that Carl would be treated as next of kin, and would be called when Nina regained consciousness.

'I'm sorry they gave you the run around, Inspector,' said the ward sister.

'I understand, Sister,' said Carl. 'I know about the rules, and that sometimes they need to be followed.'

'You don't need to wait until she regains consciousness to

come back. We've found it helps the patient if there is someone there for them, even when they're unconscious. Why don't you come back this evening? You'd only be in the way before then.'

Carl was so distracted while they waited for Nina to regain consciousness, that Chief Inspector Rankin confined him to the office. It was the chief's way of making sure someone could keep an eye on him, and of stopping him from messing up in the field.

On Friday morning, Bill Norris, from the Riverland police station, called Carl and confirmed that Nina's parents had been killed in the accident. Bill informed him that he had charged the truck driver for causing death by dangerous driving. The driver's blood alcohol reading had come in at 0.18, considerably higher than the 0.05 legal limit.

When Carl asked Bill what had happened, he told him the idiot had driven into the back of Nina's car at a stop sign, and pushed it into a tree on the other side of the intersection. Bill said he was amazed she'd survived at all. There wasn't much left of her car.

Carl asked Bill if Nina's handbag or mobile phone had survived the crash, and explained that he wanted to see if he could locate any of her extended family. After a short pause, Bill came back on the line and told him he was in luck, and asked if he wanted him to send down her keys as well. Carl agreed that was a good idea, as he'd need to get into her apartment at some stage. Bill said he'd send the package down with one of his constables, who was coming to the city on Saturday for a wedding, and added that one of the neighbours had told them that she thought Don Strong had a brother somewhere in the city. Carl said he'd ask Nina when she came round and thanked him for his help.

After the call, Carl attempted to distract himself from

thinking the worst by reading the reports of the interviews with the friends and neighbours of Michael Murphy and his associates.

All three men lived alone, in well-kept houses within walking distance of each other. Murphy and Boyle were divorced and Morris had never married. Murphy's son claimed that his father was addicted to gambling. Not only was he a bookmaker, he spent a lot of time at the casino. Apparently, although a lot of money passed through his hands, Michael Murphy didn't have much to show for it beyond the bond required to maintain his bookmaker's licence.

According to their neighbours, the three men were friendly guys who seemed to spend a lot of time together.

Murphy's ex had said she hadn't seen him for years and had no desire to. According to her statement, he was a hopeless case, addicted to gambling and booze. Boyle's ex had stated that she was still on good terms with him. She had described Charlie as a loveable rogue, impossible to live with but a great mate if you ever needed a hand. She had told the interviewing officer that she had last seen all three of them at the casino, where they'd met for lunch, a couple of weeks ago. She'd said they had been very excited, as they'd had a big day at the mid-week races and Michael had doubled their money at the tables. With half a million dollars between them, they'd talked about taking a few weeks off and flying up to the Gold Coast for some sun and relaxation.

That story would explain why they weren't home, but when Harry had checked with the airlines, after the big winnings came to light, there was no record of them having flown out of town in the last two weeks.

A search of their houses had failed to uncover any sign of forced entry at the three residences. This suggested to Carl that either they knew their attackers or whatever had happened to them had happened somewhere else. It was only the Murphy house that had been left open. None of them had driven away, as their cars were stilled parked in their garages, and the taxi companies had no record of a booking from any of the missing bookmakers in the last two weeks.

Carl was reading through the last of the reports when he spotted a reference to a grey van. One of Charlie Boyle's neighbours had told the interviewing officer that he had seen a grey van in the driveway of Charlie's house, when he'd arrived home from work on the Thursday night before last. He'd said he hadn't taken much notice, given it was eleven o'clock at night, but he did recall that it was the only time he'd seen the van in Charlie's driveway, and he hadn't seen Charlie since.

Carl wondered whether word of the big win had got out and the trio had been killed as part of a violent robbery.

That theory died when B&A bank confirmed that the four hundred and ninety thousand dollars, deposited electronically into their business account by the casino on that same Thursday, were still there.

If the trio had been bumped off, money obviously wasn't the motive, which led Carl to suspect their disappearance was connected to the Moore murders.

It was two days before Nina regained consciousness. Carl had spent two sleepless nights sitting next to her bed in the hospital, but he was snoozing in his favourite chair by the window at home on Sunday morning when the call came through. He made himself a strong coffee and caught a taxi to the hospital.

Nina was not a pretty sight. Her face was cut and bruised and swollen from where it had hit the windscreen. Her forehead was wrapped in gauze, and her left arm and leg were in plaster casts suspended from a frame above her bed. She was wearing a mask to help her breathe and was connected to several intravenous drips. Carl was tempted to whip out his phone and take a photo before she opened her eyes, but a little voice told him she would never forgive him.

He was relieved to see her eyes open when he sat down in the chair beside her bed, and took hold of her uninjured right hand.

'Hello, sweetheart. Welcome back,' said Carl, squeezing her hand.

Nina smiled at him. At least he thought she did; it was hard to tell.

'What happened?' said Nina. 'How did I end up here?'

'You were hit by a truck.'

'When?'

'Last Thursday.'

Nina took a few moments to process that information.

'What day is it now?'

'Sunday.'

'Thursday, you said.' She paused again as she searched for memories of Thursday. 'Thursday? We were taking Pedro to the vet and then going shopping. Mum wanted to buy...' Nina stopped talking and slowly turned her eyes towards Carl.

Carl could feel his heart beating and the butterflies breaking formation in his gut. He'd told a lot of people bad news but they had all been strangers at the time. Nina was the woman he loved, and she was looking at him with pleading eyes.

'They didn't make it, sweetheart. I'm sorry,' was all he could say before tears clouded his vision.

Nina looked away and closed her eyes. Carl squeezed her hand. There was no response. He checked her vital signs. The light on the heart monitor was bouncing up and down, and her chest was moving as she breathed in and out. He pressed the button for the nurse.

The nurse came in and checked.

'She's gone, again. It's pretty normal. Probably seeing you, and realising where she is, was just too much for her to take in at the moment. I suggest you let her sleep and come back later.'

Carl went home and put himself to bed. He was exhausted. He'd worked long hours before, but this was different. The worry was draining him.

It was dark outside when he awoke. He looked at the clock beside his bed: 6:24. He got up, had a shower, cooked himself a bowl of pasta and ate it with pesto sauce. Then he drove to the hospital.

Nina was still unconscious when he arrived, so he settled in to sit by her side with his weekend newspaper. At ten past nine Nina opened her eyes. She didn't want to talk, so he sat by her bed and held her hand until she went to sleep. He was amazed at how someone, who had been unconscious for the best part of three days, could still be tired. He figured her body must still be busy fixing itself, even if her mind was on holidays.

As he looked at her sleeping, he hoped the blow to her head wouldn't leave any permanent damage. He knew that broken bones repaired themselves, even if they sometimes needed a little bit of extra help from metal inserts, but you never knew what a blow to the head would do. He kissed her good hand and took himself home. He would have to be patient, like everyone else.

CHAPTER 10

STEVE GORDON STARTED his working week riding the elevator up to the eighteenth floor of the Harvey Building with Maria Mahoney, the lawyer that looked after his labour hire contracts. Steve hated elevators. They were either full of people with body odour issues or reeked of the stale smells left behind by previous riders. The fact that he was a little claustrophobic didn't help either. At least this one was an express to the tenth floor and Maria, aware of how uncomfortable elevators made him, knew it was not a good time to discuss last minute details.

On the eighteenth they were asked to wait. This always made Steve smile. It was such an obvious tactic, used to remind him that he wasn't in charge here. Steve didn't mind. He knew who held all the cards. Besides, it gave him an opportunity to recover from the elevator ride and chat with Maria. She was always up with the latest gossip from the construction industry.

After the standard fifteen minute wait, they were shown into the office of John Harvey, project manager for the company that had won the contract to convert a row of derelict warehouses into apartments, as part of the government's grand plan for redeveloping the port district.

'Sorry about the wait, Steve. Dad wanted to brief me on a few last minute details to make sure I didn't let you take advantage of us,' said John, as they entered his office.

'How is the old man?' said Steve, as he and Maria took their seats at the table opposite John, with whom they had worked on several other projects.

'Still the same. Thinks he's the only one who knows how to do anything,' said John.

'Yeah, well I know all about that,' said Steve.

'So, what's it like now that he's no longer around?' said John.

'It's early days, John. Bit scary knowing that it all rides with me but at least I have his systems to work with, and Maria here to keep me on the straight and narrow.'

Maria smiled knowingly. She'd known these two boys for twenty years and their fathers for considerably longer. While they were bantering, she extracted the contract she had drafted from her brief case and opened it on the table in front of her.

The terms of the contract were fairly standard. Steve's company would supply the labourers and tradespeople required to complete the project, and take responsibility for paying them and making sure they showed up when required. The negotiations were about how many of each type of worker would be required, the work schedule and the overall payment.

John's goal was to keep the payment low and the value of the workers high. Steve's goal was to maximise the payment and minimise the number of workers. Maria's role was to keep them on task and get the contract signed before they left John's office.

In the end, the number of labourers and tradespeople was determined by the work schedule required to complete the project on time, and this was where Steve held all the cards. If John wanted workers he had to get them from Steve's company. Steve knew that and John's father knew that, so it was no surprise that the payment terms offered by the company were sufficient to expedite the signing of the contract so that work could begin.

Steve, like his father before him, made most of his money by controlling the labour hire market in the construction industry. None of the big firms had their own workers these days. It was too expensive. It was much easier to work with a labour hire company, who took on all the employer obligation issues and responsibilities.

Con Gordon, Steve's father, had seen it all coming. Through a complex web of associated companies, and a mix of legal and illegal activities that supplied his workers with whatever they required to stay happy, Con had commandeered the available pool of construction workers into his labour hire company.

And then there was the team of enforcers Steve had inherited, along with the rest of the empire, following the death of his father.

When Steve had taken charge, he had reviewed the business and decided there were a few operations that needed to go. The Moore operation, for one, had outlived its usefulness, and Steve, who had always resented the hold Kieran Moore held over his father, decided to shut it down, and shut it down permanently. There was no way he was going to live with the threat that Kieran could exploit or expose him.

His father might have trusted Kieran, who had gone to prison to protect him, but a lot of things had changed since the days both Kieran Moore and Con Gordon had been Hells Angels pushing heroin and cocaine to rich kids.

Steve had never trusted Sean Moore either, and Sean's demand for a bigger cut of the action following Con's death had decided the issue for him.

With the kid eliminated, Steve believed he could shut the book on that unhappy chapter of the firm's business.

After dropping Maria at her office, he called Clare to confirm that she had despatched the package. His call went through to her voice mail. When she hadn't returned his call by the time he reached his office, he was somewhat annoyed. He tried Malcolm's number.

Steve didn't like Malcolm. Malcolm was one of those guys who didn't scare easily. It had amused Steve that his big tough boys, who had eliminated numerous targets for him, couldn't bring themselves to kill the kid. It was like they had some sort of code of honour. Fortunately, Clare was a cold-blooded killer who liked to spend money.

'She's not here, mate. She and the package weren't here when we got back Saturday night,' said Malcolm.

'Do you know where she is?' asked Steve.

'Maybe she's taking time out after disposing of the package. Wait up, I'll check her room,' said Malcolm.

Steve listened as Malcolm walked through the house and opened drawers and wardrobe doors in the room Clare used when she stayed with them.

'Her stuff's gone,' said Malcolm.

'Do you know where she goes to chill out?' said Steve.

'No, mate. She's not the sort of girl I ask personal questions,' said Malcolm.

'Tell her to call me when she gets back,' said Steve.

By Wednesday, when he hadn't heard from Clare and there had been no reports in the media about Toby Moore's body being found, Steve was starting to feel anxious. If Clare had done the job Toby's body should have been found by now. Leaving the body somewhere it could be found was one of the instructions he had given her for the Moore job.

He'd left several messages on her voice mail, and Malcolm had simply said he hadn't heard from her when he'd called him.

It seemed Clare had disappeared and taken the kid with her. He hoped she hadn't had some sort of conversion moment.

CHAPTER 11

WHILE LOUISE WAS EATING lunch on Thursday, the police pathologist's office called to tell her she could arrange for Kieran's and Sean's bodies to be collected for burial.

Louise rang Ron Flint. They agreed to meet at three thirty to discuss final arrangements. After speaking with Ron, Louise called Terry and asked him to come over for the meeting with the funeral director.

Terry and Helen arrived at three o'clock, with their protective services officer, who settled in for a conversation with his colleague, sitting in the outdoor setting on Louise's front veranda.

The perfect hostess, Louise made them a coffee and a plate of buttered scones.

'You boys must be getting bored with all this sitting around looking out for us,' she said, as she placed the afternoon tea on the table between them.

'Thanks, Mrs Moore. You know you don't have to do this,' said the younger of the two.

'My pleasure, love. Make sure you eat those scones before they go cold.'

She left them to it and went inside to sit with Terry and Helen to wait for Ron Flint to arrive.

'So what are you thinking, Mum? Cremation or interment?' asked Terry.

'I'm gonna burn the bastard!'

'What about Grandpa?'

'Him too!'

'Well, that simplifies it a bit. Why did you ask me to come over if you've already made up your mind?'

Louise put on her 'I am your mother' face.

'Terry, we need to work out what sort of service to have and who is going to say what. I think a few people might show up, so we need to put on a good show. Your father might have been a real bastard at times, but we can't say that. We need to find something decent to say about him, and Kieran.'

'Who do you think will come?' asked Terry.

'Your father's mates, you know, that lot he drinks with at the pub, maybe some of those bookies he spent so much time with, and maybe some of your customers,' said Louise. 'God knows who will show up for Kieran. He had a pretty colourful life. Maybe some of his friends from his Hells Angels days will turn up, if any of them are still alive. I guess that woman he stayed with up the river will come, you know, the one that came to Martha's funeral.'

'Sally Arthur,' said Helen. 'I liked her.'

One of the protective services officers escorted Ron Flint into the dining room.

'Are you in some danger, Mrs Moore?' asked Ron, as Louise stood up and shook his hand.

'The police seem to think so, Mr Flint. Let me introduce my son, Terry, and my daughter in-law, Helen.'

'Sorry to hear about your son,' said Ron, sitting down next to Helen.

'Thank you, Mr Flint. As you can see, we aren't having a very good week,' said Helen.

'Yes, well let's hope you won't be needing my services any further. There are a lot of people out there praying for his safe return.'

'Thank you.'

Ron turned to Louise, as Helen, touched by his concern, struggled to regain her composure.

'You mentioned cremation, Mrs Moore. Are you still wanting to go with that?'

'Yes.'

'Are you wanting a church service or a chapel service at the crematorium?'

'We're not church people, Mr Flint.'

'So, no priest or minister?'

'No, we just want something simple, you know, tell a bit of the story of their lives and an opportunity to say what they meant to us,' said Louise.

'I see. I can show you a few sample booklets from similar services we have conducted to give you some ideas, if you think that might help.'

'That sounds like a good idea,' said Helen. 'It's not like we've had much practice at this sort of thing.'

'And, you can probably find some others on the internet,' said Ron.

Ron pulled some papers from his brief case and outlined various approaches they could take.

Then he told them that the earliest the service could be held was two o'clock Monday afternoon, as the crematorium was booked solid until then.

Louise served coffee and hot buttered scones with strawberry jam and cream, while they considered Ron's PowerPoint presentation on the range of coffins suitable for a cremation. Louise chose the stained pinewood, only because Flinders Funerals didn't carry the cardboard version Kevin had heard about.

Before signing the paperwork, they discussed the size of the expected crowd and the number of funeral cars that would be required, in addition to the two hearses.

Louise told Ron that they really had no idea how many people would show up, so he suggested they use the bigger of the two available chapels. They decided one limousine would be plenty, since it only had to carry the three of them.

When Ron asked about payment, Louise picked up her handbag from under the table and paid him in cash.

———————

'Where'd that money come from?' asked Terry.

'Your father doesn't have any use for it where he is,' said Louise.

'That's not what I asked you,' said Terry.

'Let's just say I went through your father's pockets.'

'You want me to believe you found nearly seven thousand dollars in Dad's pockets?'

'Well, he did go to the trots on Friday night, didn't he? He had a stack of envelopes stuffed with cash in his jacket pocket. He must have had one of those good nights he was so fond of telling me about.'

Terry looked at Helen, who simply rolled her eyes.

He decided not to press it any further.

———————

On the way back to their place, Terry sat in the back with Helen, while their protective services officer drove.

'I don't know how much more of this waiting for news I can take,' said Helen.

'I know what you mean,' said Terry.

'Do you? I don't think you have any idea what it means to be a mother. You aren't the one who carried him for nine months. You aren't the one who went through all that pain to give birth to him. It's tearing me apart inside not knowing where he is or if I'll ever see him again!'

The protective services officer kept his eyes on the road and thanked God he wasn't Terry Moore.

Terry held her hand and felt tears running down his face. No, he couldn't feel her pain. He'd never been a mother but he was a father desperate to see his son again.

When Helen realised he was crying, she cuddled up to him.

'I'm sorry. I know it's not your fault. I know it's hard for you too. We need to stick together. I'm sorry.'

They rode home in silence, each lost in their own sense of loss and pain.

Kevin decided to go home early. Nothing was happening at the office and he was worried about Mary. She was still off work and hadn't answered the phone when he had called to see how she was.

He'd joked with Louise about Mary being suicidal but he hadn't really believed that she was, so he wasn't prepared for the scene that greeted him when he walked into the living room, and found her sprawled across the sofa, unconscious.

It took him a couple of minutes to notice the discarded packet, that had once held her sleeping pills, next to an empty bottle, embellished with the name of his favourite Irish whiskey, on the floor next to the arm of the sofa under her head. Then it dawned on him what she'd done.

Without thinking, he pulled out his mobile phone, dialled triple zero and asked for an ambulance.

Mary was still breathing when the ambulance arrived, so there was a good chance she would survive. It looked like he had found her in time.

As the ambulance drove away with its lights flashing and sirens sounding, Kevin wondered if he'd done the right thing. His life would be a lot simpler without Mary being in it, especially the Mary that had been in it for the last few months.

He sat in the kitchen and called Christine, Mary's sister. Then he called Helen.

Poor Helen, he thought, as he keyed in her number, now she'll have something else to worry about, as if she hasn't got enough on her plate already.

CHAPTER 12

On Friday morning, Steve had the TV news on while he was eating breakfast with Trish, his second wife.

Trish had been his mistress while Barbara, the mother of his two adult children, had been dying of lung cancer. He'd married her a few months after Barbara's death, despite his father's protestations that she was a gold digger. Steve didn't see it that way, even if she was twenty years younger than him and the same age as his older son. At least the boys hadn't said anything, and it hadn't taken Trish long to win the old boy over.

As Con's life was ending, it had been Trish sitting with him on those lonely nights when he couldn't sleep because of the chemo. That was when Con got to know her and realised she was a girl with a heart.

As they were discussing their plans for the weekend, Steve was momentarily distracted by the image of a woman dressed in black leathers displayed on the screen. Although he couldn't see her face, he knew who it was: Clare.

'Are you okay, honey?' asked Trish. 'You look like you've seen a ghost.'

'That story was about the murder of the guy who landscaped

the front garden for us, when we first bought this house,' said Steve.

'Oh.'

'I haven't seen him in ages. Guess I'll have to call someone else to redo the garden,' said Steve. 'What were you saying about tomorrow night?'

As soon as he'd left the house, Steve called Malcolm.

'Have you seen the morning news?'

'It's on the front page of the paper, mate,' said Malcolm. 'You'd have to know her pretty well to identify her from that photo though, I reckon.'

'Have you heard from her?'

'Not a peep.'

'What's it say in the paper?'

'Police don't know who she is. They're asking anyone who thinks they might know who she is to call in,' said Malcolm.

'Let's hope she's reading the paper then. If she calls, tell her to disappear and to take the package with her, if she hasn't been able to get rid of it.'

Steve ended the call. Clare was his most ruthless and trusted operative. She'd never failed him before. Then it hit him. He'd never asked her to kill a child before. He shook his head in disbelief. He couldn't picture her being the loving or motherly type. It was bad enough knowing that George and Malcolm couldn't bring themselves to kill the boy, when they knew they should have.

Clare's usual targets were nuisances like Sean Moore or the idiots who thought they didn't need to engage with his labour hire firm to get things built in the city. Why the fuck couldn't Toby Moore be a little shit like most kids, instead of being an adorable kid with puppy dog eyes. Whoever his mother was, thought Steve, she must be gorgeous to have produced a kid like that, considering the genes contributed by his father.

Shit, he thought. Terry Moore would probably be able to identify Clare from the photograph, and probably had done so already, given that it was his father she had killed. He wondered how much Terry would know about her, apart from the fact that she delivered or picked up packages from Kieran and Sean.

She'd never said anything about Terry but it wasn't like he'd asked her either. Maybe Terry had never seen her, as he was the one who actually did all the work in Sean's so-called landscape gardening service.

Steve decided there wasn't much he could do about it. There was nothing written down that would connect him to the Moores but that wasn't the case when it came to Clare, although there was nothing that could provide a direct link.

The phones used by Clare, George and Malcolm were all registered in the name of one of his companies, so that all the calls looked like exchanges between the boss and some of his employees. He had no reason to suspect anyone was listening in, and only the four of them knew who had which phone.

'I hope the bitch has enough sense to disappear,' he said to himself, as he parked his car. 'I'll fucking kill her myself, if she shows up again.'

Toby was up looking for something to eat for breakfast when Clare woke. She could hear him opening and closing cupboard doors in the kitchen, from where she lay in the bed they had shared. It was the first time she'd had another person in the bed with her in ages, and it had been a relief not to have to worry about her performance as a sexual athlete. And, unlike a lot of men she had slept with, Toby did not snore or take up more that his fair share of the bed.

She looked at herself in the mirror. Her hair was a mess and there were black smudges around her eyes, the remains of yesterday's eye makeup, she hoped. After listening to the sounds from the kitchen for a while, she got out of the bed, went to the bathroom, had a pee and washed her face. Then she pulled on some track pants and went into the kitchen.

Toby was standing at the table, dressed in his underwear and a tee-shirt, buttering himself a couple of slices of toast and waiting for a small saucepan of milk to boil. He'd found a loaf of bread in the freezer and a carton of long life milk in the pantry.

'Do we have any coffee?' he asked, as she walked in.

'What happened to good morning?' asked Clare.

'Good morning, Clare. Do we have any coffee?' said Toby, with a sheepish smile.

'Do little kids like you drink coffee?' asked Clare.

'My Dad says it's okay if I have it in hot milk.'

Toby dropped the knife and turned to the stove at the sound of boiling milk rising to the top of the saucepan. Clare watched as he expertly lifted the saucepan from the ring and placed it down on the sink.

'Do you want some jam to go with that toast?'

'Yes, thanks.'

'How about you put a couple of slices in the toaster for me?' said Clare. 'I'll find you some coffee.'

When they'd finished breakfast, Toby asked her what she was planning to do.

'George told me you wanted a holiday away from home. Is that right?'

'That was the plan. It doesn't seem like such a great idea now.'

'Why did you think it would be a great idea in the first place?'

'Did your parents ever fight?'

'Not much. My Dad was a soldier. He was away a lot. My mother always made the most of it when he was home. Do your parents fight?'

'It's been horrible. My Mum's been yelling at my Dad for months.'

'What have they been fighting about? Not you I hope.'

'Nah. Mum reckons Dad does whatever Grandpa says. She wants him to grow up and think for himself. I heard her say she was sick of having to treat him like another child, and that he couldn't be trusted with money,' said Toby.

'What's your mother do?'

'She works at a law firm, and she's studying to become a lawyer,' said Toby, with pride in his voice.

'And your Dad, what does he do?'

'He grows plants and looks after other people's gardens. Mum says he has a gift for plants.'

'And, you want them to stop fighting?'

'Yeah. I want them to get back together.'

'What, they've separated?'

'Yeah, they had a big fight. Mum was really angry. Dad's been staying with Grandma. I have to go there after school.'

'Whose idea was it for this holiday thing?'

'Grandpa Kieran. He reckoned that if I went away with him for the weekend, without telling anyone, they'd be so worried about me that they'd get back together.'

Clare smiled at his earnest telling of the story.

'Well, mate, we are going to have to lay low for a while before I can take you home.'

'Why's that? Why can't you just take me home?'

'Remember the conversation we had yesterday, when you asked me what was going to happen to you?'

Toby nodded.

'You were right. The man told me to kill you.'

Toby sat very still. Clare leant over and tousled his hair.

'Relax, I'm not going to hurt you. George was right. You're just a kid, and a pretty gorgeous one at that. If things were different, I'd keep you for myself.'

'Perhaps we can be friends,' said Toby.

'Perhaps. But for now, we need to keep a low profile so that I can keep you alive.'

'What's that mean?'

'First off, it means you need to have a shower. While you're doing that, I'll wash your clothes. Then, I'll go and buy us some fresh stuff to eat. I haven't been up here for a couple of weeks.'

'Are you going to leave me here or take me with you?'

'You'll have to stay here. Everybody in the state is on the lookout for you.'

'What if I run away?'

'We have to trust each other, Toby. I'm going to trust you to stay here and do what I ask. Besides, we are a long way from anywhere and you'd only get lost, and I'd have to come and find you. That would not make me happy.'

Toby thought about what George had said the previous day when Clare had left the room.

'What am I going to wear if you wash my clothes?'

'You can wear some of mine until yours are dry. I'll get you a tee shirt and one of my track suits. We can roll up the sleeves and the legs. At least you'll be warm. Now get out of those dirty clothes and get into the shower. I'll put some clothes on the bed for you.'

Toby went into the bedroom, stripped off his clothes and then walked into the bathroom to use the shower. Clare picked up his clothes and wrote down the size of each item. She turned up her nose at the smell of his underpants and socks, as she gathered them up and took them to the small laundry at the rear of the cottage.

The smell brought back a memory of her mother complaining about her brother's football gear, which he often left in his kit bag for several days after the game.

She stood and remembered her little brother John. He'd been killed in a helicopter crash during a training exercise, shortly after he'd been accepted into the Special Air Service regiment. Recalling that her mother had cried for weeks gave her an appreciation of what Toby's mother must be feeling. She took a deep breath and went into the bedroom to find her little man something to wear.

When Toby was dressed, Clare had a shower and got dressed in jeans and a sweater. She found her boots under the bed, where she had left them two weeks ago, checked them for spiders, and then slipped them on.

While the washing machine was doing its thing, Clare left Toby with a book and went out to the garage, where she put a cover on her bike and secured her weapons in the cellar under the garage floor. She checked her mobile phone for messages and then switched it off, and left it with her weapons. Then it was time to resume her life as Alicia Brown.

She fired up the Ford Focus she kept in the garage and backed it out. Before leaving, she went into the house to check on Toby.

'Sorry there's no TV, mate. Reception's hopeless out here in any case. I'll be back in a couple of hours. There's a clock in the bedroom, okay? If you want to draw or write things down, there's plenty of paper and pencils and things in my desk over there. Help yourself.'

'What will I do if you don't come back?'

'I'll come back. I promise.'

She took one last look at him wrapped up in her oversized

track suit sitting on the couch with a book. She smiled. It would be so nice to have a life like this. He waved to her like he didn't have a care in the world but that question he had asked told her that he was just being brave.

I hope he doesn't do anything silly while I'm away, she thought, as she closed the door and set out to resupply the cottage so they could comfortably stay for a week or so.

Once Clare had driven off, Toby decided to take a look around the cottage. Apart from the living room, which was by far the biggest room, there was the bedroom they had shared - that had been something different, sleeping in the same bed with a woman who wasn't his mother. He wondered what his mother would have to say about that when he told her.

The bathroom was an en-suite to the bedroom, and then at the far end of the living room, there was the kitchen, which had a door leading to a small laundry, where the washing machine was washing his clothes. It looked to Toby like this was a place designed for one.

After wandering through the house, Toby slipped on his shoes and went outside to see the place in daylight. He found himself standing at the end of a very long track, leading back along the floor of a valley that seemed to go on forever. He looked up and down both sides of the tree lined valley. He couldn't see any other houses. The only sounds were courtesy of Mother Nature. Looking up into the sky, he spotted a vapour trail moving across the clear blue, as if a piece of invisible chalk was drawing a straight line for him to see. He felt very small and vulnerable, as if he was standing at the bottom of a very deep well.

He went back inside and locked the door. When the washing machine stopped, he took his clothes out and put them in the dryer. Then he sat down with the book he had found on her bookshelf to wait for Clare to come home.

After what had seemed like forever to Toby, he heard a car coming down the track leading to the house. He looked out the window and was relieved to see Clare's Ford Focus approaching. He waited until the car had stopped in the space between the house and the garage before opening the door and going out to meet her.

Clare greeted his appearance on the veranda with a wave and a huge smile. She was relieved he hadn't run away, and pleased he had decided to trust her with his life.

Toby helped her carry in the shopping, just like he did with his mother. Clare showed him the clothes she had bought for him - a pile of underpants and socks, a pair of jeans and a couple of tee-shirts.

'Is that the clothes dryer I can hear?' said Clare.

'The washing machine stopped, so I put my clothes in the dryer. That's what Mum does when it's not sunny outside.'

'Okay, let's take the tickets off these and we can give them a quick wash, so you'll have something to change into tomorrow.'

Clare handed him the scissors, so he could cut off the labels attached to the clothes, while she put away the food items she had purchased. Then she showed him the paper.

There was a front page story about him, with his school photograph, and a plea from his parents for whoever had him to bring him home. At the bottom of the story there was a telephone number for anyone who thought they had seen him to ring.

'Looks like the first part of your plan is working,' said Clare, as Toby read the story again. 'Your parents sound worried to me.'

CHAPTER 13

Terry was waiting for the water to boil so he could cook pasta for tea, when the telephone rang. He looked at Helen sitting dejectedly in the living room and decided he'd better answer it himself.

'Moore residence.'

'Terry, it's Kevin. Mary's tried to top herself. I've just packed her off in an ambulance. Fuck, Terry, I didn't see this coming.'

'Shit.' Terry was momentarily dumbfounded; then his mind kicked into gear. 'Which hospital?'

'They're taking her to City,' said Kevin.

'Okay, I'll tell Helen and we'll meet you there.'

'Thanks. Tell Helen I've called Christine.'

Terry put the receiver back on the wall mount and went into the living room. The ramifications of what Mary had done hit him. It was bad enough with Toby being missing, and his father and grandfather being killed. Now that stupid, stuck-up bitch that hated his guts was claiming her moment in the spotlight.

He looked at Helen. She looked like death warmed up.

'Who was that?' she asked, in a faraway voice.

'Your father.'

'What did he want?'

'He's in a bit of a state.'

She turned and looked up at him with 'please explain' written across her face.

'Your Mum's tried to kill herself.'

'What?'

'He didn't give me any details. Just said he'd sent her off in an ambulance to City Hospital.'

Helen felt instantly awake, like a student of Zen whacked by her master for falling asleep during meditation.

'Tell the guy out the front we have to go to the hospital and turn off the stove. I'll just go to the loo.'

Bloody hell, she thought, as she sat on the toilet. First, I lose my son and now my mother tries to kill herself. What have I done to deserve this, she wondered.

If there is a God, she mused, he sure has a twisted sense of humour.

Kevin was pacing up and down the waiting room, speaking to Louise on his mobile phone, when Terry and Helen got to the hospital.

'Got to go, the kids are here.'

Helen rushed over and embraced him.

'Is she going to be alright?' she asked.

'She might survive, but I doubt she's going to be alright,' said Kevin.

'Is Auntie Christine coming?' asked Helen.

'Said she'd be here as soon as she could get away. She was still at work when I called her.'

'Thanks for coming so quickly,' said Kevin, turning to Terry.

'No problem,' said Terry, although hospitals always gave him the creeps. He was not comfortable in places that seemed to treat people like machines, and insisted that you complied with their routine. Terry had hated hospitals ever since he'd been admitted as a kid with appendicitis. He was always amazed that, in a place where you needed to sleep to recover, they made so much noise and woke you up to stick some instrument into you to see if you were still alive.

The last time he'd been in a hospital was when Martha was sick, and that hadn't ended well - she'd died, and she wasn't even sixty. The time before that had been when Toby was born and, if he hadn't been so excited about becoming a father, he doubted whether he'd have been able to stay until the very end of Helen's long labour.

They sat on the seats and waited.

'What did she do?' asked Helen, to break the silence.

'Looks like she swallowed a whole box of her sleeping pills and washed them down with a bottle of my favourite whiskey,' said Kevin, wondering whether she'd done that bit to taunt him. 'She hasn't been herself lately. She's been depressed about work, she was worried about you and Terry breaking up, and then with Toby going missing, maybe I should have seen this coming.'

'I don't think she was worried about us breaking up, Dad. I think she was more worried that we'd get back together,' said Helen, remembering some recent lectures, she could hardly call them conversations, she'd listened to her mother deliver over the phone or across the kitchen table.

'I tried to get her to speak to someone about all the things she was worked up about. She wouldn't listen to me though. Told me I didn't know the first thing about women or menopause. I agreed with that, but she still wouldn't go and see anybody, except that quack she's been going to for years. And what did he do? Gave her anti-depressants and sleeping pills. Fat lot of good that did!'

Kevin put his head in his hands. Helen put her arm across his shoulders.

'Don't blame yourself, Dad. We all know how pig-headed she can be. She's always right, according to her. That's why I gave up arguing with her years ago,' said Helen.

'Yeah, sometimes I think you did the right thing getting out early. I might follow your lead,' said Kevin.

Helen was a little taken aback. She'd never considered that her parents would split up.

'You can't be serious, Dad. You guys have been together for thirty years.'

'We're not as close as we used to be. She's changed over the last few years. She'll drag me under if I stay. I've got to think of myself sometimes. I can't take any more of her mood swings. If she pulls through this, I'll help her get back on her feet, if she'll let me, and then, then we'll see.'

Terry didn't say a word. Mary wasn't his favourite person. She had made it abundantly clear to him over the years that she regarded him as Helen's biggest mistake. Mary doted on Toby, not out of love as most grandmothers do, but as a strategy designed to win him away from his father. The fact that she had failed only made her loathe Terry all the more, and redouble her efforts to get Helen to leave him.

Initially, Mary had been overjoyed when Terry had retreated to his parents' house following the massive fight he'd had, and lost, with Helen. She'd moved in for the kill with all guns blazing, only to be shot down in flames by Helen, who had told her she had no intention of leaving Terry, and that she only wanted him to grow up and get out from under his father's shadow. Still, Mary had kept at it right up to the weekend, when Toby had run off with Kieran.

Helen looked at Terry and could almost read his thoughts from the look on his face. She laughed to herself, as it struck her that here they were, the three people that Mary loved to torment the most, worrying about whether she would wake up from her self-induced coma.

They were on their second coffees when Christine arrived.

'Sorry, Kevin, a few emergencies of my own today. Any news?'

'We're still waiting,' said Kevin.

'I'll see what I can find out,' said Christine.

After ten minutes, Christine re-appeared from within the labyrinth of the emergency department into which she had walked to find out about her sister, and sat down next to Kevin.

She placed an arm around his shoulders and leant in close.

'Sorry, Kevin. She must have taken the pills some time before you found her. They've tried everything. It didn't work. We've lost her.'

Christine looked over at Helen and Terry, who were holding on to each other as if they each needed the other for support to stay up. What a week those kids have had, she thought. She hoped to God that Toby was going to come home, soon. She couldn't bear to think what would happen to Helen if he didn't come home. She'd seen too many women destroyed by the loss of a child to believe Helen would come through unscathed.

Helen noticed Christine was back, and the tears on her father's face. She looked at her auntie.

'She's gone,' said Christine.

Mary looked peaceful, as if she was sleeping, as they stood around the gurney holding her body for a brief farewell. None of them were prepared for this.

Helen had believed her mother would always be there, telling her what to do whether she wanted her advice or not.

Terry was nonplussed. He simply couldn't compute the fact of another death.

Kevin was in a state of shock. There had been times when he had hated who she had become, but he had tried to support her, despite all of her rebuffs. Now she had walked out on him, before he'd mustered the courage to walk out on her.

Christine thought of all the good times she had shared with her sister growing up, and the desolate perspective Mary had chosen to take of life. So much potential for goodness lost in all that envy and jealousy that she had allowed to consume her, and all that anger she had directed at Terry, refusing to see that Helen loved him for who he was, not for what Mary wanted him to be. What a waste, she thought, as she gazed at her sister's lifeless body. It all could have turned out differently, if she'd only seen the good instead of the bad in people.

At home Helen just sat. She didn't want to talk. What was there to say anyway, she thought, as she watched Terry twisting a tea towel endlessly in his hands and staring into space. She could feel her lights going out but it looked like Terry's were already extinguished.

It had been around eight o'clock when they had returned from the hospital. Now, here they were at midnight, still sitting in the kitchen with uneaten, stone cold pasta in the plates on the table between them.

Terry came out of his trance and noticed the time, and then Helen, who was sitting at the table opposite him.

'Come on, sweetheart. Time for bed,' he said, helping her up from her chair.

She followed him meekly to the bedroom, where he undressed her and put her into the bed.

Shortly after ten on Friday morning, they were woken by the sound of the telephone ringing. Terry rolled out of bed to answer it. Helen pulled the covers up over her head and stayed put. She didn't want to talk to anyone.

'Terry, it's Mum. I've just heard about Mary. Is Helen alright?'

'Rock bottom, I'd say, Mum. It's been the week from hell and it's not over yet. Who knows if the worse news is still to come?'

'Don't go there, love. Stay strong, and hang on to the hope that whoever's got him will give him back. Don't give up. If you give up, you could end up like poor Mary.'

'I wasn't expecting her to do that.'

'I think she had some serious issues on her plate. A few things hadn't gone her way and Toby being abducted was just the last straw, according to Kevin.'

Well, that explains how she knows, thought Terry. Kevin, obviously, had called her. A little voice in his head told him that something wasn't right here, as he was under the impression that the relationship between his parents and his in-laws wasn't that close, given Mary's dismissive attitude towards him and his parents. As far as he could recall, they had only ever spoken to each other during those times they had been drawn together by the events in Toby's life. He wondered what had prompted Kevin to reach out to Louise, but wasn't game enough to ask.

'Keep me posted, love. I'll let you go to look after Helen. Give her my love.'

'Bye, Mum.'

Despite Terry's efforts to coax her out, Helen couldn't find the strength required to get out of bed. She knew she should do something but she just couldn't face Terry or anybody else. It was so much easier to just stay where she was and not bother with anything. She didn't even want to eat. The food Terry had brought in for her sat untouched on the tray, where he had left it.

She had been so strong since Toby had disappeared. Even after they'd learnt that Kieran and Sean had been killed, she'd been the one keeping them going with her belief that Toby would come home safe and sound. But now, all those doubts and fears she had pushed away were back, along with a massive dose of guilt.

She knew there was no way she could have prevented the murders of Kieran and Sean. They'd somehow brought that on themselves with the drug stuff. But if she hadn't had that big fight with Terry, if she'd only been happy to accept him the way he was, instead of insisting he change, there would have been no separation and Toby would not have run off with Kieran.

In Helen's mind, it was all her fault. She'd married Terry, despite her mother's opposition, and she'd defended her choice in the face of her mother's recent campaign to make the separation permanent. Now her mother had committed suicide.

Helen couldn't help but feel responsible for that as well. If she'd listened to her mother, she would never have married Terry, and even if she'd still gone ahead and had Toby, he would never have met Kieran, and if he'd never met Kieran he wouldn't have run off with him. He'd be here with her and her mother would still be alive.

Terry came in to see how she was feeling. She didn't want to look at him.

'I just want to die. Leave me alone.'

She heard him leave the room but, when she opened her eyes some time later, he was sitting in a chair next to the bed reading.

Terry smiled when he noticed she was looking at him.

'Thought I told you to leave me alone.'

'You've told me to do a lot of things that never got done,' said Terry.

Wasn't that the truth, she thought.

'What time is it?'

Terry looked at his watch. 'It's nearly five o'clock.'

'I'm famished.'

'I'm not surprised. You haven't eaten anything since lunch yesterday. I've got a chicken in the oven. Why don't you get up and have a shower, while I make some veggies to go with it?'

'Can you get me a drink? My mouth tastes like shit.'

Terry handed her the water bottle he had placed on the bedside cabinet.

Helen took a swig from the bottle. 'Thanks, you're a lifesaver.'

After they had eaten, Terry suggested they go and see how Kevin was doing. He didn't tell her that he had spoken to Kevin earlier, and told him that she had dropped her bundle, or that Kevin had told him he had found a suicide note of sorts.

Helen agreed. She knew she had to do something, otherwise she'd sink into that dark hole of self-loathing again.

They arrived at Kevin's, with their protective services officer, just after seven o'clock, to witness the exodus of a group of Kevin's mates, who had spent the better part of the afternoon consoling Kevin and drinking his whiskey.

'Feeling any better?' Kevin asked Helen, as she embraced him.

'It's all got on top of me, Dad. It's bad enough with Toby being missing, without all this other stuff. I never thought Mum would kill herself. Why do you think she did it? Did she leave a note or anything?'

'Take a seat. I'll just get it.'

Helen sat next to Terry on the sofa, without realising that it was the place Mary had chosen to end her life.

'Wonder how much whiskey he's had today?' she asked Terry. 'Sure smells like he's been hitting the bottle.'

'You saw who was leaving as we arrived. I only see those guys with Kevin in the pub,' said Terry.

Kevin came back into the room with an envelope.

'I found this in the bag she takes to work.'

Kevin handed the envelope to Helen. It looked like something official from the council Mary had worked for. She turned the envelope over with the intention of extracting its contents. On the back were some words in Mary's handwriting:

I guess you'll find this if I'm dead. You'll be wanting to know why. Well here's the why - I've lost my daughter to that idiot - Terry, I've lost my grandson to some crazed murderer, I've lost you to some bimbo - don't think I didn't know, and now they're taking away my job. There's nothing left for me to live for.

I was going to say sorry but I'm not. Fuck the lot of you!

Helen passed the envelope to Terry.

'Shit, Dad. What's been going on over here?'

'Have a look at the letter inside,' said Kevin.

Terry pulled out the letter and handed it to Helen, who read it, and then gave it back to him.

'I thought she hadn't gone into work this week because she was upset about Toby. I had no idea she had been terminated last Friday for harassing her colleagues. She didn't say anything about it to me,' said Kevin.

'What's this bit about a bimbo, Dad?'

Kevin squirmed in his seat and looked at his hands.

'Things haven't been good between me and your mother for some time. It got worse when she started getting all those mood swings and hot flushes. We've been sleeping in separate rooms.'

'Is there a bimbo?' asked Helen.

'There's another woman. I wouldn't call her a bimbo, though. She's not much younger than Mary.'

'It's Mum, isn't it?' said Terry.

'Louise?' Helen was incredulous. 'Why on earth did you say that?'

Terry looked at Kevin, who looked as if he'd been caught with his pants down. 'I'm right, aren't I?'

'How did you know?' said Kevin.

'What? You're saying it's true?' Helen was on her feet standing over her father. 'What the fuck have you been doing?' She didn't wait for an answer. She turned on Terry. 'How long have you known about this?'

'I only worked it out this afternoon, and I still wasn't sure until those words popped out and Kevin looked like he'd shit himself.'

An uneasy silence settled on the room.

'How long has this been going on for, Dad?'

'About six months. Started after Toby's last birthday party,' said Kevin.

'And there I was thinking I was responsible for Mum killing herself. Shit, Dad. It's like you gave her the pills yourself.'

'You don't know what it's been like living with her since you two got married. Something changed after that.'

'What changed, Dad, was she found out she couldn't control my life.'

'Yeah, well she tried her hardest to control mine. As I said last night, I was on the verge of leaving her, she'd become insufferable to be with. Nothing was ever right as far as she was concerned. If she was like that at work, it's no wondered they fired her. She'd turned into a real bitch.'

Kevin was crying now. The combination of pent up emotions and too much whiskey effectively removing any resistance he had to tears. In one way, it was such a relief that she was gone, but that didn't stop him from feeling guilty for betraying her behind her back with someone she hated, or feeling the sadness flowing from the realisation that he had once loved her.

Once his tears started, they couldn't get any sense out of Kevin. It was the first time Helen had seen her father as a blubbering drunk, although as Terry helped her put him to bed, she realised it wasn't the first time she'd put a blubbering drunk to bed.

Once they'd tucked him in they headed home.

'How did you know it was your mother?' Helen asked, as they drove home, followed by their protective services officer.

'Remember the phone ringing this morning?'

'I think so.'

'That was my mother. She wanted to know how we were seeing that your mother had died.'

'Why did that make you think she was Dad's bimbo?'

'She let it slip that Kevin had told her about your mother,' said Terry.

'You got it from that?'

'Well, there were a couple of other things floating around inside my head that sort of came together when your father said his girlfriend was not much younger than your mother.'

'Like what?'

'Like the new twinkle in my mother's eye every time she was in the same room as your father, her renewed interest in keeping herself in shape. Did you know she's joined a gym?'

'Yeah, Curves, it's for women. I was thinking of going with her. What else?'

Terry turned the car into the driveway and pulled up behind his truck.

'The final bit was a memory of Toby telling me he had seen a car, 'like Grandpa's', driving away from Mum's place one after-noon as he was arriving there after school.'

'You're quite the detective,' said Helen, opening the door to get out of the car.

'No, I don't think so. It all sort of came together without any help from me.'

Toby read the story of his kidnapping and asked Clare when she was planning to take him home. He told her that he and Kieran had only intended to stay away for the weekend.

'Well, your parents don't know that do they? So, if you stay away for a bit longer, they'll be really pleased to see you when you get back, won't they? They don't hit you, do they?'

'No. My Mum's not into hitting. It's only big boys at school that hit me,' said Toby.

'Why's that?'

'Dad says its because I'm smart and some kids don't like that. He says they have to let me know how tough they are, so I'll see being smart isn't the only thing you can be good at.'

'Is it a big problem for you, these big boys hitting you?'

'I try to stay away from them, but it might be a problem when I go back to school though.'

'Oh, why's that?'

'Grandpa Kieran caught two boys hitting me on the way home from school. He picked them up and banged their heads together.'

'I bet that hurt.'

'Yeah, they were the ones crying.'

'And, did Grandpa Kieran get into trouble?'

'No. He took me back to school and made me tell the Principal who the boys were. They got suspended for a week.'

'And they've left you alone since?'

'Pretty much, but Grandpa Kieran's not going to be around, is he?'

'You can always tell the Principal. You don't need Grandpa Kieran for that, do you?'

'I suppose.'

When Toby's clothes were dry, he got dressed in his own clothes, while Clare put the clothes she had bought for him into the washing machine. Then Clare took him for a walk up into the hills, where they shared the picnic lunch she had purchased in town with Alicia Brown's credit card.

'Is that your house we're staying in?' Toby asked, as he chewed on the ham and salad sandwich Clare had handed him.

'No, the house belongs to a friend of mine. She's working overseas and lets me use it,' said Clare, thinking there was no point in telling him the truth, since she was sending him home to his mother.

'Do you come up here often?'

'When I can.'

'It's nice up here. My Dad would love a place like this.'

'Why's that?'

'He's into plants. He likes growing them.'

Clare thought of Terry Moore standing in the plant nursery at the back of Sean's office, smiling at her when she had dropped in to leave a parcel for Kieran.

'I suppose he would then. Come on, let's go and see how much water's in the waterfall.'

They got up from the fallen tree they had used as a seat while eating their lunch. Toby followed Clare along the barely visible path that wound its way up the valley to a tiny waterfall, where the stream dropped over a boulder and splashed down to the floor of the valley below them.

Toby and Clare spent the week reading books, trekking through the bush and sleeping in the same bed. On Wednesday night, Clare erected her two-man tent in a clearing by the stream and they spent a night camping out, eating burnt sausages Toby had cooked over a camp fire.

After that night, when they'd slept together in Clare's sleeping bag, Toby wondered just how much of this adventure he'd be able to disclose to his mother. It had felt good being snuggled up alongside Clare's warm, soft body inside the sleeping bag.

On Thursday morning, they went back to the cottage for a hot shower and a warm breakfast. Toby spent the morning working on crosswords in a book Clare found for him on the bookshelf, while Clare drafted the note she was planning to add to the iPhone she had in a sealed box in the garage.

Steve would regret ever having come up with his smart communications strategy, she thought, as she wrote the note.

In Clare's mind, if George and Malcolm had done the job properly, she would never had been put into the position of being expected to kill Toby. She would never have known him. On the other hand, she thought, if they hadn't put her in that position, would she have woken up to what she'd been doing for the last couple of years, since her discharge from the army.

She'd drifted into becoming a hired gun, simply because after being in a war zone, civilian life was boring. She'd killed so many people in the name of world peace or the war on terror or whatever they chose to call it. What did it matter what they called it, she thought. It was all about people with guns shooting each other, and anybody who got caught in the crossfire, to get their way.

She'd been introduced to George and Malcolm by a mate who'd gone over to the dark side before her. The only piece of advice that he'd given her was to use a handle, a trade name, so that no-one would know her real identity. She was fairly certain George and Malcolm were common, garden variety thugs, who'd done a lot of work for Steve. Getting rid of the bookies had been her first real assignment with them.

Prior to that, Steve had used her to eliminate a couple of business rivals and to keep an eye on the Moore operation, while he waited for his father to die of the cancer that had finally terminated his life six months ago.

She'd enjoyed taunting Sean with her sexual charm but he wouldn't touch her. He was scared of Con. That had been funny, his thinking she belonged to Con when all the time she was Steve's enforcer. At least Steve hadn't tried to fuck her like that idiot Malcolm, who thought he was God's gift. She'd given him a set of black balls he would never forget.

Pity about George though, underneath his tough boy image and history of brutal murders, he was a likeable sort of guy, who had looked out for her. She could understand how George wouldn't have been able to kill Toby.

Toby, she thought. Wouldn't it be great to have a kid like him? She was tempted to take him with her when she disappeared but the knowledge of what losing a son had done to her own mother stopped her. She didn't even know Toby's mother but she figured she'd have to be a loving mother to have produced a kid as wonderful as Toby.

She looked at Toby absorbed in the crossword puzzles and sighed. She'd be handing him back in a few days and she'd probably never see him again. No doubt he wouldn't want to see her again either, once he found out she had killed his grandfather.

Funny, she thought, he talks about Kieran a lot but he hasn't said much about Sean.

'Do you like your grandfather, Toby?'

Toby looked up and scratched his head with the end of the pencil he was using. 'Which one?'

'Grandpa Sean.'

'He's alright.'

'What's your other grandfather's name?'

'Grandpa Kevin.'

'What's he like?'

'He buys me stuff. He's going to get me an iPad for my next birthday.'

'He's got plenty of money then?'

'I suppose. He sells houses.'

'And, what are your grandmothers like?'

'Grandma Louise doesn't work. I go to her place after school, until Dad picks me up on his way home. She only lives a couple of streets away from school, so I can walk there when it's not raining. She spoils me. I like her.'

When he stopped, Clare waited a couple of moments before asking, 'What about the other one?'

'She's not very nice.'

Toby went back to the crosswords.

Late Monday night, Clare sat in the car in the garage. Toby was asleep in the cottage. She keyed the details of her message to the police into the Notes app on the iPhone Steve had given her, after disconnecting the device from the iCloud account it had been signed into. There was no point in giving Steve an opportunity to read and delete her note before she could get the iPhone into the hands of Inspector West, the policeman the radio told her was in charge of the case.

She'd also heard on the car radio that the police were looking for a woman dressed in black motorcycle leathers, who had been caught on CCTV at the warehouse where a body had been found on Wednesday. Clare had laughed to herself when she heard that. She'd known about that camera and had taken adequate precautions to make sure her face wouldn't be photographed. They'd be hard pressed to prove it was her once she'd gotten rid of the bike and the leathers. And, even if someone had recognised her, they'd be looking for someone called Clare, someone without a last name or any valid documents. Even her motorbike licence was in the name of Maria Smith.

Satisfied with her note, Clare shut down the iPhone and went to wake up Toby.

'Time to go home, mate.'

CHAPTER 15

ON MONDAY MORNING, Chief Inspector Rankin relaxed his curfew on Carl, who spent the morning in the Incident Room with Bob Reid, discussing the fact that they had three bodies, a kidnapped boy, three missing adult males and no idea who was responsible.

'If what Terry Moore told us is correct, these bookies must have been in cahoots with Kieran and Sean. All of Sean's so-called winnings could have been nothing more than a round robin of cash. Lose it to the bookies on Wednesday and win it back on Saturday,' said Bob. 'The bookie records it as winnings on the Wednesday and as a loss on the Saturday. Sean only records the winnings, claiming he's a lucky punter every week.'

'I wonder who handled the distribution of the drugs and the collection of the money into this little funnel,' said Carl.

'Kieran must have dropped them off somewhere on his way back into the city, and if he did, he sure as hell didn't record it in his manifest, unless it's hidden there among the obvious,' said Bob. 'We've been through his records with a fine-tooth comb. He wasn't making enough from his little courier business to keep his van on the road, despite what he reported to the tax office, so he was obviously getting funds from somewhere else.'

'Bob, what if that stuff you found at Sean's office wasn't a plant? What if Sean was organising the distribution as well?'

'Vice reckon they haven't had anything on either Sean or Kieran since Kieran got out. That's twenty something years. If they were dealing all that time, we would have known. Besides, Rankin's had Kieran under surveillance for years, looking for the Mr Big he reckons Kieran took the fall for.'

'Something must have happened. Maybe there's been some sort of falling out. Who did the chief think Kieran took the hit for?'

'Thought you knew'

'No, he's never told me, even though he did introduce me to Kieran years ago, when I first joined his team. Tough bastard, was my impression. Built like a brick shithouse,' said Carl. 'Do you know?'

'Some guy called Constantine Gordon,' said Bob. 'Heard of him?'

'You mean Con Gordon, the one that's always in the papers for giving money to worthy causes?'

'The same.'

'Why would the chief suspect him?'

'Mr Gordon might be a big shot now but, according to Rankin, he's got a bit of a murky past. He was with the Hells Angels back in the days when the chief arrested Kieran. Had a different name back then too, something like Giorgiopolos.'

'Hang on,' said Carl. 'Didn't this guy die recently? I think I remember reading it in the paper, maybe six or seven months ago.'

'Surely the chief would have noticed that,' said Bob.

'Well, I suppose if he thought he was the Mr Big, the game would have been up when he died.'

'So, why is he so interested in Kieran's murder?'

'Maybe his interest is sentimental, after all, Kieran was his first big arrest,' said Carl.

'I don't think so, Carl. The only person Rankin seems to be sentimental about is you. You'd think he was your father with the way he's been looking after you since Nina had her accident.'

Carl thought about that. 'I've known him a long time Bob, ever since I made detective. I guess he's the closest thing I've had to a father.'

Bob took in his friend's wistful expression.

'Come on, I'll buy you a coffee and we can come back and look at this with fresh eyes.'

After coffee, Carl went to see Chief Inspector Rankin.

'How's Nina?' said the chief, when Carl walked into his office.

'She's awake but she's not a pretty sight,' said Carl.

'Does she know?'

'She does now. I had to tell her.'

'That must have been hard,' said the chief.

'You're not wrong there, Chief. Doubly hard because I'd only just met them. They were good people.'

'Not the same when it's people you know, is it?' The chief took off his glasses. 'It's even harder when you're telling the wife or parents of an officer who's lost his life on the job, but you've done that too, haven't you?'

Carl thought back to the day when he'd had to tell the young wife of Peter James, the detective who had been his constant shadow for the three years before Harry.

They'd gone to an address down at the port to arrest a man accused of raping a fifteen-year old girl. He'd answered their knock at the door with a shotgun blast that had thrown Peter across the landing into the wall behind them. Carl had shot him before he could reload, but that hadn't made it any easier to tell Peter's young wife.

Chief Inspector Rankin broke into his thoughts.

I guess you didn't want to see me to talk about that. What's on your mind?'

'Want to tell me about Con Gordon and Kieran Moore?'

The chief leant back in his chair.

'I always thought Con was the brains behind the heroin ring Kieran claimed was his operation. I just couldn't prove it, and that bastard Kieran wouldn't spill his guts.'

'Is that why you've kept tabs on Kieran all these years?'

'I guess you could say it became a bit of an obsession. We didn't have an open case, so I had to keep it informal, nothing official. That's why I'd drop into places where I knew Kieran went to drink, to catch up and say hello.'

'I remember one of those visits,' said Carl. 'It was a couple of months after I joined your squad. Did you have any idea what Kieran was up to?'

'As far as I could tell, he wasn't doing anything apart from operating a private courier service between here and the Riverland. I even got Sean to redesign my garden, so I would have an excuse to see what he was up to. His son still comes around every couple of weeks to do the maintenance. My wife thinks he's a nice young man, very courteous, and certainly knows his plants.'

Carl smiled. He knew Mrs Rankin was a hard person to please.

'Did you know about Sean's betting on the horses?' said Carl.

'Yes, I knew about the horses. I don't think Sean would have been able to support his lifestyle without the money from the horses. He had a bit of a reputation as a punter with the golden touch. Wouldn't disclose his secret though.'

'Well, Chief, as it turns out his secret, I think, had more to do with money laundering than any golden touch or special knowledge about horses. As you've no doubt heard, I've got three missing bookies, and young Moore says they're the same three bookies Sean did most of his betting with.'

'Do you think young Terry is caught up in all this?'

'I don't think so, Chief. He's been very helpful to date and, according to his wife, he's clueless when it comes to business.'

'Any progress on finding their boy?'

'No. Looks like he's disappeared into thin air. Not one positive sighting. Plenty of false ones though. You know how it is. We put out a photograph and every kid out there in the same age bracket with brown eyes and dark hair is suddenly Toby Moore.'

'Why did you ask me about Con Gordon?'

'When Bob told me that was who you thought Kieran was protecting, I remembered reading something in the paper a while back about him dying.'

'He died around six months ago. I went to the funeral. It was a big deal, plenty of powerful people there. The who's who of the construction industry, the premier and a couple of ministers, including our own. Seems Con had come a long way since the days when he'd been a mate of Kieran's.'

'Who's taken over the running of his business empire? I understand he had cornered the labour market in the construction industry.'

'Steve, his son. I gather he had been running the business, anyway. Con was in his seventies, like Kieran, and sick for a long time before he died. Steve's in his early fifties. He's got a couple of lads of his own. One's a lawyer and I think the other one is some sort of stockbroker.'

'Does this Steve have a record?' asked Carl.

'Why'd you ask that, Carl?'

'I've heard a few rumours that things are not squeaky clean in the construction industry.'

'What sort of rumours?'

'That there's a bit of corruption around overpricing on government projects, with Gordon splitting the proceeds with the developers,' said Carl.

'Bit out of our jurisdiction, Carl.'

'I was just wondering whether there was any connection between the death of Con Gordon and the mess we have on our hands.'

'That's why I've got you on the case, Carl. It struck me as a bit odd that Kieran was killed six months after Con was out of the picture.'

'What do you mean, Chief?'

'If I'm right that Kieran took the fall to protect Con, and let's assume that I am, then you'd think Con would owe him big time, wouldn't you?'

'I'd certainly be pretty pissed off if I'd spent ten years in the slammer for someone and they didn't look after me when I got out,' said Carl.

'What if Kieran's little operation was funded by Con? Con was an organiser for the construction workers union when Kieran got out. I've never been able to prove it, but word on the street back then was Con could get you anything you wanted to keep you happy, if you were part of his union. It was that pool of workers that he eventually turned into his labour hire firm.'

'So, Con would have had a use for Kieran's product, and a way of repaying him for doing the time for him and, I guess, Kieran would have had a hold over Con,' said Carl.

'That's feasible, but does it help us work out why anyone would want to liquidate Kieran's operation?'

'Chief, what if Kieran's usefulness expired with Con's death or the new management simply saw him as a long-time threat that needed to be removed?'

'We need to tread carefully, Carl. Steve Gordon has a lot of influential friends. We'll need a watertight case before you can do anything. Get this one wrong and you'll spend the rest of your career, if you have one, in Traffic, and I'll be taking early retirement.'

———

At lunch time, Carl went to visit Nina. He took her mobile phone, which Bill Norris' constable had delivered.

Nina was awake when he walked into her room and smiled at him as he sat down beside her bed. She was still wearing the mask to help her breathe and used her good hand to lift it off her face.

'Hello, sweetheart. How do I look?'

'Think you might need to touch up your face. Looks like your mascara has run a bit,' said Carl.

'You got a mirror?'

'No, but I've got your phone. I can take a picture.'

'Why don't you do that?'

Carl took her mobile phone out of his pocket.

'What's the password to open this thing?'

'Six, six, six, six.'

'That sounds real secure.'

'What's secure got to do with it when you need to open the bloody thing in a hurry?'

Carl pressed the six on the screen pad four times and then pushed the camera icon on the screen. He got out of his chair and walked around to the foot of the bed and took her photograph. He took a close up of her face before handing her the phone.

Nina scrolled between the photos he had taken and decided her face looked as bad as it felt. She closed the screen and handed the phone back to Carl.

'How you'd get hold of that?'

'Bill Norris sent it down with your handbag and your keys.

Your car might be a write off but at least we can get into your apartment.'

'Oh.'

'Bill said one of the neighbours told him that your father had a brother down here somewhere. Do you have any way of contacting him?'

'Uncle Robert. His number's in my phone.'

'I need to call him. Is there anybody else?'

'No.'

'Do you want to talk to him?'

'After you've spoken to him. I don't think I'm up to telling him.'

Carl went out into the corridor and located Robert Strong's number in Nina's contacts, and then pulled out his own phone and keyed it in.

'Robert Strong?'

'Yes. Who's this?'

'Detective Inspector West, I work with your niece, Nina. I'm afraid I have some bad news for you.'

'Oh, what sort of bad news, Inspector?'

'Nina's been involved in an accident,' said Carl.

'Is she alright?'

'She's in City Hospital. They're telling me she's serious but stable. I'm with her now.'

'Why are you telling me? Surely you've contacted her parents.'

'Mr Stone, I'm sorry but your brother and his wife, who were in the car with her, didn't survive the accident.'

'Oh.'

Carl noticed the loss of energy in the tone of Mr Strong's voice and waited.

'When did this all happen, Inspector?

'Thursday. You might have seen it on the news. It happened in the Riverland.'

'How come you're telling me now?'

'I had to wait for Nina to regain consciousness to find out how to contact you.'

'Is she alright? Where is she?'

Obviously, thought Carl, he's in a state of shock, so he simply repeated the information he had already given him.

'She's in City Hospital. Are you able to come in and see her?'

'Can I talk to her?'

'Sure. I'll just walk back to her room, but let me warn you, she's pretty fragile.'

Carl handed Nina the phone.

After Nina had reassured her uncle that she was indeed alive, she handed the phone back to Carl.

'He wants to know how he can contact someone in the Riverland.'

Carl gave Nina's uncle the details for contacting Bill Norris in the Riverland. Robert told him he'd start the funeral arrangements once he had contacted Inspector Norris. Carl knew Bill would be relieved that he could finally release the names to the press.

As he ended the call, Carl felt the weight of being the only next of kin lift from his shoulders. All he had to focus on now was helping Nina pull through.

'How long do you think I'll be here, Carl?'

'Dr Tran told me you'd be here for a few weeks, and then you'd need to recuperate somewhere for probably another six to eight weeks, before you could even think of going back to work.'

'God, I'll be an old woman by then.' She attempted a smile

but her face muscles didn't cooperate. 'Who's going to look after me when I get out of here? I doubt I'll be able to look after myself for a while.'

'Well, you could always get a nurse or go into one of those private hospitals that offer recuperation services, or there's me.'

'You'd take time off work and look after me?'

'Why not? I love you and besides, there's nobody else, unless you'd prefer Uncle Robert to wipe your arse.'

'Oh, Carl, I love you.' She squeezed his hand and let the tears roll down her face.

CHAPTER 16

Harry sat in the chapel at the crematorium, along with the small group of mourners that had gathered to farewell Kieran and Sean Moore.

There didn't appear to be too many family members, and there were only about twenty friends and associates.

He could see Sean's widow, sitting next to a man he didn't recognise, who looked like he'd been drained of all signs of life. Next to them sat Terry and Helen. Terry kept fidgeting with his hands and looking at the coffins, while Helen sat immobilised, as if she'd been pumped full of sedatives. They'd been a depressing sight when they'd entered the chapel, with Terry holding onto Helen and directing her to her seat.

God, it must be awful not knowing if your son was going to come home or not, or wondering if he would be permanently scarred by his ordeal, thought Harry. He hated kidnap cases, they were so emotionally draining. He preferred working homicide cases involving adults, where it was a lot easier not to get emotionally involved. Anything involving kids was always gut-wrenching when the ending was unpleasant.

Harry had bumped into Sally Arthur and May Butterfield as he arrived, and Sally had asked him if they'd had any luck finding young Toby. Neither of the women had asked if they'd caught Kieran's killer.

Everyone's focused on the boy, thought Harry. Maybe that's why the killers took him, so we'd be distracted from the murders. Obviously, they didn't know much about DI West if they'd convinced themselves that would work, he thought.

This was the first funeral Harry had been to that didn't involve some sort of priest or minister. According to the program, the service was being conducted by a woman from the funeral home, and it didn't look like there would be any religious overtones either.

A woman in a white suit stood up and addressed the mourners. She read a brief statement covering the details of Kieran's life, and a slightly longer one describing Sean's.

Harry decided that she'd obviously been given the sanitised version, as there was no mention of Kieran's life as a known drug dealer or the fact that both men had been murdered.

At the end of the reading, the woman invited anyone who wanted to say a few words to step forward. There were no takers.

The service concluded with the mourners being invited to drop a flower onto the coffins, before they were lowered through the opening in the floor to start their journey to the cremation chamber, located below the chapel.

When the coffins had disappeared, the mourners gathered in an adjacent room for afternoon tea and conversation before dispersing.

Harry stood next to Sally and May and learnt that most of the mourners were either long-time customers of Sean's gardening business, or his drinking mates from the local pub.

Sally and May were the only mourners for Kieran.

Terry and Helen rode in the limousine with Kevin and Louise back to Louise's place, then they retreated to their own house.

Kevin and Louise drank whiskey and talked into the early evening. Kevin told her how he felt so guilty about Mary's suicide, as if he was in some way responsible for it, despite all the other things that had gone wrong in her life and her fits of depression.

Louise decided she didn't like a sad drunk any more than the abusive one she'd just been liberated from, so after they'd had a bite to eat, she rang a cab and packed him off home.

She hoped he'd get over it after they'd buried Mary on Wednesday, otherwise she'd have to find a new lover.

When they got home from the funeral, Helen went to lie down and Terry sat brooding in the living room. The police had cancelled the protective services' surveillance of their house that morning, advising them that they no longer believed their lives were in danger. Terry hoped they were right but that wasn't what was bothering him.

None of his mates had shown up at the funeral. He wondered if that meant they thought he was involved in the drug stuff as well, and that they no longer wanted to be associated with him. He was hurt. He'd been friends with some of them since high school. He was tempted to get drunk and blot it all out, but the thought of fighting with Helen about that later was enough to help him restrict himself to one beer.

As he sat drinking his beer, he realised they'd be doing it all again on Wednesday, when Mary was buried. He wondered what that was going to be like. Helen's parents were more religious than his.

Kevin and Mary were regular church goers. That had been

one of Mary's issues, that Helen had stopped going to church once she'd married him. She'd pressured them to get Toby baptised, but the only time Toby had been to a service since was when he'd stayed with Kevin and Mary, and they'd taken him to church with them.

Whenever Terry had asked Toby about it, he'd only ever said that it was boring.

Terry had only ever been to church twice. The first time was when they got married, and the second time had been when Toby had been baptised.

His father certainly hadn't had a high opinion of priests, 'bunch of pedophiles' was how he'd described them, and his mother had agreed. She had been so paranoid about priests when he was growing up that she wouldn't even let him walk past the Catholic Church on the way home from school, 'just in case'. The memory made him laugh, and he thought of the heated discussions they'd had when he'd told his parents that he was marrying Helen Sloan, in a Catholic Church.

In the end, they'd come anyway and fallen in love with their daughter in-law, well at least his mother had, and then Toby. Even his father hadn't been able to resist the pull of his grandson. And, somehow, Toby had captured Kieran's heart as well. Big tough Kieran, with his tattoos and deep voice.

Terry had loved Kieran too. He knew Kieran was a big softy underneath that gruff exterior he had shown the world. Now they were both gone, his father and his grandfather, and it seemed neither of them had been totally honest with him. What was it about him that had stopped them from trusting him with their secret, he wondered. Or was it they had decided to keep him out of it for his own good. Maybe he should be grateful. If they'd drawn him into it he'd probably be dead too.

Being the one left behind didn't make it any easier. What the fuck was he supposed to do now, he asked himself. He had no idea how the business worked and doubted whether he could continue with it on his own. And what if the court decided everything he had worked for was really the proceeds of crime, despite what Helen thought. Thanks for nothing boys. Helen had been right, like she always was. He should never have gone to work for his father.

He was so pissed off with them that he didn't hear Helen come into the room and sit down in the recliner opposite him.

'You okay?' said Helen. 'You look annoyed.'

Terry looked up, startled.

'What did you say?'

'I just wanted to know if you were okay. You look upset.'

'I was just thinking how Dad and Grandpa have landed me in the shit.'

'At least they didn't get you killed.'

'Yeah, there is that to be grateful for.'

Helen came over and sat down next to him on the sofa and snuggled up.

'Don't know if I'd want to keep on living if I'd lost both you and Toby.'

'Let's hope you haven't lost Toby either.'

'It's been more than a week, Terry. I don't know if I can take any more of this waiting, but I can't bring myself to accept that he's never coming back either.'

'I know.'

'But we can't stay stuck here either. At some point, we have to try and move on, get back on with our lives, otherwise we'll starve.'

'What do you mean, we'll starve?'

'Terry, we haven't got much money left in the bank. If we don't go back to work we'll have to start begging, and I don't want to do that.'

'When?'

'After Mum's funeral. You're already a week behind with your customers. If you don't go back soon you won't have any. You might lose some anyway, now that all this has happened.'

'Hadn't thought of that.'

'And, we'll have to decide if you want to stay with the business or whether you want to do something else, now that your father isn't around.'

'Like what?'

'You might want to get a job and let someone else worry about things.'

Terry looked out the window at the fading light of day turning into night.

'What about your studies?'

'I've decided to withdraw for this semester. I think it would be a waste of time anyway. I'll see how I feel before the next semester starts.'

'Fair enough.'

'And, what about your work?'

'I'll call them after Mum's funeral. They told me not to feel like I had to rush back, but going back to work might make it easier. I don't know. We'll just have to wait and see.'

'Do you feel like something to eat?'

'Let me fix something. It's about time I looked after you for a change, don't you think?'

Terry kissed her on the cheek.

'Okay. I'll close the curtains and come in and set the table.'

CHAPTER 17

Carl waited with Nina until her uncle arrived at the hospital with his wife, Nancy, who got excited when she realised Carl wasn't just one of Nina's colleagues. After the introductions, Carl headed back to the office, promising Nina that he'd call in later on his way home.

Carl met Harry in the elevator on the way up to his office.

'How was the funeral? Anyone interesting show up?'

'Strangest funeral I've been to, Boss. Hardly anybody there. A few of Sean's drinking mates, some of his customers, those two women we met up the river, Helen's father, who looked like a corpse himself, and the family. No eulogy or anything, apart from a couple of prepared statements telling the stories of their lives that left out more than they put in, read out by a woman from the funeral home, and an opportunity to put a flower on the coffin. Service took less than half an hour.'

'Sounds like they just wanted to get it over with,' said Carl.

They got out of the elevator and walked towards the Incident Room.

'How's Nina?'

'She's awake. I reckon you'll be able to visit her in a couple of days. She'd love you to drop in. Mind you, she looks a sight. And, we called her uncle, so I'm off the hook for being the only next of kin.'

'What's the uncle like?'

'Younger version of his brother. Uncle Robert and Auntie Nancy,' said Carl, with a grin spreading across his face. 'Nancy almost had kittens when she realised I was the boyfriend, as you so diplomatically put it the other day.'

'Worked, didn't it?'

'I owe you one for that, Harry.'

'Perhaps you can ask me to be your best man at the wedding, I reckon that would settle the account.'

'You're on, if we get that far.'

Carl told Harry what he had learnt from Chief Inspector Rankin earlier in the day.

'Shit. Con Gordon, who would have thought?'

'Only those people with long memories, like the chief,' said Carl. 'Apparently, he'd even changed his name while Kieran was inside.'

'This Steve, the son that's taken over the business, what's he like?'

'I have no idea, Harry. That's where you come in. See what you can find out about the workings of the Gordon labour hire business, and, while you're at it, find out what you can about this Steve Gordon. I want to know if there were any connections between Gordon and Kieran Moore.'

Harry stood up to leave Carl's office.

'By the way, have we made any progress on identifying the woman captured on the CCTV at the warehouse where Sean was shot?'

'Nobody seems to know anything about her, apart from Terry Moore.'

'He claimed she was some sort of motorbike courier, didn't he?'

'DI Reid's had one of his people check with all the motor-cycle courier companies in town. The best they can come up with is she must be a private operator, like Kieran was.'

Harry took out his notebook and flipped the pages until he found the notes he'd made the day they had shown the photograph to Terry Moore.

'Terry told us that sometimes Sean gave her a parcel that Kieran had left for her. I wonder if she's the connection we need between the Moores and the Gordons.'

'We need to find her first, and it doesn't sound like we're having much luck there. She must have known the camera was there, and I'd say she was no fool given the way she managed to get Sean inside his own storage unit to shoot him.'

'There's something about the bodies that's bothering me, Boss. The Moores were left where they were killed, as if the killer wanted us to find the bodies. There was a token effort to hide Bob Butterfield's body. I mean, they could easily have hidden that more effectively by burning it, along with all the other rubbish they incinerated. If they've also killed the three missing bookies, why haven't we found their bodies?'

'Good question, Harry. Carl ran his hand through his hair. 'Why would they want the world to know that the Moore's had been killed? Who is that message for? I'm pretty sure it wasn't meant for you or me.'

'Maybe it's a message for the chief. You know, with Kieran no longer around the chief will never know for certain who he went to prison for now.'

'You could be right, Harry, but whoever it is hasn't factored in our obsession with connecting the dots, has he?'

Carl thought about their dots. He drew four black dots representing the Moore operation on the white board in the Incident Room. He could form a picture of the way the operation worked but he knew his picture was incomplete. He knew where the drugs came from, who made them and how they got from the lab in the Riverland into the city. What he didn't know was how the drugs got into circulation.

He drew in a red dot representing Clare. She was a bit of a mystery but he thought she might be the essential link that could lead him to the mastermind. What if she moved the drugs from the Moores to their ultimate distributor and brought the money back for Sean to pass through his money laundering operation with the bookmakers, he wondered.

Then he asked himself why the operation had been shut down, if it was making money. Perhaps it hadn't actually been making money at all. What if the whole operation had been a sham set up by Con Gordon to keep Kieran quiet. That might explain why Vice knew nothing about it, because no-one was actually distributing the drugs. Con could have just been repaying Kieran for taking the fall, and letting him think that the money was coming from the sale of the drugs.

He wondered what had gone wrong following Con Gordon's death and why had it taken six months to manifest. Carl decided he'd let that thought go, too much speculation required at this point.

He drew a blue dot representing Toby Moore and wondered why they hadn't found his body. It just didn't make any sense. Carl couldn't see why Kieran's killers had taken the boy, unless there was something they wanted from Terry Moore in exchange for his life. But that didn't make any sense to him either, as there had been no demands from the killers. Perhaps they had gotten whatever it was they wanted when they had broken into Kieran's, he thought, in which case the boy would have become expendable.

Carl was not hopeful Toby Moore would be found alive. Most cases of child abduction did not have happy endings, especially when the child was missing for more than a week. He wasn't looking forward to telling Terry and Helen that sort of bad news.

He stood back from the board and looked at his dots. Then he drew in two more dots to represent the two men in the grey van. They seemed to have vanished along with the boy they had taken. He placed another dot on the board, when he remembered that someone had driven Sean's truck back to his office, sometime after the time of death nominated by Mike Jonas, who had completed the autopsy on Sean's body.

Finally, he drew a dot representing Steve Gordon, and wondered how he was going to connect any of the other dots to that one.

CHAPTER 18

CLARE MADE TOBY a hot chocolate and, while he got dressed and drank the hot chocolate, she packed his clothes into the backpack she had purchased for that very purpose, along with the iPhone she had prepared for Inspector West.

After he had finished the hot chocolate, she handed him his woollen hat and made him pull it down over his ears. There was no point in risking some passing motorist recognising him on the way.

'Ready?'

Toby hugged her. He'd felt safe with her and had enjoyed the bush walking and camping out. In some ways, Clare had been a lot more fun than his mother. She sure knew a lot more stuff about nature and finding her way around in the dark than his mother did.

'Thanks for not shooting me, Clare,' he said, releasing her from his hug.

'My pleasure, sweetheart. Come on, let's get you home.'

Although Toby was excited, he soon fell asleep as Clare made her way out of the valley and onto the freeway that led down from the hills into the city.

It was approaching eleven o'clock by the time they reached

the street Toby lived in. Clare drove past the house. There was a light on in the front room, and there were no cars parked in the street in front of the house.

Clare drove around the block and pulled up two houses back from Toby's. Then she leant over and woke him up.

'You're home, sweetheart.'

Toby looked around. It was his street. He smiled at Clare, as she reached into the back seat, dragged over his backpack and handed it to him.

'Make sure your Dad gives the packet to Inspector West, okay?'

Toby nodded.

'Now off you go. I'll wait here until they open the door.'

Toby got out of the car, lifted up the backpack and ran down the street to the front door of his house, where he rang the doorbell.

'Mum! Mum! I'm home!'

When he heard the door being opened, he looked back up the street. Clare was gone.

———

Terry was watching TV when he heard someone run up the driveway. He nearly jumped out of his skin when the doorbell rang and Toby called out.

He rushed to the front door and opened it, to find Toby, wearing his red parker and a blue woollen hat pulled down over his ears, standing on the other side of the security door, looking over his shoulder into the street. Terry opened the security door and Toby rushed into his open arms.

'Dad! Dad! She brought me home like she promised.'

'Who?' asked Terry.

'Clare.'

Terry looked out into the street. There was no-one there.

'Where's Mum?'

'In bed.'

Toby broke from his father and pushed past him to get to his mother, who collided with him in her bedroom doorway as she came out to see what all the noise was about.

'Mum!'

Toby buried himself in the folds of his mother's embrace.

'Toby! Toby!' Helen hugged him tight.

They stood in the doorway, a family re-united, almost unable to believe they were all standing in the same place.

'Where have you been?' asked Helen, pulling off his hat. 'You must be hot in that lot.' She helped him take off his parka, and then they sat on the bed.

'We've been hiding up in the hills.'

'Who's we?' said Helen.

'Me and Clare. They wanted her to shoot me but she didn't.'

'Thank God for that,' said Helen, rolling her eyes at Terry.

'Who's this Clare?' asked Terry, wondering if it was the same one that had apparently killed his father.

'She was at the house George and Malcolm took me to.'

'Who are George and Malcolm, honey?' said Helen.

'They're the ones that killed Grandpa Kieran, I think,' said Toby. 'They took me to a house that looks like Grandpa Kevin's place. Clare was there,' said Toby.

The mention of Kieran reminded Helen that Toby had initially run away from home.

'Honey, why did you run away?' said Helen.

'I didn't run away. I went on a holiday with Grandpa Kieran. We were just going for the weekend. He said it would help get you back together.'

'Yeah, well he was right about that bit,' said Terry. 'Too bad he didn't stop to think about all the trouble taking you away, without telling us, would cause.'

'He said he'd take care of that when we got back,' said Toby.

They stopped talking.

'Dad, Clare gave me a package you have to give to someone called Inspector West. It's in my backpack. Do you want me to get it?'

'No, leave it where it is. It might have her fingerprints or something on it. Guess I'd better call him, then,' said Terry. 'Where did I put his card?'

'It's by the phone in the kitchen,' said Helen.

Terry went to the kitchen, located the card and keyed in Inspector West's number.

'Inspector West.'

'Inspector, it's Terry Moore. Toby's home.'

'That's great. How is he?'

'He seems to be okay. Says he has a package for you, from Clare,' said Terry.

'Clare?'

'Yeah. I thought that too.'

'Terry, I'll be right there, and Terry, don't touch the package, it might be our only chance of getting something to identify the woman.'

'I understand, Inspector.'

Terry went back to the bedroom, where Toby was telling Helen about his holiday with Clare.

'We even went camping. Clare let me cook the sausages over the fire and we slept in a tent.'

Helen looked up as Terry walked in.

'Might want to save your story until the inspector gets here, Toby. I'm sure he'll have lots of questions.'

Terry went back to the telephone in the kitchen to call Louise and Kevin. His mother was still up watching TV but he had to leave a message on Kevin's answering machine.

Louise was beside herself with joy and wanted to come over straight away. With the police coming, Terry persuaded her to wait until the next morning by putting Toby on, so she could satisfy herself that he was alright.

When Terry told Helen he'd had to leave a message for Kevin, she surmised he'd probably drunk himself senseless after the funeral. She hoped their news would help him snap out of his black mood.

Carl, just home from the hospital, was pouring himself a nightcap when his mobile phone rang. The call from Terry Moore was the best bit of case related news he'd had all day.

He called Harry.

'You still up, Harry?'

'Yeah, what's up?'

'Toby Moore's turned up.'

'He's alive then,' said Harry.

'How'd you know?'

'There's enough excitement in your voice to light the city.'

'I'm going to see him. Want to come?'

'You bet. Want me to organise child liaison?'

'You do that while I call the chief. I'll meet you at headquarters in ten to fifteen minutes.'

'Okay, Boss.'

Carl called Chief Inspector Rankin.

'Hello Carl. Don't you know an old man like me needs to sleep?' said the chief.

'Sorry, Chief, but I think you'll get a good night sleep after what I have to tell you.'

'That sounds promising. Well, come on, don't keep me in suspense.'

'Just had a call from Terry Moore. Young Toby has turned up at home.'

'Thank God for that.'

It was eleven thirty five by the time Carl, Harry and Constable Judy Stringer, from the Child Liaison Unit, arrived at the Moore's.

Carl decided to conduct the interview in the living room, where there was enough room for everyone to sit. He asked Toby to sit next to his parents on the couch, and sat in the armchair facing them. Harry and Constable Stringer sat on chairs from the kitchen.

After introducing himself, Harry and Constable Stringer to Toby, Carl explained to Terry and Helen that Constable Stringer's role was to make sure Toby got any support he might need after his ordeal. Then he started the interview.

'Toby, Detective Fuller and I, and a lot of other police officers, have been looking for you since the Saturday before last. Can you tell me where you've been all that time?'

'I went up the river with Grandpa Kieran for a holiday but it didn't work out like I thought it would.' Not sure what to say next, Toby looked at his hands.

'What happened up the river with Grandpa Kieran?' said Carl.

'We went to this shack. Two men arrived when we were having breakfast. Grandpa said they were probably there to pick up a package and told me to wash up the breakfast dishes, while he went out to see them.'

'And did you wash the dishes?'

'I washed the dishes. Then I went out to see what Grandpa was doing.' Toby stopped talking.

'We know that Grandpa Kieran is dead, Toby,' said Carl. 'You know that too, don't you?'

Toby nodded his head.

'Did you see what happened?' asked Carl.

'Grandpa was on the ground when I went outside. Malcolm was feeling his neck, like you see people do on TV when they're checking to see if a person is still alive.'

'Was there anybody else with Malcolm?' asked Carl.

'George.'

'What happened after that?' asked Carl.

'George made me get in their van and Malcolm went into the house to make sure there was no-body else there. He came out with my parka and then we came back to the city.' Toby looked at Inspector West. 'They thought it was funny when the story about me running away from home came on the radio.'

'I bet they did. Where did they take you?'

'To a house that looked a lot like Grandpa Kevin's.'

'Do you know where it is?'

'I was asleep when we got there,' said Toby.

'He quite often falls asleep in the car,' said Helen.

'Is that where you've been all this time?'

'No. I only stayed there until that night.'

'What happened?'

'I asked Clare what was going to happen to me. She told me I'd have to wait and see what their boss decided.'

'Who's Clare?' asked Carl.

'She was at the house when we got there. She wasn't very happy with George and Malcolm for bringing me, but she made me something to eat and let me watch TV. Then she went out and I watched the football with George.'

'So who took you from the house?'

'Clare. She woke me up in the middle of the night and we went to her friend's place in the hills. She took me on her motorbike!'

The look on Helen's face was enough to tell Carl she was petrified at the thought of that bike ride.

'Where about in the hills?'

'I don't know. It was dark and scary. I had to hold on real tight. She made me wear a helmet and I couldn't see a thing.'

'Do you know why she took you to the house in the hills?'

'She said we had to hide, because her boss wanted her to kill me.'

'And she had decided not to, is that it?'

Toby looked at his mother. 'She said I was too cute to kill. She wanted to keep me but she said that would really upset Mum, so she brought me home.'

'Did she bring you home on the motorbike?'

'No. We came in a car but I went to sleep again. It was a long way.'

'Your Dad said something about a package Clare sent for me.'

'It's in the backpack she gave me.'

'Is there anything else in the backpack?'

'The clothes Clare got for me.'

'Can you get the backpack for me, Toby? Don't open it, just bring me the backpack.'

Toby got up and retrieved the backpack from where he'd left it on the floor in his parents' bedroom, and handed it to the inspector. Carl passed it to Harry.

'Thank you, Toby. Now, one last question for tonight, okay?'

Toby yawned. It had been a long night and his sleep had been disrupted twice.

'Did Clare look after you?'

Toby nodded.

'We'll talk again tomorrow, Toby. I'll ask Mum and Dad to

bring you into my office in the morning, where we can show you some photographs to see if we can work out who these people are. You've been a very lucky boy. Will you promise me that you won't run away from home again? Your parents have been very worried about you.'

Toby looked sheepish. 'I know. We read it in the paper.'

Carl turned to Terry. 'Shall we say ten o'clock in the morning?'

Terry looked at Helen and nodded.

'Just go to the reception desk on the ground floor and tell them you're there to see me.'

Carl was eating breakfast at his desk when Chief Inspector Rankin walked into his office. The chief looked like he'd had a good night's sleep.

'You been to bed, Carl?'

'I got in at six thirty. Couldn't sleep.'

'What did young Toby have to say for himself?'

'The most interesting part of his story is that the woman, who was supposed to kill him, was the one who brought him home. Said she told him he was too cute to kill.'

'Lucky boy. What else did you get?'

'Apparently two men, Malcolm and George, brought him back to the city after Kieran was killed. I don't think he saw them kill him, though.'

'What makes you think that?'

'Told me he was washing the breakfast dishes and that Kieran was already on the ground when he went outside. Chief, what do you think the name of the woman is?'

'I don't know.'

'Clare, and she rides a motorbike.'

The chief inspector looked at him, disbelief in his eyes. 'You're kidding. She kills Sean but can't bring herself to kill the boy. He must be some cute kid.'

'He's cute alright. He'll be in with his parents around ten. Hopefully, he can give us enough details to identify some of them.'

'Anything else? I've got to brief the Commissioner at nine.'

'Clare sent us a package. Harry's taken it to Forensics for testing. I'll give you a call once we know what's in it or if we get anything that might identify her.'

A little after nine o'clock, Harry returned holding a brown envelope with an iPhone in it.

'Forensics reckon this is clean. No prints, no nothing. Looks like she wiped it with a wet one before she put it in the envelope.'

'Anything on the envelope?'

'Nothing biological but it's got some writing on it.'

'What's it say?'

'The passcode is four three five eight. Read the notes app.'

'What's keeping you?'

Harry entered the passcode and opened the only note in the notes app.

'Read the call log, call one zero one and listen to the voice mail, find out who owns this number and those in the call log. 281 East Terrace, Portside.'

'What's at that address?'

Harry logged on and opened Google Maps.

'It's a house.'

'See if you can get a picture of the house from Street View to show Toby.'

While Harry located the house in Street View and set it up so

Toby could see it when he came in, Carl rang the desk sergeant to get an armed patrol on standby to raid the house.

———

Terry and Toby Moore arrived just after ten o'clock without Helen, who had gone to attend to a distraught Kevin.

Carl asked Toby to take a look at the pictures of the house from Street View.

'Looks like the house I went to with George and Malcolm. I remember those bricks. It's the same pattern as on Grandpa Kevin's house, and the garden. Yeah, I think that's the house. It was near a main road. I remember that from the ride on the motorbike.'

Carl picked up his desk phone and pushed the button for the desk sergeant.

'Tell them to go.'

Then he turned to Toby and showed him the photograph of the woman taken from the CCTV footage from the warehouse where Sean's body had been found.

'Do you recognise this woman?'

Toby studied the photograph for a few minutes.

'Looks a bit like Clare,' he said, 'but I'm not sure. You can't see her face. She has clothes like that. Who is she?'

'We think this is the woman who killed Grandpa Sean,' said Terry.

Toby's eyes opened wide. 'Clare?'

'Remember when you told me she went out on Saturday, while you were watching football with George?' said Carl.

'Yes.'

'That's when your grandfather was shot.'

'Oh.'

The phone on Carl's desk rang.

'DI West.'

'Senior Constable Head, Inspector. I'm at your East Terrace address. The place is empty. There's no-one here. One of the neighbours reckons the two men that live here haven't been home since Saturday morning.'

'Get descriptions of the men and find out if a woman with a motorbike has also been living there, and if the men were seen driving a grey Mercedes van.'

'We've only spoken to one of the neighbours so far, Inspector. I'll call in my report when we've spoken to everyone.'

Carl took a deep breath. It was early days.

'Toby, Detective Fuller is going to take you to meet some of our sketch artists. I want you to tell the artists what Malcolm, George and Clare look like. Do you think you can do that?'

'I think so.'

'Do you remember Constable Stringer from last night?'

Toby nodded.

'After you've finished with the artists, she wants to ask you a few questions to make sure you're okay. She'll talk to your Dad while you and Detective Fuller go and see the artists.'

Constable Stringer explained to Terry that she was a psychologist and that her job was to assess Toby's state of mind after his ordeal.

'Is he likely to suffer long term damage?' Terry asked.

'That will depend on what actually transpired while he was with his abductors and whether he actually saw his grandfather being killed.'

'His great grandfather actually,' said Terry.

Constable Stringer made a note.

'Has he said anything to you about how he was treated?'

'He talks about Clare as if she's his best friend. Sounds like they had a great week together. She bought him some new clothes and took him hiking in the woods near where they were staying. They even went camping one night. He's so excited about her letting him cook sausages over a campfire, and sleeping in a tent.' Terry shook his head. 'Even I haven't taken him camping.'

'It's not uncommon for a child to bond with his abductor, especially when he thinks that person has saved him from a worse fate.'

'He's pretty adamant she saved him from getting killed.'

'You find that hard to believe?'

'The bit that's hard to believe is that this Clare seems to be the same woman Inspector West thinks shot my father, Toby's grandfather.'

'That's certainly an inconsistency but maybe what Toby told us is the key. Maybe it's a lot harder to shoot a cute little boy, even if you're a paid assassin.'

Toby spent an hour with the police artists, answering their questions and picking out features from the computer screen. At the end of the session they had three faces and body forms.

The body form Toby had selected for Clare closely matched the one of the woman in the CCTV footage, while he could only describe George as being really big and strong, and Malcolm as tall and skinny. When they had finished, he told Harry that the picture of the woman's face looked a lot like Clare but he wasn't so sure about the one's they had come up with for George and Malcolm.

'We'll see if we can match them with any faces in our database and, if we get any matches, I'll get you to have a look at any photographs we have. Okay?' said Harry.

'Okay.'

Harry took Toby to talk with Constable Stringer, and asked Terry to come and have a look at the mock ups based on Toby's descriptions.

'That's Clare alright,' said Terry, 'but I have no idea who those two are.'

'We'll see if they match any known offenders. Hopefully, Toby will be able to recognise them if we have a clear photograph.'

'What happens if they're clean skins?' said Terry.

'I beg your pardon?'

'You know, if they don't have a record?'

'Then we'll have to ask the public to help us identify them. At least now we have a better idea of what this Clare probably looks like,' said Harry.

Carl examined the call log on the iPhone Clare had sent him. It contained very few numbers. Nearly all the recent calls were either to or from the same number, listed under 'The Man' in the contacts list. The other number recently called was listed under 'Malcolm', while the only other number was listed under 'George'.

He keyed in 101 and listened to the recording of a male voice asking her to call him and confirm that the package had been despatched as requested. Telstra conveniently informed him of the number of the caller, which he wrote down, and that the call had been placed on the previous Monday.

He wasn't surprised to discover that it was the same number as the one listed under 'The Man' in the contacts list.

Carl went to organise the warrant required to get Telstra to provide the details of who owned the four numbers.

CHAPTER 19

CARL LISTENED while Senior Constable Charlie Head, who had led the raid on 281 East Terrace, gave him a verbal update from the scene of the raid.

'According to the neighbours, Inspector, there were two men and a woman living in the house. Apparently, the men had been living there off and on for months, and the woman with the motorbike was in and out. The only description I have of the woman is tall, slim, in black leathers and with a helmet on.'

'What about the men, Charlie?'

'One is described as being a giant and the other as a tall, skinny guy with long hair in a ponytail. Both probably in their thirties.'

'Anything else?'

'The old man across the street says the garden was maintained by Moore's Garden Services. Isn't that the name of the company of the guy that was killed down at the port, Inspector? I was there when we fished his truck out of the harbour.'

'That's interesting, Charlie. Could mean Terry Moore might know who they are. He's the one that actually did most of the garden service work from what I can gather.'

'Don't think so, Inspector. The old man I spoke to reckoned it was an older man that did the garden. Isn't Terry Moore a young guy?'

'Still won't hurt to ask,' said Carl, more to himself than to the senior constable. 'What about the house itself?'

'We haven't been in yet, Inspector. I'm still waiting for Forensics to arrive.'

'Anything on the vehicles these people are using, Charlie?'

'The men were using a grey Mercedes van until a week or so ago, now they're driving a white one.'

'What about the motorbike?'

'All I've got on that, Inspector, is that it's big, black and makes a lot of noise. Apparently, no-one has seen it, or heard it, since it roared out of the place late at night, Saturday before last.'

Bob Reid walked into Carl's office.

'I hear we've had a few developments on the Moore case. The chief's just told me young Toby was delivered to his parents last night.'

'He's just been in speaking to the sketch artists. Looks like he's spent the last week with the woman I think shot Sean Moore.'

'You're kidding?'

'Look at this.'

Carl turned his computer screen so that Bob could see the picture.

'Terry Moore reckons this is the same woman that's in the CCTV shot from the warehouse.'

'Get anything useful from the kid on who killed Kieran?'

'This is the best the artists could do with the descriptions he gave them.' Carl pulled up the pictures for Bob to see.

'Put them on the screen together.' He waited while Carl

adjusted the size of the images. 'I reckon I've seen those guys somewhere. I think I know these guys. Did the boy give you any names?'

'He said the big one called himself George. The other one goes by Malcolm.'

'Nah. Those names don't go the with the pictures. I reckon we did these guys for roughing up customers at a night club a few years back. They were door security. Where was it?'

While he was waiting for Bob to scan his memory banks, Carl heard the ping that announced the arrival of a new email in his inbox. He glanced at the pop up message and noticed the email was from one of the officers in Forensic Art. He opened the email.

'James Bennett and Stephen Falter,' said Carl, reading the information in the email message.

'That's them. They got a good behaviour bond and lost their security licences for twelve months, I reckon,' said Bob. 'How'd you know the names?'

'Toby's description got us a few matches. Looks like our artist friends over in Forensics did what you did. Put them together and bingo!'

'What about the girl?'

'Nothing. She's the one we have the best picture of but it appears we don't know who she is.'

'Guess we'd better get someone over to Motor Registrations to see if they have face on a licence application that matches. Did you get anything from the iPhone?'

'I've just sent Harry over to Telstra. There's only a handful of numbers on the phone, and we've got a good recording of a voice message. Could be useful but we'll need to see where it leads us. No doubt the chief told you he wants a watertight case, if we're going to move in on Steve Gordon.'

'Twice actually.' Bob smiled. 'John on the desk told me he'd sent Charlie Head on a raid for you down at Portside. What was that about?'

'Charlie's still there. She gave us an address and Toby confirmed it was the place they'd taken him to on the Saturday Kieran was killed.'

'How did the kid know that?'

'Street View on Google Maps. Harry showed him the pictures of the house.'

'Whatever would we do without Google?'

'Like we did in the good old days, Bob. We'd either take the kid to the house or send someone out there with a camera. Same result, only quicker today.'

Bob shook his head. 'Charlie find anything?'

'No-one home. Seems they've done a runner but the descriptions provided by the neighbours fit. Forensics are giving the place the once over as we speak.'

'Want me to do anything?'

'How about you get one of your guys to visit the Portside Post Office to see if he can find out if any mail was delivered to that house, and can you find out who owns the house? And that idea you had about Motor Registrations, can you follow that up? If she has a motorcycle licence, we might get lucky. I'll go and see what young Toby has to say about these two.'

While he was driving to the Moore's, Carl got a call from the sergeant heading the Forensics team at 281 East Terrace.

'Inspector, you remember that place up the river we looked at for you? You know, the one that had been sterilised after they killed the guy in the bathroom.'

'The place where we found the body in the orchard?'

'That's the one. Well, this place is like that, Inspector. Everything's been wiped clean, even the gym equipment in the garage. There are no items of clothing, no bed linen or bathroom towels, or anything like that in the place. It looks like they've steam cleaned the carpets, the mattresses on the beds and all the soft furnishings. I don't think we're going to find anything useful for you here, Inspector.'

'Do what you can, Sergeant. Remember, you did find enough in the other place to work out where they'd killed him.'

'Don't worry, Inspector, we'll give the place a thorough going over. I just didn't want you getting your hopes up.'

'Thanks.'

When he arrived at the Moore's house, Carl showed the photographs to Toby, who took a brief look at them, before confirming they were of the men he knew as George and Malcolm.

Carl thanked him and let him run back to his grandmother.

As he was leaving, Carl asked Terry to step outside with him.

'281 East Terrace, Portside. Ring any bells for you, Mr Moore?'

'We've got some customers down that way, Inspector, why do you ask?'

'That's the place where Toby was taken by those two men. One of the neighbours told us that the garden was looked after by Moore Garden Services.'

'Just a minute.' Terry walked over to his truck in the driveway and opened the driver's side door with Moore Garden Services painted on it. He took a book from between the seats and flipped through its pages until he'd found what he was looking for.

'I've been there, about three years ago. We redesigned the front garden. I put all the plants in. Dad did the maintenance on that one though, special favour for Helen's father.'

'What do you mean?'

'Kevin's company is the property manager, at least it was

when we redesigned the garden. You'd have to check with him to see if it's still on his books. He's always complaining about the turnover of rental properties.'

'How is he, by the way? I heard his wife committed suicide last week.'

'That's where Helen is. He's a bit of a mess, actually.'

'Do you have a number for his office?'

'Sure.'

––––––

'We lost that property when the house was sold last year, Inspector.'

'Do you know who bought it, Connie?'

'Sorry, we don't have that information on file. We didn't handle the sale, Inspector.'

'Okay, thanks, Connie.'

Carl realised they'd have to do a formal search of the title after all. At least he had some decent pictures, with names, to release to the public for help in tracking down 'George' and 'Malcolm'.

CHAPTER 20

KEVIN AND LOUISE sat on the sofa in the living room, with their grandson between them, listening to Toby recounting his adventures. The joy of having him back let some light into the dark spaces they had lived through in his absence.

'Were you scared?' asked Louise.

'A bit but they didn't hurt me. They just said they couldn't do anything about Grandpa Kieran and we had to leave.'

'Did you realise they had killed Grandpa Kieran?' said Kevin.

'Yeah. I didn't believe them when they said he had just fallen over and hit his head.'

'What were they like, these men?' asked Louise.

'George was alright. He watched the football with me. He's a Power supporter. He teased me a bit when they beat the Crows. I didn't like Malcolm. He gave me the creeps.'

'What did they say when they found out you had run away from home?' asked Kevin, who wanted to see if what Terry had told him was true.

'They thought it was funny, and when I told them why I had gone away with Grandpa Kieran, they said they'd give me a holiday that would really make my parents worried.'

'What about this woman that took you up into the hills?

What's she like?' asked Louise, intrigued after being told by Helen that Toby was infatuated with his abductor.

Toby paused for a few moments before answering her question.

'Dad says the police think she killed Grandpa Sean, so I guess she must be a bad person. She was supposed to kill me too but she told me I was too cute to shoot.'

Louise smiled at him.

'She was right there, darling.'

'Did she hurt you? Did she tie you up so you wouldn't run away?' asked Kevin.

'In the first house, she locked me in the house, and after tea she locked me in a bedroom.'

'Couldn't you climb out the window?'

'There were security screens.'

'What about in the second house, the one up in the hills?' said Kevin.

'She didn't tie me up, not even when she went to do the shopping.'

'Why didn't you run away when she was out?'

'Grandpa, I didn't know where I was. I looked outside and I couldn't see any houses, and it was cold. Besides, she told me she'd bring me home when it was safe.'

'So, what did you do for a week?' asked Louise.

'We went for walks in the forest, she took me to a waterfall to show me where the stream started. I read some books and did some crossword puzzles. She had a really big book of crossword puzzles.'

'I heard you went camping,' said Louise.

'We slept in a tent and we cooked sausages on a camp fire. She let me cook the sausages.'

'Was it cold in the tent?' asked Kevin.

Toby looked at his hands. He hadn't told anybody, not even

the policewoman who had asked him a lot of questions, that he had slept in the same bed and sleeping bag as Clare. Something told him it would be better to keep that information to himself.

'Not really. I slept with my clothes on in a sleeping bag.'

'Come on, tea's ready,' called Helen from the kitchen.

The church was packed when they arrived for Mary's funeral.

If only she'd realised just how many friends she had, thought Kevin, as he walked down the aisle behind the casket, maybe we wouldn't be here doing this today.

Toby had a good view of the altar from his seat alongside his parents in the front pew. He'd never been to a funeral service in a church before. The service for Grandma Martha, the only other funeral he had attended, had been held in a chapel at the crematorium.

Mary's sister Christine gave the eulogy at the end of the service. Kevin, angry at how Mary had chosen to end their relationship, and filled with shame at her suicide, couldn't bring himself to stand in front of their friends and talk about her life.

After the service, a lot of people made a big fuss over Toby being home. Fortunately for Toby, the story of his abduction by Kieran's killers had obliterated any trace of the original story about him being a runaway.

At the cemetery, Toby watched his first interment and wondered what it would be like to be dead.

Thursday morning was a 'reset' moment in the Moore household, as normal daily life resumed.

Toby went back to school.

Helen and Terry returned to work.

Terry had a list of gardens that needed his attention, even if the police were still sifting through his father's books.

Helen had her job and her father, to worry about. She was glad that Louise hadn't dropped into a black mood like Kevin had, and she hoped that Louise would help her pull him out of it.

Toby got to tell the story of his adventures to his school friends. Even the bullies, who had made his life a misery at times, wanted to hear all about it.

By Friday, Toby was old news in the school yard, Terry was feeling the pressure from trying to catch up on all the gardens he had missed in the week or so since Toby had run off, and Helen had cleared her email inbox.

Somethings would never be the same but it looked like they would survive the ordeal, unless something came out of left field.

CHAPTER 21

HARRY KNOCKED on the door of Carl's office. Carl looked up and signalled for him to come in.

'The media unit's released the photos from Toby's session this morning' said Carl.

'Any luck with the face matching?'

'Got names and photos for the two guys. James Bennett and Stephen Falter. Seems they've worked together before. Conviction for belting up some kids at a night club. DI Reid remembered them.'

'Hopefully someone will know where they are, then.'

'How did you get on with Telstra?'

'Those numbers are all registered in the name of a company called MG Cleaning Services, and the accounts are paid from a B&A bank account.'

'What do we know about this company?'

'Nothing, yet.'

'Well, I guess you know what you need to do then, Harry.'

'On it, Boss. You going to see Nina tonight?'

'Thanks for reminding me.' Carl stood up. 'I'd better get going. I'll see you in the morning.'

Carl headed for the basement, while Harry started an online search of company registrations.

Nina was still awake when Carl arrived at her bedside, despite having expended most of her energy with her uncle and aunt, who had been in to see her during the day.

'Think you might get some competition from Auntie Nancy when they let me out of here, sweetheart,' said Nina, as Carl leant over and kissed her cheek.

'I might let her help but she's going to be disappointed if she thinks I'm stepping aside.'

Nina smiled at him, although it wasn't obvious to Carl. Her face was still puffed up and bruised. He thought she looked like some of the faces he'd pulled out of the gutter after fights at the football, when he'd first joined the force. He didn't want to think about some of the more recent beaten and bruised faces he'd seen on corpses.

'Making any progress on that case?'

'The boy was dropped off home last night. At least, I can stop worrying about him,' said Carl.

'That's good. What did he have to say for himself?'

Carl shook his head. 'You won't believe this.'

'What?'

'He spent the week with the woman I think shot Sean Moore, and it sounds like they had a good time together.'

'You're kidding?'

'He told me she thought he was too cute to shoot.'

'Any idea who she is?'

'Not really. He calls her Clare but I doubt that's her real name.'

'Did you at least get a description from him?'

218

'I've got a sketch based on his description, and his father claims she looks like the motorbike courier that picked up parcels from Kieran and Sean. He knows her as Clare as well.'

'Nothing in the database?'

'Nothing. DI Reid's got someone going through the licence application photographs over at Motor Registrations. We might get lucky.'

Nina squeezed his hand.

'Thanks for coming, sweetheart, but I can't keep my eyes open.'

'You go to sleep. I'll just sit here for a while. Then I'll go and get something to eat. Not sure when I'll be in tomorrow.'

'Come any time. I'll be here.'

Carl let her sleep and hoped her face would recover its beauty. Some part of him wanted to bash the living daylights out of the idiot that had driven his truck into her car, and damaged her without a thought. Just as well Bill Norris has that idiot under lock and key, he thought.

He took a few deep breaths and let his anger subside. He had enough experience from his twenty odd years in the force to know that anger only clouded his thinking, and he needed a clear head if he was going to find this Clare.

Carl read the words on the post-it note Harry had left on his computer screen - Maria George Cleaning Services.

When he logged on to his computer, there was an email from Harry informing him that the directors of the company were a Maria Smith and a Malcolm George, and that the company was a subsidiary of Gordon Construction Labour Hire, Steve Gordon's privately held company. He smiled as he read Harry's reminder about Toby telling them the two men called themselves George and Malcolm.

He called Chief Inspector Rankin.

'Chief, we might have our first chink in the Gordon armour. The company that pays for the phone Clare sent us is part of Steve Gordon's empire.'

'Keep at it, Carl. I want more than a chink. I want the bastard with his pants down. And Carl, it's possible this woman is setting us up or sending us on a wild goose chase to give herself time to disappear. We need to find her before we can go after Steve Gordon.'

'Let's hope he doesn't have any sources inside Telstra or B&A,' said Carl.

'You'll have to deal with the shit as it happens, Carl.'

Carl wondered whether they could get the information from B&A without raising any suspicions that they were trying to link Steve Gordon to a crime.

He called Harry.

'Harry, don't worry about the bank just yet. See what you can find on those directors without asking anybody face to face. I don't want anybody tipping off Gordon that we're looking into his affairs.'

'Okay, Boss.'

After lunch, Harry came into Carl's office.

'Malcolm George and Maria Smith listed their residential address as 281 East Terrace, Portside in the company registration.'

'Any news on who owns that place?'

'Wayne's just sent me an email about that. It belongs to MG Cleaning Services.'

'Well, according to Forensics, they're pretty good at cleaning. That house is spotless. Sterilised is the word they used.'

'The question is, where are our cleaners?'

Bob Reid joined them.

'Take a look at this.'

Bob placed a sheet of paper on Carl's desk. It was a screen print from Motor Registrations, with the details of a motorcycle licence issued to a Maria Smith of 281 East Terrace, Portside. The photograph of the woman associated with the licence looked a little like the sketch they had of Clare.

'The only match we could find but, as you can see, it's not very close,' said Bob. 'Forensics gave it a less than ten percent chance of being the same woman.'

'Any idea who this Maria Smith is?' said Carl.

'Not yet.'

'The chief might be right.'

'What do you mean?' asked Harry.

'Whoever this Clare is, she's playing us for suckers.'

Carl released the photograph of Maria Smith to the media.

They waited for the public to respond.

While they were waiting, Harry studied the hills behind the city on Google Earth, using the satellite imagery, to see if he could locate an isolated house, next to a stream in a wooded valley. It was a huge area to search but it had to be there somewhere, if Toby's story was true.

He initiated the search by concentrating on the margins of the several national parks located in the hills, figuring they would be the most likely places to find a house that fitted the description.

After two tedious days, he had three locations that appeared to fit the description Toby had given them.

'How do you want to go about this, Boss?'

'Let's go for a drive tomorrow, Harry, and play tourists. There will be lots of them in the hills tomorrow. I hear it's going to be a fine, sunny day.'

'Probably take us all day. These places are not close together, and we might need a four wheel drive to get to one of them.'

'That one might not be the one, then. Young Moore told us he came home in a Ford Focus,' said Carl.

'Yeah, I think you're right. If we leave, say around eight, we could be back by lunch time. I'll bring my camera.'

'Okay, pick me up at eight.'

The first house they visited, after a two hour drive, belonged to an elderly couple that had lived there for forty years. They told Carl they had arrived home from an overseas trip on Wednesday, after spending six weeks on a cruise, and that they hadn't noticed anything out of place on their return.

When they joined the couple for morning tea, Harry realised that the house had too many rooms to be the one described by Toby.

They left the first house, drove back to the freeway, crossed over, took the third dirt road on the left and followed it down through a series of forks until they were on a dirt track. The dirt track led them to a small cottage, surrounded by trees, next to a stream.

Harry knocked on the door. There was no response. Carl checked the garage and opened the side door, which was not locked, and looked in. It took his eyes a couple of moments to adjust to the low light inside the garage. When he could see through the gloom, he realised that the garage held a white Ford Focus and a motorbike under a dust cover. He lifted the dust cover to reveal a black Suzuki GSX-R1000.

Carl walked back to where Harry was photographing the house.

'Harry, you're a genius. Come and look at this.'

After looking in the shed, they looked in all the windows of the house, and tried the back door. It was open, however, as the house was a potential treasure trove of evidence, they did not go inside.

'Where do you think she is?' asked Harry, after they had called in to request Forensics.

'Long gone, I'd say. Probably walked out.'

'She could be hiding in the forest. It covers most of the hills. She could easily hide in there.'

Carl made a call to the Dog Squad and asked them to bring up a tracker to see if they could pick up her trail.

It took Forensics two hours to get to them.

'You could have picked an easier place to find, Inspector,' said the sergeant, as he stepped out of their four wheel drive van.

'Took us two days to find it,' laughed Carl.

'How are we getting in?' asked the sergeant.

'Back door's open, and the side door on the shed. Guess people don't lock up way out here.'

'Hard to believe the city is only over those hills,' said the sergeant, pointing back up the track.

Carl and Harry suited up in plastic and went inside with Forensics. The cottage matched the description Toby had given them. Carl noted there was only one bed.

'Boss, look at this.'

Harry pointed to a book of crossword puzzles on the table next to one of the armchairs. He used his pen to flick it open and looked at the round lettering someone had used to fill in the answers.

'I'll bet this is Toby's handwriting,' said Harry.

Carl nodded. The sound of another vehicle approaching

caught his attention. With the amount of noise the Dog Squad's vehicle made as it moved along the track to the house in low gear, Carl realised that anyone in the house would hear a vehicle approaching long before it came into sight. He wondered if Clare had simply bolted as they were arriving.

The dog's handler used the dirty clothes in the laundry to give the dog a scent. The dog picked up a trail from the back door of the cottage and led his handler along the track that followed the stream up the valley to a small waterfall. The dog stopped and sat at the edge of the pool at the base of the waterfall. Clare had obviously stepped into the water.

The handler led the dog up and down both sides of the stream and let it explore the area around the house. The dog failed to find another trail.

'Think you're dealing with someone who knows how to disappear, Inspector. I'd say she set up that trail and obliterated her scent from the area around the house,' the handler said to Carl, before he put the dog back into his vehicle.

Carl went back into the house to speak to the Forensics team, while the dog handler made his way out of the valley.

'Any luck, Sergeant?'

'This place hasn't been cleaned. Think we'll have plenty of stuff for you by the time we've finished. There's hair all over the place and at least two sets of fingerprints, one belonging to a child I'd say.'

Harry was looking through the drawers in the desk located on the side of the living room next to the bedroom.

'Boss, the gas accounts in here are in the name of Alicia Brown, and there's a credit card here in that name as well.'

'Guess you better find out who she is, then.'

'Too bad it's Saturday.'

'Let's go back to that village we passed on the way in. Maybe someone there will know who this Alicia Brown is, or will remember seeing our Clare.'

They left Forensics at the house and drove back up the track to the village. It consisted of a few houses, and a shop that was a cross between a general store and a coffee shop, with a petrol bowser and a sign for Australia Post.

They went into the shop. A middle-aged man sat on a stool behind the counter reading the paper.

'Can I help you, boys?' he said, as Carl and Harry entered the shop.

'Police,' said Carl, showing his badge.

'You boys lost then? We don't see too many coppers up here.'

'What's your coffee like?' said Carl.

'Haven't had too many complaints. Do you want some?'

'Yes, thanks.'

'Black or white?'

'White, thanks.'

'Clare, can you get two coffees? We've got some thirsty coppers out here.'

'I guess you want more than coffee, otherwise you wouldn't have shown me that badge. I'm John,' he said, coming out from behind the counter and joining Carl and Harry at one of the tables. 'Clare's the wife.'

'Detective Inspector Carl West and Detective Harry Fuller,' said Carl, shaking hands with John.

'So, what's on your mind, Inspector?'

'Harry, show him the photos.'

Harry placed the photographs and the sketch of Clare on the table.

'Do you know any of these people?'

'Never seen either of those two,' said John, pointing at the photographs of James Bennett and Stephen Falter, 'but that woman looks familiar. I reckon she's been in the shop. Clare might know. Don't recognise this Maria Smith, don't think I've ever seen her.'

A short woman with greying hair approached the table with two cups of coffee on a tray.

'This is my wife. These guys are policemen, love. Want to know if we know any of these people.'

Clare smiled, served the coffees and looked at the photographs on the table.

'I don't know the men or that woman, but that's Alicia.' Clare pointed at the sketch. 'She has a place down in the valley.'

'Alicia Brown?' asked Carl.

'I don't know her last name.'

'When was the last time you saw her?'

'Couple of weeks ago. She dropped in to buy some eggs and the Sunday paper.'

'Is she a regular?'

'No, we don't see her much, mainly on weekends. I think she uses that cottage as weekend hideaway,' said Clare. 'She's not a local.'

'Why are you looking for her?' asked John.

'Did you read about the boy that was missing for a week?'

'Little Toby Moore?' said Clare.

Carl nodded.

'We think this woman may have abducted him. This picture is based on the boy's description of the woman, and he told us he was kept in a small house next to a forest,' said Carl. 'We've just come from Alicia's and it looks like the place.'

'I guess she's not there then?' said John.

'No, but her car and motorbike are.'

Carl and Harry drank their coffees.

'She could have taken the bus,' suggested Clare. 'There's a bus that goes to the city in the morning and comes back at night Monday to Friday. Here, I'll give you one of their brochures.'

It was Monday morning before they could speak to anyone at the local council or the office of the bus company that operated the small commuter service.

The house in the valley did indeed belong to someone named Alicia Brown, but she was a woman in her sixties, according to the birthdate in the council's records. She had purchased the cottage about eight years ago, but no-one in the council office had actually ever her. All they could tell Carl was that her rates were up to date, and that they were paid electronically from a bank account.

Carl wrote down the details of the account number and thanked them for their assistance. He hoped Harry was having better luck with the bus company. The sound of his mobile phone ringing disrupted his thoughts.

'Boss, she caught the bus into the city the morning after she dropped Toby off,' said Harry. 'The driver remembered her. Said she was the only female passenger that morning, and she had a heavy backpack. He dropped her off near the city bus terminal. I'm on my way there now to see if they have any CCTV for that day.'

'Good work, Harry. By the way, according to the woman I spoke to in the council office, Alicia Brown is someone in her sixties.'

'Wonder if she's still alive, given what Clare's been up to,' said Harry.

'Guess that's a possibility, Harry. Keep me posted.'

Carl turned his attention to the report from Forensics on his desk. They had matched one set of fingerprints to Toby Moore but they couldn't find a match for any of the others they had lifted from the cottage. It looked as if at least three people had been inside the cottage besides Toby. They had plenty of material to extract a DNA sample from and had sent it off to be sequenced. If we ever find her, at least we'll have the evidence to nail her, thought Carl.

Obviously, she wasn't part of the cleaning team. That must be Bennett and Falter, who still hadn't been located either.

He read the report again, and focussed on the list of items found at the house. Then it struck him. There were no weapons in the list. Maybe that's why she had the heavy backpack when she caught the bus, he thought. She was armed. He already knew she was dangerous. What if she wasn't on the run, he wondered. What if she was settling scores? Might explain why they hadn't found Falter and Bennett. If Steve Gordon was the mastermind, as the chief believed, maybe his life was in danger.

Carl called Chief Inspector Rankin.

'Carl, deal with the shit as it happens. I don't want anybody alerting Gordon that we're on to him.'

An email arriving from Bob Reid triggered a notification ping on his computer. Carl opened the email and read that, according to Motor Registrations, the Suzuki was registered to the same Maria Smith as the motorcycle licence they had provided, and that the Ford Focus was registered to a sixty-three year old Alicia Brown, residing at the cottage where they had found it.

CHAPTER 22

GOLF WAS Steve Gordon's passion and he took every opportunity to indulge in the game, often using an early morning round to clear his head before going into the office. He liked playing his early morning games on the tree lined public links in the parklands on the edge of the city centre, so that he could have a quick breakfast in the city on his way to work.

Steve had persuaded John Harvey to get out of bed early and join him for nine holes on Tuesday mornings. He enjoyed the challenge of playing with John, and the opportunity to discuss things with him away from listening ears. This cold Tuesday morning, the course was all but deserted.

Deep in discussion about the next infrastructure project Harvey Construction was planning to tender for, as they walked from the green of the third hole to the tee box for the fourth, neither of them noticed the small green light that briefly flickered on Steve's white jumper, a moment before the sharp report of a rifle shot broke the still, cold air.

John looked up, startled by the sound. Steve fell backwards and crashed into his golf buggy, spilling his clubs onto the ground. John turned and saw a red stain spreading across Steve's white jumper, as Steve lay motionless on top of his scattered clubs, his eyes staring into the grey overcast sky.

John looked around. There was no-one in sight. He dropped to his knees beside his friend, and felt for a pulse. He couldn't feel one. Frantic, wondering whether he was about to be shot, John threw himself flat onto the ground, fumbled for his mobile phone in his trouser pocket and called for an ambulance, hoping that it wouldn't be too late.

The ambulance arrived within minutes, but it did not leave until the police pathologist and his team had arrived.

Carl pondered his breakfast choices. He knew the healthy option was to prepare something but the easy option won out. He decided to get something on the way to the office.

He had just ordered a bacon and scrambled eggs roll when his mobile phone started vibrating in his pocket. He stepped outside to take the call. The girl behind the counter, recognising him as a regular morning customer, finalised his order while he took the call. By the time the Operations Centre had told him that Steve Gordon had been shot dead on the city golf course, she had his coffee and roll ready for him to take with him.

'Have a good day,' said the girl, as he collected his order.

Carl sat in his car and ate his breakfast. Steve Gordon wasn't going anywhere. The pathologist would still be doing his preliminary investigation and, if it was Clare, he reasoned she'd be long gone by now.

He called Harry.

'Fancy a round of golf, Harry?'

'Not really my game, Boss. What's happening?'

'Someone's cut short Steve Gordon's morning round with a

bullet. Better meet me at the city golf course. You know the one, north of the city?'

'Yeah, my Dad plays there.'

'Meet you at the clubhouse.'

'On my way, Boss.'

'Have some breakfast, Harry. This could be a long day.'

Carl drank his coffee and headed for the golf course. Carl hated golf. It was one game he just couldn't get the hang of, no matter how hard he tried, and why anybody would get out of bed early to hit a little white ball into nine or eighteen holes before going to work, was beyond Carl's appreciation of the finer points of life.

Judging by the small number of people gathered in the club-house, Carl guessed not too many people had ventured out for a game of golf on this particular Tuesday. Maybe it had something to do with the grey, overcast sky threatening rain.

The constable standing outside the entrance to the clubhouse pointed Carl in the direction of John Harvey, who had been with the victim when he was shot.

Carl crossed over to the table where John Harvey sat, immersed in a conversation on his mobile phone. Carl heard him telling, whoever it was he was talking to, that he couldn't leave until he had spoken to some Inspector West. John ended the call when he noticed Carl standing at his table.

'Mr Harvey? Inspector West. I'm with Major Crime. Sorry to keep you waiting.'

'Call me John. I guess we're not all up at the crack of dawn playing golf, hey, Inspector?'

'Something you do often, John?'

'Steve was obsessed with beating me at all sorts of things, Inspector. We had a round most Tuesday mornings before work. It was the only thing I knew I could win without an argument, or a team of lawyers.'

'So, business associates or friends?' asked Carl.

'Both, Inspector. I've known Steve for a long time.'

'Can you tell me what happened this morning?'

'We hit off just before seven. We'd decided to play the front nine. You don't get enough time to do the full course on a winter's morning.'

'Many other players out this morning?'

'Only us fanatics, Inspector. I think there was a threesome behind us, those guys sitting over there.' John pointed to a table across the room, where three young men sat eating breakfast. 'I didn't see anyone in front of us. There might have been some others on the back nine. I don't know.'

'Where were you when Steve was shot?'

'We'd just finished the third and were walking through the trees around to tee off for the fourth. You have to walk over a little hill and then down to the tee. We'd just reached the top of the hill when I heard a loud bang, like a rifle going off. I remember looking up and then I heard Steve crashing into his buggy. I looked around and he was on the ground. I nearly shit myself. I thought I'd be next, but nothing happened.'

'Did you see anyone?'

'I didn't even see a flash. There was just that one bang and then silence.'

'Think carefully, what were you actually doing when you heard that bang?'

'Talking. We were talking business. That was another reason we played together.'

'So, you weren't paying that much attention to your surroundings?'

'Not until I heard that shot. Then I was looking everywhere.'

'Do you have a business card with you, John?'

John pulled out his wallet, extracted a card and handed it to Carl.

'Any idea who would want Steve Gordon dead, John?'

'I think there'd be a long list of candidates, Inspector. Steve had the construction labour hire market cornered. There's a lot of people who stand to gain if his company collapses. I'm not sure any of them would go as far as shooting him though.'

'Did he have any enemies outside the construction industry?'

'Not that he mentioned to me.'

'Thanks for your help, John. If you think of anything else, give me a call on this number.' Carl handed him his card. 'Sorry about your friend.'

While John Harvey made his way out of the clubhouse, Carl crossed over to the table where the three young men were finishing their breakfast.

'Will we be able to go soon? We've got lectures,' the one closest to the windows said, as Carl approached.

'I'm Inspector West. I'm with Major Crime.'

'Morning, Inspector,' they chorused, like school boys.

'Any of you see anything?'

'We saw the two guys in front of us walk off the green on the third. Simon here,' he pointed to the man across the table from him, 'had just teed off with a mighty whack when there was a loud bang. Sounded like it had come from somewhere over on the fourth. Then it was quiet, until we heard that guy you were just talking to calling out for help,' said the man by the window, who had obviously been elected as their spokesman.

'What did you do then?'

'We went to see what the problem was. Took us about five minutes to get there. The other guy was dead when we got there.'

'What happened after that?'

'That guy you were talking to had a mobile phone. He called an ambulance but I knew the other guy was already dead. We're med students. The guy had a hole where his heart should have been.'

'Did you see anybody else on the course?'

'We asked the guy where he thought the shot had come from. He had no idea. We looked up and down the fairway. We didn't see anyone.'

Carl turned to the other two, who hadn't spoken.

'You guys see anything different?'

'Nah. Peter's pretty well summed it up,' said Simon.

'Same,' said the third young man at the table.

'Have you given your details to that constable over there?'

'Yes, Inspector.'

'Thank you for your help. If you think of anything else give me a call.'

Carl handed them each one of his cards and went outside to find Harry.

He found Harry talking to Mike Jonas, the pathologist, who was explaining that it looked like the shooter had used a hollow pointed round, given the amount of damage inflicted on the body of the victim.

'Whoever it was, Harry, they knew what they were doing to have taken him out with a single shot,' said the pathologist, as Carl joined them.

'So, cause of death is beyond doubt, Mike?' said Carl.

'No argument there, Inspector.'

'We haven't been able to determine where the shooter fired from yet, Boss,' said Harry.

'Any idea on direction, Mike?'

'Somewhere across from the tee off spot, further down the fairway. If you stand where the victim was when he was hit, and basically follow your arm, you end up in the trees across from there.'

'Uniform are searching that area now,' said Harry.

'How far is that from where he was standing?' said Carl.

'A good three hundred paces, Inspector. I think you're dealing with a marksman,' said Mike.

'Or someone who got in a lucky shot,' said Harry.

It took the searchers all morning to locate the spot used by the shooter, and it was only after they'd stopped looking at the ground and started looking up into the trees that they spotted the marks, where the shooter's boots had scuffed the bark, on a tree directly opposite the tee box along the line of fire suggested by the pathologist. Despite an intensive search of the area beneath the tree, the search team was unable to locate the casing of the round that would have been ejected from the shooter's rifle. Carl concluded that either someone had inadvertently stepped on it, and buried it, or the shooter had removed it when leaving.

Shortly after midday, a member of the public, who had been driving into work at around seven thirty, called the Crime Stoppers number in response to Carl's request for help in identifying anyone acting suspiciously near the golf course that morning. The caller told the operator he had seen a tall woman in a black track suit, wearing a black baseball cap and carrying a black sports bag, walking along the road that led from the golf course into the city, just before the lane that went down to the railway station.

The news was several hours old by the time it got to Carl but it was the best lead he'd had since the morning, and it confirmed his suspicions about the identity of the shooter. He called Chief Inspector Rankin.

'Chief, sounds like our shooter might be Clare.'

'What makes you think that, Carl?'

'We've had a call from a Harry Pentin, describing someone,

matching our description of Clare, walking away from the golf course carrying a sports bag,' said Carl.

'Keep me posted and, Carl, there's no reason why you can't talk to Gordon's people now. After all, he's a victim of crime now.'

Carl thought he detected a smile in the chief's voice.

He put down his phone and went to see Bob Reid in his office.

'Bob, I've got Harry interviewing this Harry Pentin to see if he can confirm the woman is Clare. Need you to get someone onto checking the CCTV recordings for movement at the railway station. It's a long shot, but if she caught a train, we might be able to narrow down our search zone.'

Ten minutes after Bob had left to organise the review of the CCTV recordings at the railway station, Harry called to let Carl know that Mr Pentin, an advertising executive, was fairly sure that the woman he'd seen was the woman in the photograph they'd taken from the CCTV recording from the warehouse, where Sean Moore had been shot.

Carl wondered if she'd take out Bennett and Falter or whether she'd stop with Steve Gordon.

Bennett and Falter might be harder for her to find. Steve Gordon had been a creature of habit, and that had made him an easy target for someone like Clare. Besides, as far as Carl knew, Steve Gordon hadn't been hiding. Obviously, he'd seriously underestimated the threat. Perhaps he hadn't seen her as a threat, even after Toby Moore turned up alive.

Carl took Constable Jane Priest with him to interview Steve Gordon's wife.

Trish Gordon and Steve's sons from his first marriage, Conrad and Trent, had gathered at the family home in anticipation of the visit. Carl couldn't help but notice that Trish Gordon was in the same age group as Steve's sons.

Conrad, the older of the sons, was standing beside the chair in which his step-mother sat, with his hand on her shoulder, when they entered the room. Conrad left his step-mother's side and extended his hand to Carl.

'I'm Conrad, Inspector. This is my brother Trent, and this is my father's wife, Trish.'

'My condolences,' said Carl, taking Trish's offered hand. 'Sorry to have to call at a time like this but, given the circumstances, I guess it's no surprise that we have a few questions.'

All three heads nodded in agreement. Conrad returned to his position beside his step-mother.

'Where would you like to start, Inspector?' asked Conrad.

'Do any of you work in the family business?'

'I'm only involved with the charitable foundation, Inspector,' said Trish. 'Basically, I organise our social calendar. I have nothing to do with whatever it is that Steve does during the day.'

Carl looked at Conrad.

'Dad was getting ready to float the business, Inspector. We aren't interested in it really. I'm a lawyer and my brother is a stockbroker. We've discovered there are other ways of making money that don't involve keeping hundreds of people happy.'

'So, what do you think will happen now?' asked Carl.

'The float will go ahead,' said Trent. 'The firm I work for is doing the underwriting. Dad had a good management team, so it was never about him. The firm has plenty of work, so its income stream is secure for the foreseeable future. It's a good investment. You should look into it.'

'I'll have to consider that with my financial advisor,' said Carl, 'but right now, what I need to look into is why your father's been shot. Any ideas?'

'It's a mystery to me,' said Trish.

'I'm sure he had enemies,' said Conrad. 'You can't be that successful without stepping on a few people's toes.'

Carl handed the photograph of the woman from the warehouse CCTV recording to Conrad. 'Do you know this woman?'

Conrad shook his head and passed the photograph to his brother.

'Isn't this the woman that you think killed that man down at the port, Inspector?'

'It is. Do you know her?'

Trent shook his head. 'No. I've only seen her picture on the TV.'

Carl noticed the colour draining from Trish's face as she studied the photograph.

'Inspector, I don't know who she is but a couple of weeks ago, when this picture appeared on the TV, Steve took a lot of interest in the story. He told me he knew the man who had been shot. Apparently, he'd designed the garden for one of Steve's houses, when these two were still living at home.'

'Yeah, I think that's right. It was the garden for this house actually, about fifteen years ago,' said Trent. 'I remember now, he was a mate of Dad's. They used to go to the races together. That was before Dad discovered golf.'

'Why are you showing us this woman's photograph, Inspector?' asked Conrad.

'I think she shot your father.'

'Why?'

'I haven't worked that bit out yet. You mentioned your father may have stepped on a few toes. Anyone in particular?'

'I wouldn't really know, Inspector,' said Conrad.

'You probably already know, Inspector, that the business was started by our grandfather and Dad worked for him.' Trent glanced at his brother. 'Grandpa was a firm believer in the theory that the third generation only destroys any business it inherits, so even the float idea was his. He died six months ago, before they could get the float organised. I guess there will be another delay now, while the probate and all that stuff gets worked out, but then it will go ahead.'

'If you want to get an insider's perspective on the business, Inspector, I suggest you talk to Maria Mahoney,' said Conrad.

'Who's she?' asked Carl.

'Dad's lawyer. She's been the firm's contract law specialist ever since Grandpa got into the labour hire business. If Grandpa or Dad stepped on any toes, she'd know,' said Conrad. 'Of course, she might not want to tell you.'

On the way back to the office, Carl asked Constable Priest what she had made of the interview.

'Pretty cold lot, if you ask me, Inspector.'

'What makes you say that, Jane?'

'The guy was only shot this morning. If it had been my father or my husband, I'd be pretty upset. She didn't even look like she'd been crying and the sons seemed fairly disinterested to me.'

'I've interviewed a lot of people in similar circumstances, Jane, and it never ceases to amaze me how people respond to someone close being murdered. What intrigued me was not so much the lack of emotion, that could simply be shock, but the degree of intimacy between Conrad and his step-mother.'

'I did notice that he was always touching her.'

'Yes. What I'm wondering is whether it was out of endearment or control. Was he simply showing support or making sure she didn't say too much?'

'Now I know why you're the detective, Inspector, and I'm still in uniform,' said Jane.

'Why's that, Jane?'

'Suspicious mind, sir.'

Carl laughed. He liked Jane, she was a straight talker.

CHAPTER 23

NINA SPENT most of Tuesday crying, after looking at the photographs of her parents' funeral service that her uncle had taken for her. She still couldn't believe her parents were dead, and she was touched that Carl, who had hardly known her parents, had attended their funeral.

After ten days in the hospital, Nina was spending more of her day awake than asleep, and the swelling on her face had subsided. Now, when she checked her face in the hand mirror her aunt had left for her, she saw a washed-out version of the image she recalled from before the accident, instead of the heavily bruised monster Carl had captured on her iPhone.

Her body hurt in places she hadn't imagined a body could hurt. Earlier in the day, the nurses had loaded her into a wheelchair and taken her to see a physiotherapist, who had given her a series of daily exercises for the muscles in her unbroken limbs. Although her ribs hurt whenever she moved her arms, the physiotherapist insisted she do the exercises. She'd protested, but he'd said she'd regret it, when it was time to get out of bed and move around on crutches, if she didn't do them now.

The trip to the physiotherapist was the first time Nina could remember being out of her room, since she had woken up in the hospital. She'd visited people in this hospital on several occasions, but she was stilled amazed at how anybody could find their way around the maze of corridors and arrive at their destination. The place had so many people powered vehicles moving through its corridors that it had its own traffic jams.

As she watched the evening news on the TV above her bed, the story of Steve Gordon's murder caught her attention, not because she knew much about Steve Gordon, but simply because she knew it would take up more of the time she wanted Carl to spend with her.

Carl arrived to visit her just after seven thirty. He looked exhausted.

'Are you looking after yourself?'

Carl looked mystified.

'You look like you haven't slept for a week.'

'Bit of a long day. Did you see the news?'

Carl sat down on the chair beside her bed.

'You mean the Steve Gordon murder?'

'I've been on it since before breakfast.'

'Can't DI Reid take it?

'We're all on it. The whole force is trying to locate this bloody Clare woman.'

'What, the same one you think took out Sean Moore?'

'Yeah, and we still don't know who she is. Anyway, enough about me. How are you doing?'

'I went on a field trip today.'

'A field trip?'

'Watch this.' Nina demonstrated her new exercises.

'That looks like it hurts.'

'Everything I do hurts.'

'You'll get better.'

'That's what everybody keeps telling me.'

'You certainly look a lot better than you did the first night you were in here. I don't need to check the name plate anymore to know it's you.'

Nina watched the smile spread across his face.

'It's nice not having to breathe through that mask thingy anymore.'

Carl leant over and kissed her lightly on the lips. Nina reached up with her good arm, held him in place, and kissed him back.

'Hmmm. Obvious signs of improvement in this patient's condition,' said a familiar voice from the doorway.

Nina and Carl looked up to see Harry holding a box of Nina's favourite chocolates.

'Thought the whole force was out searching for this mystery woman?' said Nina.

'Well, not this part of it,' said Harry, passing Nina the chocolates and sitting down next to Carl. 'The chief said we could have the night off.'

'So how are you boys planning on spending your night off?'

'We thought we'd come and visit you and then go out on the town,' said Carl.

'Yeah, right,' said Harry, 'as if you'd be able to keep your eyes open. I don't know about you but I'm going home for a decent night's sleep. My head hurts.'

'Perhaps you should try some of my painkillers, Harry?' said Nina.

'I want to wake up tomorrow, Sarge.'

'In that case, I guess I'll have to go home to bed then. It's not much fun having a wild night on your own,' said Carl.

At ten thirteen on Wednesday morning, the Crime Stoppers number received a call from a Mr Ming, the manager of the Crazy Dragon Motel, a sleazy establishment on the edge of the city's entertainment district, opposite the railway station. The operator passed the details of the call through to the Incident Room set up for the Gordon case outside Carl's office.

Carl and Harry accompanied the Forensics team to the motel. On arrival, Carl took a look at what had been discovered in room 309, before interviewing the manager and a very distraught housekeeping maid.

The maid told Carl that she'd found a black sports bag on the bed in room 309, obviously left behind by the guest who had used the room. She'd tried to lift the bag off the bed so she could change the sheets. However, as it was rather heavy, she'd looked inside to see what the guest had left behind, and was shocked to find a disassembled rifle, two pistols and several boxes of ammunition.

Fortunately for Carl, she hadn't cleaned the room but called the manager, who had called Crime Stoppers.

'Who was the guest in room three zero nine?' asked Carl.

Mr Ming gave him a print out of the invoice for payment on the room. It was made out to a Maria Smith and revealed that she had stayed for eight nights, starting on the Tuesday before last, and had paid cash in advance.

'Did she have ID?' asked Carl.

'Driver's licence,' said Mr Ming.

Carl took out the photographs and sketches he had of Clare, including the one on the licence from Motor Registrations, and placed them on the counter.

'Did she look like any of these?' he asked.

'That one.' Mr Ming pointed at the sketch based on Toby's description. 'And that one.' He pointed at the shot from the warehouse.

'When was the last time you saw her?' asked Carl.

'Yesterday, in morning, eight o'clock. She come in with bag. Come back from gym, next door.'

'What did she do while she was here?' said Carl,

'What you mean?'

'Did she stay in her room or did she go in and out?'

'Oh, she in and out. No restaurant here, she go out to eat, sometimes she out all day, come back late at night.'

'Do you have a security camera?' asked Carl.

'No camera. Not good for business. Our customer not want camera. Not everyone like police.' Mr Ming smiled apologetically at Carl.

'When did she check out?' asked Carl.

'She no check out, leave key in room.'

'Thank you, Mr Ming. When my people have finished with the room, they will let you know. Shouldn't be very long.'

Carl and Harry left Forensics to gather what information they could from the room, and went next door to the gym. The woman at the desk told them that a young woman, that looked like the woman in their sketch of Clare, had used the gym two or three times over the last week and had paid the casual rate in cash.

'Was she in yesterday morning?' asked Carl.

'I don't think so. I do the morning shift. We open at six thirty. I don't recall seeing her yesterday, Inspector.'

When they got back to the office, Carl had the team review the information they had collected on Clare.

Their examination of the CCTV recording from the railway station had not identified anyone meeting Clare's description entering the station, or catching a train, within the seven thirty to eight window they had reviewed after yesterday's reported sighting.

From what they knew now, it looked like Clare had gone from the golf course back to the motel, and then slipped out without being seen. Either she had found a rear exit or she had walked out without being recognised. Maybe she had simply waited for the front desk to be unmanned, and then left the motel.

Carl's mobile rang. He answered it, and found himself talking to the sergeant who had led the forensic examination of the cottage in the hills where Toby had been held.

'Inspector, got some interesting results for you from that material we sent for DNA.'

'What makes them interesting?' said Carl.

'Apart from the boy, we have a mother and daughter,' said the sergeant.

'Well, that could explain a few things. Thanks.'

Carl returned to the Incident Room and shared what the sergeant had told him.

'Reckon we need to find this Alicia Brown, now that we know we're looking for her daughter,' said Bob Reid.

'How about we run a check at Births, Deaths and Marriages,' said Harry.

'You might need to run one in every state. Who knows where she was born?' said Bob.

'I wonder if she's still armed,' said Carl. 'She left a small arsenal in that motel room.'

'Think we might want to keep that to ourselves, for the moment,' said Bob. 'Might help us flush out Bennett and Falter, if they still think she could get to them.'

'Good idea,' said Carl.

'God, Carl, she's got a nerve. She's been sitting right under our noses for a week,' said Bob.

'What's that saying? The best place to hide is in plain sight. The question is, Bob, is she still out there or has she left town?' said Carl.

'I've got people going through the CCTV from the airport, the bus station and the interstate rail terminal. We've got her picture plastered all over the city. It's in the papers and it's doing wall to wall on the TV news channels,' said Bob. 'And, she still managed to walk around the city for a week.'

'Either she doesn't really look like that sketch or people don't give a shit,' said Harry. 'Maybe we're the only ones interested in finding her. I certainly didn't get the impression Mr Ming had any idea who she was, or that woman in the gym. Just took her money and didn't pay her any attention.'

'Take a deep breath, Harry. You'll blow a fuse,' said Carl.

He waited for Harry to take a few breaths. 'Now go and see what you can find out at Births, Deaths and Marriages.'

'We're covering all the official gateways out of the city, Bob. What if she drove?' said Carl. 'I wouldn't be surprised if she had another vehicle or she simply took one. Seems to be a woman of many talents, not just a good shot.'

'That was a bloody top shot that took out Steve Gordon. I wonder if we're dealing with someone the army has let loose on society. I gather there are some pretty mixed up vets out there,' said Bob.

'Worth a try. Give them a call and see if anyone recognises our girl,' said Carl. 'Better check with the desk sergeant. There'll be some bloody protocol you'll have to follow.'

Shortly after midnight, Carl was roused from a deep sleep by the ringing of his mobile phone, which he had plugged into its charger and left on the floor beside his bed.

'Sorry to disturb you, Inspector, but I thought you'd like to know Bennett and Falter have just been taken into custody,' said the night desk sergeant from Police Headquarters.

'What happened?'

'Patrol pulled over their vehicle for speeding on the causeway leading out of the port.'

'Where are they now?'

'In transit to the City Watch House. They should be there within the next half hour or so.'

'Thanks,' said Carl.

Carl called Harry when his alarm went off at six thirty. After a shower and a quick breakfast, he dressed and then headed to the City Watch House. Harry was waiting for him when he arrived.

'Morning, Boss. Duty lawyer hasn't arrived yet,' said Harry, when Carl walked in. 'Who do you want to see first?'

'Let's start with Falter.'

As they waited, a young woman dressed in a smart grey business suit and carrying a brief case, joined them in the interview room.

'Hello, Harry. I was hoping the next time I saw you it wouldn't be this formal.'

Carl looked at Harry and raised an eyebrow.

'Hello, Jessika,' said Harry, a slight blush creeping across his face. 'Maybe we can catch up after we get this sorted. Do you know Inspector West?'

'Only by reputation.' She extended her hand. 'Jessika Walsh, Legal Aid.'

Carl shook Jessika's hand, noting her firm grip.

'Been keeping tabs on young Harry here, have you Jessika?'

Jessika's smile in Harry's direction told Carl more than she had intended to convey.

'Just friends, Inspector. We were at uni together, but that was before he crossed over to the dark side. I'm still trying to convert him to the light.'

'Good luck with that. Shall we begin?'

'Do you mind telling me why these two have been arrested?' asked Jessika. 'Is this connected to the Moore case or the Gordon case?'

'Both, actually. These two match the descriptions given by Toby Moore of the men that removed him from the scene of Kieran Moore's murder. They're also suspects in the murder of Bob Butterfield, who had been working with Kieran Moore. And, they might be able to tell us something about the woman I suspect killed Sean Moore, and more recently, Steve Gordon. Ready?'

Jessika nodded her head. She wasn't here to defend them, only to protect their rights until either they hired a lawyer or the court appointed one, if they were charged.

Carl pressed the button under the desk to let the guard know they were ready.

Stephen Falter was led into the interview room and hand-cuffed to the chair, bolted to the floor, on the side of the table opposite Carl. Harry pushed a button to start the video recording of the interview, stated the names of those present, and asked Stephen Falter to state his full name for the record.

Falter glared at him and then said, 'Stephen Malcolm Falter.'

Harry read him his rights from the card stuck to the table, and explained that Ms Walsh was a Legal Aid lawyer, who was there to protect his rights during the interview, seeing as he hadn't asked for a specific lawyer to represent him.

Falter gave Jessika an appraising look.

'I hope you're not just another pretty face, Ms Walsh.'

'Any idea why you're in here Mr Falter?' asked Carl.

'I read the papers, Inspector. I gather you think I had something to do with that kid that was missing.'

'And, did you?' asked Carl.

'You don't have to answer that question,' said Jessika.

Falter remained silent.

'Mind telling us where you were going in such a hurry, last night, Mr Falter,' asked Carl.

'Going up the coast fishing.'

'What was the hurry?'

'Shit, I was only doing ninety in the eighty zone, and there was nobody else on the road, except those clowns in the patrol car.'

'Harry, show Mr Falter the pictures.'

Carl watched Stephen Falter's face as Harry placed the photographs and sketches of Clare and Maria Smith in front of him. His face remained impassive, but the tiny flicker in his eyes was enough to tell Carl he'd recognised Clare.

'Do you know any of these women, Mr Falter?' asked Carl.

Stephen Falter shook his head.

'Can you answer the question for the record, please?' said Harry.

'Don't know them,' said Falter.

'Are you sure you don't know this one?' said Carl, pointing to the photograph they'd taken from Maria Smith's licence application.

'Don't know her,' said Falter.

'What can you tell us about Maria George Cleaning Services, Mr Falter?

Falter's face blanched. 'It's my company.'

'What exactly does your company do, Mr Falter?'

'Specialist cleaning of industrial sites. We clean up spills and stuff like that. Make places look like new again after accidents.'

'Who is the we?'

'James and me.'

'Is that James Bennett?' asked Carl.

'Yes.'

'How long have you been in the cleaning business? The last time you visited us you were in the security business.'

'Yeah, well thanks to you lot, we lost our security licence. That's when I started the cleaning business.'

'Harry, show Ms Walsh the results of the company search for Maria George Cleaning Services.'

Harry placed the sheet of paper in front of Jessika Walsh, who read it and then placed it where Stephen Falter could read the names of the company directors and the address given for the company's office.

Carl placed his pen on the photograph taken from Maria Smith's licence application.

'According to Registrations, this is a photograph of the Maria Smith that lived at 281 East Terrace, Portside. We lifted it from her application for a motorcycle licence. Registrations also told us she is the registered owner of a black Suzuki GSX-R1000. Are you certain you don't know her?'

'I've never seen that woman.'

'Mr Falter, we have several witness statements placing you, and a woman with a black motorbike, at 281 East Terrace, Portside.'

'I don't deny living there but it wasn't with that woman.'

'Who is the woman with the motorbike, Mr Falter?'

Stephen Falter remained silent.

'What's your mobile phone number, Mr Falter?' asked Carl.

'You've got my phone, work it out for yourself.'

Harry placed an evidence bag on the table.

'I'm placing on the table the mobile phone, taken from Mr

Falter when he was arrested, and now I'm going to call each of the numbers we obtained from the mobile phone Toby Moore delivered to us.'

Carl noticed another twitch in Falter's eyes.

Harry keyed in a number and a mobile phone in another evidence bag under the desk started ringing. He ended that call and keyed in a second number. The iPhone in the bag on the table started ringing.

Carl pushed the sketch of Clare towards Stephen Falter.

'She dropped you in it. She's taken care of your boss, and she's probably out there looking for you. Who is she?'

Falter's head dropped.

'Her name is Clare. She's the one with the Suzuki.'

'Clare who?' asked Carl.

'I don't know. You'd have to ask Steve, but you can't do that now, can you?'

'Anything else you can tell me about her?' asked Carl.

'She scares the shit out of me.'

'Why's that, Mr Falter?'

'She's a cold-blooded killer.'

'Is that why you broke cover and tried to get out of the city last night?'

'She knows all the safe houses. She set them up. We had to go somewhere she didn't know about, otherwise we'd end up like Steve Gordon.'

'What made you think she'd killed Steve Gordon?'

'Inspector, she's a crack shot. She never misses. Who else do you think it was?'

'Why do you think she shot him?' asked Carl.

'Steve told her to kill the kid. She must have flipped.'

'How did she get the kid?' asked Carl.

Jessika Walsh cautioned Falter about continuing to answer

their questions, as he was incriminating himself, and reminded him that the police would use anything he said against him in court.

'I'm probably safer in prison, if she's still out there.'

'Do you want to give us a statement?' asked Carl.

'Where do you want me to start?'

Stephen Falter talked for close to an hour. He claimed that Clare had killed Bob Butterfield and Sean Moore, and blamed James Bennett for the accidental killing of Kieran Moore. According to his statement, James had only meant to scare Kieran, but the old man had fallen back and hit his head on the floor of his own van.

Falter claimed they'd only taken Toby because they couldn't leave the kid in the middle of nowhere, and it was Steve Gordon who had decided that he had to be killed, simply because he knew too much.

Falter explained that their role was to clean up after Clare, if Steve wanted the evidence removed, and confirmed that he and Bennett had cleaned the Butterfield place after Clare had killed him, and that they had cleaned 281 East Terrace to remove all trace of their presence in the house.

When pressed on the use of names, he said that it was all about keeping things secret. They always referred to Steve as 'the man' when talking about him or to him, especially on the phone, and it was a way of protecting themselves from Clare, who only knew them as Malcolm and George, like they only knew her as Clare.

He denied any knowledge of the three missing bookmakers.

Once he had signed his statement, he was escorted back to the cells, while Carl, Harry and Jessika adjourned for a coffee.

Following their coffee break, they interviewed James Bennett.

Once James Bennett had been secured into the chair previously occupied by Stephen Falter, Harry introduced Jessika Walsh, and started the video recorder. Jessika explained her role to him.

Carl started the interview by showing him the photographs.

'Do you recognise any of these women, Mr Bennett?'

'That one is Clare,' he said, pointing to the shot of the woman coming out of the warehouse where Sean Moore had been killed. 'I don't know who this is but that looks like a drawing of Clare.'

'Does Clare have a last name?' asked Carl.

'I'm sure she does, Inspector, but I don't know what it is.'

'How long have you known her?'

'I wouldn't say I know her. We've worked with her for a couple of years.'

'In the cleaning business?'

'Clare didn't do cleaning, Inspector. Malcolm and I did the cleaning.'

'Malcolm?'

'Falter. Malcolm's his working name.'

'And, do you have a working name, Mr Bennett?'

'George.'

'Before we go any further, Mr Bennett, I must warn you that your colleague has made certain admissions concerning the murders of Bob Butterfield and Kieran Moore, and the abduction of Toby Moore. As Ms Walsh has explained to you, anything you say can be used as evidence in court, do you understand what I'm saying?'

'What's the little prick said? He doesn't take the blame for anything. What's he blamed me for this time?'

'What do you know about the death of Kieran Moore?' said Carl.

'Gordon wanted him dead. I hit him. He hit his head on the van when he fell. Falter didn't even need to use the knife on him.'

'What about Bob Butterfield?'

'The guy who made the stuff?'

Carl nodded.

'He lived in a garbage dump. He was a real pain in the arse. Falter slit his throat. We buried him in the orchard and burnt all his stuff. Took us two days to clean his place.'

Carl put the photographs of the three missing bookmakers on the table in front of him.

'What about these three?'

'Clare shot them. We put them in the foundations of the new hospital. Gordon reckoned no-one would find them until they demolished the hospital in a hundred years' time.'

'How much did Steve Gordon pay you guys?'

'We got a hundred thousand up front, and we were meant to get a shitload of shares when he floated his business. I don't know what he promised Clare.'

'Why didn't you kill the boy?'

'Toby? Why would I want to kill him? He's just a kid.'

'How did he end up with Clare?'

'I thought she'd taken him out somewhere to kill him, like Steve wanted. I never thought she'd send him home to his mother.'

'Why's that?'

'She's one cold bitch, that one.'

On the Friday after Bennett and Falter had confessed to some crimes and accused each other of others, some of the more tedious work involved in solving a crime exposed a few of Clare's secrets.

The search of the records held by Births, Deaths and Marriages had revealed that an Alicia Brown (nee Smith), a nurse, had married a John Adam Brown, a soldier, thirty three years ago when they were both thirty. She had given birth to a daughter, Alicia Maria, thirty two years ago, and a son Adam John, thirty years ago. Both the son and the husband were deceased.

Inspector Reid had released the photograph of the older Alicia Brown, taken from her driver's licence, to the media with a plea for her to come forward or for anyone who knew her to contact Crime Stoppers.

Around midday on Friday, the same day the photograph had appeared in the papers, a nurse employed at the Seaview Nursing Home contacted Crime Stoppers, and told them they had a Mrs Alicia Brown, that looked like the lady in the paper, in residence, and that she was visited every week by her daughter, who had last been in on Monday.

Carl took Harry with him to interview the nurse. She had already told him on the phone that there would be no point in talking to Mrs Brown, as she had been admitted to the nursing home by her daughter, after suffering a debilitating stroke that had left her bedridden and unable to speak.

'Does Mrs Brown have any photographs of her daughter in her room?' Carl asked.

'She doesn't have any photographs at all. She used to have some, but she always got upset when she noticed them, so her daughter took them away,' said the nurse.

Carl placed the photographs and the sketch of Clare on the table.

'Does the daughter look like any of these?'

The nurse pointed to the shot of her leaving the warehouse.

'That one looks like her. She rides a motorbike, and that one, the one that looks like a drawing, that looks like her, though her hair is a bit longer and a lighter colour.'

Carl had just sat down behind his desk when Bob Reid walked in with a sheet of paper in his hand.

'What's up, Bob? You look like you've won the lotto.'

'Take a look at this. Just came through from the Department of Defence.'

Carl looked at the sheet of paper Bob had given him.

It was a print out of the summary page of a personnel file for a Corporal Alicia Maria Brown. It contained two elements that caught Carl's attention. A photograph, taken three years ago when she had been discharged, and an entry under skills. She was rated as her unit's top marksman.

'I've released the photograph along with her name,' said Bob. 'Hopefully, that will make her easier to find.'

Bennett and Falter were taken before a magistrate and charged with the murders of Bob Butterfield and Kieran Moore, the abduction of Toby Moore, and as being accessories to the murders of Michael Murphy, Charlie Boyle and Chris Morris. The Magistrate remanded them in custody to await trial.

An investigation into the workings of Gordon Construction Labour Hire and its relationships with the major construction companies got underway, but Carl and his team from the Major Crime Unit were not involved.

The media mounted a campaign to have the bodies of Murphy, Boyle and Morris recovered from the foundations of the new hospital. The State Government rejected their call on the grounds of cost, and proposed that a memorial garden be established in the vicinity of the spot where James Bennett claimed they had been buried. The three murdered bookmakers became part of the investigation into Sean Moore's money laundering activities, that was being conducted on the fringes of the Gordon case, to see if Sean Moore had any connections with the Gordon empire.

CHAPTER 24

FOUR WEEKS AFTER HER ACCIDENT, Nina was released from hospital. She was wheeled out to Carl's waiting car in a wheelchair, although she could make her way around on crutches. Her left arm, still encased in plaster, was in a sling, and her lower left leg sported a blue moon-boot. Apart from its pallid colouring, her face had returned to normal, and although most of the bruising had faded, her ribcage still hurt when she exerted herself.

Nina hopped out of the wheelchair, swivelled on her good leg and slid herself into the backseat of the car. It was good to be going home, she thought, after four weeks of institutional care, but she wondered what level of service her new carer would be providing.

Carl placed her bags in the trunk and got in behind the wheel. The nurses waved as they drove away.

Carl eased the car out into the traffic and drove home. They had decided that his apartment was the better choice, as it had no stairs and two bedrooms. Carl had spent the previous day clearing out the second bedroom and setting it up for his patient. He'd gathered all the things she'd listed for him from her apartment, and installed them in the room she'd be using for sleeping, while her limbs were still encased in plaster. He'd made room for her toiletries in the bathroom vanity, and paid his cleaning lady to do an extra clean of the apartment in readiness for Nina's arrival.

Nina insisted on walking in under her own steam, while Carl carried her bags. Given that she had arrived at the hospital with nothing of her own, she had been surprised when Carl had arrived with two sports bags to carry her stuff out to the car.

Carl finished setting up the wifi network that would allow Nina to use her laptop from anywhere in the apartment, while Nina inspected her room.

Satisfied that she could find the things she was most likely to need, Nina hobbled back into the living room and eased herself into the armchair by the window.

'Any chance of a decent cup of coffee, sweetheart?'

'You're expecting decent coffee?'

'Anything would be decent after the stuff they called coffee in that hospital.'

'Guess you have a point. I'll see what I can do. Would madam like an espresso, a long black or a latte?'

'An espresso would be nice.'

Nina wondered what he was playing at, as Carl's move into the kitchen that adjoined the living space, was followed by some serious coffee making sounds.

After a couple of minutes, Carl presented her with a steaming espresso.

'Where did you get that?' she asked. Carl's previous best effort for coffee had been an instant coffee made with milk.

'There have been some improvements since madam's last visit,' said Carl.

'What? You finally bought a coffee machine?'

'Thought you might like a welcome home present.'

Carl went back into the kitchen and picked up the coffee he had made for himself.

'I could get to like this,' said Nina.

'What, the coffee?'

'No, having a servant.'

Carl smiled. He didn't mind in the least. She was alive and that was all that mattered to him.

Just before six o'clock, Nina's Uncle Robert and Auntie Nancy arrived, with a hot lamb roast in a casserole dish, for Nina's welcoming home meal.

Robert and Carl opened a bottle of red, while Nancy and Nina fussed around in the kitchen transferring the hot meal from Nancy's casserole dish to Carl's plates.

'How long before those casts come off?' asked Robert.

'The doctor said maybe another six to eight weeks, and then I'll have to work with a physiotherapist for a few weeks,' said Nina.

'And, what are your plans, Carl?' asked Nancy. 'Do you have enough holidays?'

'I've got plenty of holidays, Nancy.'

'He never takes them when he should,' said Nina.

'Well, I've got a good excuse now, haven't I?'

'Six to eight weeks?' said Nancy.

'More than that,' said Carl. 'I've decided to take a month's annual leave for the first bit. I figure Nina will be pretty mobile in three to four weeks, so she may not need constant support, but if she does, I've still got another five weeks of annual leave and fifteen weeks of long service leave to fall back on.'

'I see what you mean, Nina,' said Robert. 'You realise there's a reason why they call it annual leave, don't you, Carl?'

'Tell that to the criminals, Robert. As it is, even if I take more leave, I may still need to be around to testify in court. Anyway,

Nina and I have some decisions to make before I settle on how much leave I'll take.'

After a shared meal and an evening of conversation, Nina was tired, and retired to her room as soon as Robert and Nancy went home. Carl looked in on her to make sure she had everything she needed, and then let her enjoy her first night of uninterrupted sleep since she had regained consciousness.

Carl discovered that the strain of being attentive to Nina's every need was almost as stressful as some of the cases he'd worked on. He was caught in the tension between wanting to look after her, and show her that he could, and being on his best behaviour.

Over the years that he had lived on his own, Carl had developed some personal habits, of which he was largely unconscious, that came sharply into focus now that he was sharing his personal living space with Nina.

It hadn't taken them long to revisit the seat up or down discussion, which they'd had on previous occasions when they'd shared a bathroom. Carl knew he'd lost that one when Nina, like Virginia before her, pouted and said, 'What's your issue? You don't have to stand up to pee.'

He also had to deal with Nina sitting in his armchair, soaking up the winter sunlight, when he wanted to do that, and wishing he'd bought another armchair instead of the couch. In the end, they compromised and shifted the couch, so they could sit in the sunshine together.

It was several days before Carl could relax enough to simply be himself, and let his love for Nina take care of everything else, despite the fact that they had spent several weekends together in his apartment.

There was one thing Carl could relax about doing, without

thinking or worrying that Nina would give him advice on how he should do it, and that was cooking. Nina was not a cook.

Carl's grandmother had made sure he could cook before she let him leave her house to live at the Police Academy. Even Virginia had been grateful for that gift, but it had not been enough to balance the other stresses of living with a policeman.

Each afternoon around three, Carl went to the gym. It gave him an opportunity to work out his anxieties and allowed Nina some time to herself. On the way home from the gym, at least once a week, Carl called into Nina's apartment to attend to her forest of plants, in accordance with her strict instructions. Amazingly, he hadn't killed any of her plants, even when he had taken it upon himself to look after them while she was still too sick to worry about them.

Nina found that there was a range of things, like doing up a bra, that she just couldn't do for herself with one functioning arm. She was grateful she had one arm she could still use, and thought she would have died of embarrassment if she'd had to rely on Carl, as he had joked in the hospital, to wipe her arse after using the toilet. It had been bad enough in the hospital with the nurses, but at least they were professionals and didn't have a personal relationship with her. She wondered whether that was only pride and not independence. She had no doubt Carl would have done it, if she'd needed him to.

Nina had learnt to look after herself following her first husband's betrayal of her trust, and although she wanted to be with Carl, she also liked her independence.

In the second week, Nina found herself overwhelmed by tears. The first wave was triggered by Carl bringing her one of the quilts she had asked him to fetch from her apartment, so that she could sit in the sunshine without turning the heater on.

Her mother had made the quilt for her, and a lot of the other things that decorated the walls of her apartment. That had been a major factor in her decision to spend the first few weeks of her recuperation with Carl, instead of moving into her own apartment.

Carl came home from the gym one afternoon and found Nina curled up on the couch with her quilt, crying her heart out. At last, he thought, the dam has broken. He sat down beside her on the couch.

'It's not fair. Why am I still here? Why did I have to survive? I should be dead too!'

Nina's red, raw eyes told him she'd been crying for some time, probably since he'd left to go to the gym.

'We don't get to write the rules of the game, sweetheart, but I'm glad you survived.'

Nina turned and snuggled into his side.

'I miss them so much.'

Carl wrapped his arm around her. He couldn't think of any words to say that wouldn't sound glib, and decided that silence was the best way he could show her that he understood.

He thought of what it had been like when his mother had died, and then his grandfather. Those had been the saddest two moments in his life. Carl didn't pretend to understand God or how life worked. He'd decided long ago that it was all too hard to work out, and that his best option was to go with the flow. Shit happened, and you simply had to deal with it or you went under, was his survival philosophy.

Coping with death was part of the daily grind for Carl, as it was for every member of the Major Crime Unit. A lot of people died for some very stupid reasons, as far as he could tell. Arguments over money, jealousy, revenge, power struggles, imagined slights or because of the influence of drugs.

The deaths of Nina's parents fitted that pattern. In a way, it was the lucky ones that died from what the medical profession called natural causes. But no matter how stupid or trivial the reason, when someone died there were always others left behind to mourn their passing. He didn't envy Nina; he knew what it was like to be the one to survive. He'd lost several partners to the irrational acts of crazy people in the twenty or so years he'd been in the force, and it never got any easier.

When she had composed herself, Nina showed him the form requesting a victim impact statement, which had arrived in the mail.

A week later, Nina asked Carl to take her up the river to visit her parents' graves and take a look at their house. She needed to decide what to do about the house, and to speak to her parents' lawyer about winding up their estate.

Given that it was a three to four hour trip from the city to Nina's parents' place, they decided they'd spend a few days in the Riverland.

At the cemetery, Carl stood alongside Nina as she said her silent farewells. It was a moment of closure for Nina, who hadn't been able to attend their funeral.

After the cemetery, they dropped in to see Bill Norris, and took a look at the pile of twisted metal that had been Nina's Ford Focus. Bill informed them that the trial of the driver, who had driven his truck into the back of Nina's car, was scheduled for next Wednesday, and asked Nina if she intended to attend.

'I have no recollection of the crash, Inspector. The last thing I remember is stopping at the stop sign. Then I woke up in a hospital bed and saw this guy,' she pointed at Carl, 'looking at me as if the world had come to an end.'

'My world damn near had,' said Carl.

'I hear he's pleading guilty, in any case,' said Bill Norris.

'Yes, I know. I was asked to provide a victim impact statement,' said Nina.

They had lunch with Bill and then continued on to her
parents' property, another half hour's drive upriver.

'Who's the executor of the estate?' asked Carl, as he turned
the car into the driveway that led down to the cottage.

'Me, according to the letter from Dad's lawyer,' said Nina.
'She's offered her services to help me sort it out. I called her
yesterday to accept her offer, and I made an appointment to see
her tomorrow.'

'Not too early, I hope,' said Carl.

'Think you can handle eleven o'clock? We'll have to leave
around ten thirty.'

'Sounds good to me.'

Carl parked the car in front of the house. The gardens looked
as though someone had been watering them.

'Who's been watering the garden?' asked Carl.

'I guess Dad's automatic sprinklers are still working,' said
Nina. 'Did Uncle Robert mention who was looking after Pedro?
I'd forgotten all about him.'

'Pedro was in the back seat of your car, sweetheart.'

'Oh, yes, I remember now. That's why we were going into
town. We were taking him to see the vet.'

Nina sat staring at the mat on the front porch that had been
Pedro's favourite spot.

'You okay, sweetheart?'

Nina came out of her trance and smiled at him.

'Come on, let's get our stuff and go inside.'

Nina opened her door and waited for Carl to bring her
crutches around to her, then she made her way around to the
back entrance, while Carl got their bags out of the trunk.

Carl had to make two trips to transfer their luggage and
provisions into the house.

He found Nina in the kitchen. She was cleaning out the fridge so they could restock it with the fresh produce they had brought with them.

'Carl, can you open some windows? This place needs a good airing, and then can you change the beds? Bring the dirty sheets out to the laundry so I can wash them.'

Carl spent the afternoon cleaning, under Nina's supervision.

'I can see why you have a cleaning lady,' said Nina, as she pointed out places he had missed.

By early evening, Nina was tired. She retired to the sitting room and watched the TV news, while Carl heated up the pumpkin soup he had made the previous day, and toasted several slices of the thick country loaf they had purchased on their way to the cottage.

After the meal, they put on their coats and went outside and sat on the outdoor furniture in the courtyard behind the house, and looked at the night sky.

'This is one of the things I miss the most, living in the city,' said Nina.

Carl, who had grown up in the city centre, never took much notice of the night sky. In the city, it was either daytime or night-time. In the daytime, the light came from the sky. In the night-time, any light there was came from street lamps, and even when you looked up, the glare of the city lights obscured any stars that there might have been.

'It sure is an amazing sight, isn't it? I had no idea there were so many stars until I visited my uncle's farm when I was a kid. My cousins used to laugh at me, when I stood outside looking at the sky.'

'Do you think you could ever live in a place like this?'

'It would take a bit of getting used to. It's a long way from anywhere, and it's so quiet it doesn't seem quite right.'

'I think that's what I was running away from when I left

home. It's even this quiet in town. When I was a kid, we lived in a house a couple of streets back from the Resort Hotel, although it was only called the Riverland Hotel then,' said Nina.

'Would you want to come back here?'

'Only for a holiday. I'd get bored living here. I like being with people, going to the theatre, walking through the shops, catching up with friends for coffee. It's more of a closed world up here. There's a downside to knowing everyone and being known to everyone.'

'I can imagine. Bit like being in the force, I suppose. Seems it's hard to keep things secret there, too.'

'Are you really upset about everyone knowing about us?' said Nina.

'Too late now even if I was?'

'Answer the question.'

'No. In a way I'm glad it came out. Now we don't have to worry about being seen together, however, I'm a bit pissed that DI Reid's going to be getting the benefit of your smarts.'

'I'll take that as a compliment, Inspector.'

Carl kissed her on the back of the neck. 'When do you think they'll let you go back to work?'

'Doctor Tran says I should be able to start on light duties in a couple of weeks. No field work for a couple of months. Not until I have full mobility back in my leg.'

They sat for a while listening to the silence.

'What are you going to do with this place?' said Carl.

'I'd love to keep it as a country retreat, but it's a long way from the city. Guess I'll sell it.'

'You could rent it out,' said Carl.

'I think a clean break from the place would be best. There would always be memories whenever I came back here. I think selling it is the best option.'

'Guess you're right.'

'That's what I want to sort out with the lawyer tomorrow.'

'Fair enough. I'm getting cold, can we go inside and fire up that heater?'

'Sounds like a good idea to me.'

The meeting with the lawyer was productive. As Nina was the only beneficiary of the estate, it was a simple matter for her to commission the lawyer to wind up the estate and transfer the proceeds. They agreed to drop in the key to the house on their way back to the city, after they had spent a few days going through her parents' personal effects.

By the end of their stay, they had contacted Don's accountant, and arranged for him to finalise her parents' tax affairs, and given him the contact details of the lawyer who was overseeing the winding up of the estate.

When they returned to the city, in a car loaded down with Alice's handiwork, Nina moved into her own apartment, to give herself some time and space to consider the new depth of their relationship.

CHAPTER 25

With Nina being mobile enough to take care of herself, Carl returned to work. In the month that he had been away from the office, the team had made no progress on locating Clare or Alicia Maria Brown, as they now knew her to be. It appeared that she had disappeared without a trace.

Despite all their reviewing of CCTV recordings from the bus station, the railway station and the airport, all the public portals to interstate travel, they had not come up with a positive sighting of her.

No record of anyone resembling her description renting a car had surfaced either, but Carl was wary of that outcome, as car rental firms were not required to maintain photographic records, and CCTV was not common in their offices.

'Either she left by private means or she's still here somewhere,' said Bob Reid, after he had briefed Carl on the team's activity in his absence. 'And, we've had no reports of anyone seeing her interstate.'

Carl shook his head. Not only was she a crack shot, it appeared she was also a master of the art of blending into the background.

'What have we found out about Alicia Maria Brown?' asked

Carl.

'She hasn't touched her bank account since the week before young Moore came home.'

'How much is in it?' asked Carl.

'Just under fifteen thousand dollars.'

'Any idea where the money came from?'

'Looks like it's what's left of her army pay. There are no deposits into the account since she was discharged,' said Bob.

'She must have some accounts in another name. Have we tried the Maria Smith angle?'

'You got any idea how many Maria Smiths there are?'

'Can't be that many with a 281 East Terrace, Portside address?'

'Harry's checked with every bank in town. There's a grand total of none.'

'I wonder if there's a paper trail from Steve Gordon through MG Cleaning Services.'

'Been down that rabbit hole, Carl. Appears Gordon Construction Labour Hire paid MG Cleaning Services close to a quarter of a million dollars this year, for specialist cleaning services. Problem is, MG Cleaning Services only paid one account electronically.'

'Their phone account.'

'Spot on. Looks like everything else got paid in cash. Our girl might have access to around a hundred thousand dollars.'

'I doubt she's carrying it around in her handbag,' said Carl.

'She may as well be.'

Carl was frustrated with their lack of progress but there was little he could do about it. Like everyone else in the team, he was dependent on the eyes and interest level of the general public, who'd let her walk around the city for a week between the time she had released Toby Moore and shot Steve Gordon.

'Somebody must have seen her. It's not like she's invisible.'

Two weeks after Carl returned to work, the trial of James Bennett started in the Supreme Court. Although both Bennett and Falter had made statements admitting varying degrees of guilt and accusing each other, the inconsistencies in their statements, and Bennett's willingness to testify against Falter, had persuaded the state prosecutor to start with Bennett.

The trial caused a round of concern in the Moore household. Toby was called as a witness, and asked to tell the court what had happened to him, and what role James Bennett had played in his abduction.

The prosecutor, who had spent several hours talking to Toby, and rehearsing the questions he would ask, in the days leading up to the trial, started by asking him if the man he knew as George was in the court.

'Yes, sir. That's George over there,' said Toby, pointing to where James Bennett sat in the dock.

Bennett smiled at Toby. He liked the kid and was glad Clare hadn't killed him, even if it meant Toby could identify him.

'Did you see who hit Grandpa Kieran, Toby?' asked the prosecutor.

'No, sir.'

'Can you tell the court what you saw when you went out to see what Grandpa Kieran was doing that morning?'

'Grandpa Kieran was on the ground near his van, and George was standing next to him. Malcolm, the other man, was squatting down next to Grandpa, feeling his neck.'

'What happened after that?'

'I asked Malcolm what was wrong with Grandpa Kieran. He said that he'd fallen over and hit his head.'

'And, did you believe him?'

'Not really, but he looked like he was dead to me.'

'What made you think that?'

'He wasn't moving. He'd wet his pants and you could smell pooh. Dad says that's how you know someone is dead.'

The judge looked up as a few smiles spread across the faces of the people sitting in the gallery.

'What happened after that, Toby?'

'Malcolm told George to put me in their van while he checked the house. When he came back, he drove us to a house in the city.'

The prosecutor handed Toby a photograph.

'Your Honour, I am showing the witness a photograph of 281 East Terrace, Portside,' said the prosecutor. 'Toby, is this the house you were taken to?'

'Yes.'

'Can you tell the court what happened to you there?'

'When we went inside there was as a lady, called Clare. She told off George and Malcolm for bringing me to the house, like she was their boss. Then she made me some lunch and let me watch TV. I had to stay in the house. She said all the doors were locked and there were security things on the windows. I watched the football with George, and Clare and Malcolm went out somewhere.'

'Did they go out together?'

'No. Clare went out on her motorbike and someone came in a car to pick up Malcolm.'

'What happened when they came back?'

'I don't know if Malcolm came back. When Clare came back, she locked me in her bedroom. There wasn't anything to do. I was scared. I thought they were going to kill me.'

'What made you think that?'

'Clare said I watched too much TV.'

A wave of chuckling rippled around the courtroom, including across the bench.

'Obviously, they didn't kill you, so what happened?'

'Clare woke me up in the middle of the night. Then she took me to a house somewhere in the hills, on her motorbike.'

'Thank you, Toby. Your witness,' said the prosecutor, turning to the lawyer representing James Bennett.

'No questions, Your Honour.'

Terry and Helen Moore sat in the gallery as Toby gave his testimony. When Toby had finished, they went out into the foyer to collect him from the Sheriff of the Court.

As they were leaving the building, they met Carl, who was on his way in to wait for his turn in the witness box.

'Hello, Inspector,' said Toby, when he saw Carl walking up the steps towards them.

'How did it go, Toby?' asked Carl.' Not too scary?'

'It was all right,' said Toby. 'Have you found Clare yet, Inspector?'

'Still looking,' said Carl. He wasn't sure, but the momentary smile in Toby's eyes left him with the impression the boy was relieved she hadn't been found. Carl turned his attention to Toby's parents.

'Life getting back to normal?'

'We're back to being a family again,' said Helen. 'Toby's settled back into school and I've gone back to work.'

'That's good. How's the business going without your Dad, Terry?'

'Mum's sold the business. I've got a job lined up at the Botanic Gardens. I'm starting on Monday,' said Terry.

'How'd you pull that off? I've heard it's pretty hard to get a job there,' said Carl.

'One of the guys I studied with works there. They had an

opening, and he asked me if I was interested.'

'And, I said, yes,' said Helen.

'Congratulations, I hope it works out,' said Carl.

Carl watched the family make it's way down the steps, and then went to sign in to the witness waiting room.

As it transpired, James Bennett did not contest anything in the statement he had made to Carl, when it was read to the Court, and Carl was not required to take the stand.

James Bennett was sentenced to twenty five years with a non-parole period of fifteen years. A week later, Stephen Falter, despite protesting he had no role in the murder of Bob Butter-field, received a similar sentence for his part in the murders and abduction.

The assertions, made during their trials, by Bennett and Falter that Steve Gordon was behind the killings, severely tarnished the solid citizen image Steve Gordon had built up with the media. A lot of high profile players in state affairs, from the Premier down, found themselves fielding awkward questions, from that same media, about their relationships with Steve Gordon.

Fortunately for those asked, the fact that Steve Gordon was dead, apparently executed by his own assassin, allowed people to say whatever suited their purposes. He wasn't there to defend himself or contradict them.

The media reported on the rumours, circulating in the city, that Steve Gordon had been set up and silenced, by un-named parties, in a planned operation to devalue his company prior to its initial public offering.

Carl and his team had plenty of evidence, and the testimonies of Bennett and Falter, implicating Alicia Maria Brown, also known as Clare, in the murders of Sean Moore, Michael Murphy, Charlie Boyle, Chris Morris and the abduction of Toby Moore. She was also their prime suspect for the murder of Steve Gordon. Carl's only problem was he couldn't find her, despite a nation-wide appeal to the public for assistance.

'Do you think she's still out there or has someone bumped her off?' Harry asked Carl, as they sat in a pub two streets from the office, enjoying a beer before calling it a day.

'Who would have killed her, Harry? She seems to have had the upper hand once she decided not to kill the boy. Pretty obvious from the messages Steve Gordon left on her voice mail that he didn't know where she was, and Bennett and Falter had obviously been ordered to go to ground, probably by Gordon. The phone records show he was in contact with them right up to the day before he was shot.'

'What if they weren't running from her but from having killed her?' asked Harry. 'Falter did his best to pin the blame for all the murders, besides Kieran's, on her, and Bennett only fingered Falter for Butterfield. We only have their word, for what that's worth, that she had anything to do with any of the other killings. If she's dead she can't argue with their statements.'

'We have young Toby's story of how she saved him from them, but we also have the CCTV from the warehouse where Sean Moore was killed,' said Carl.

'I wonder if there's someone else in the Gordon empire that would benefit from her not being found,' said Harry.

'That would depend on what she might know. As I see it, Steve Gordon was cleaning up some dirty business left over from his father's association with Kieran Moore, so his company would survive the due diligence studies required to facilitate its public float.'

'Well, you'd think he'd have wanted these three out of the way before that went ahead,' said Harry.

'That would mean he'd have had to eliminate them himself, wouldn't it? Otherwise he'd only have shifted his problem. And, if he was planning to kill his hit team, why go to the trouble of using them in the first place? There's probably something bigger here, but right now it's not my problem.' Carl drained his glass. 'Another one?'

'One more should be okay,' said Harry.

Carl signalled to the waitress to bring them another round.

'Obviously, something went wrong between them, otherwise why would she shoot him?' said Harry. 'Why do you think she left her weapons behind for us to find?'

'She might have been trying to tell us that she had finished or, on the other hand, she could have been lulling us into a false sense of security. Who knows how many other weapons she has access to, or safe places to hide for that matter? Besides, it's a lot easier to walk away if you're not carrying a rifle and a couple of hand guns in your handbag.'

Harry took a pensive sip of the fresh glass of beer the waitress had put down on the table in front of him.

'She's got to be somewhere, alive or dead. People just don't disappear off the face of the earth.'

'I guess we'll have a better chance of finding her if she's still alive. There's a lot of country out there to hide a body,' said Carl.

Carl read through the summary report of the investigation into the Gordon empire. The report revealed very little of use to Carl. It confirmed that MG Cleaning Services had been acquired by Gordon Construction Labour Hire a little under two years ago, just after Con Gordon had handed over operational control of the enterprise to Steve.

The paper trail had revealed very little about what type of

specialist cleaning services MG Cleaning Services provided. It only confirmed that they were expensive.

He noted that the only property MG Cleaning Services owned was the house at 281 East Terrace, Portside. It appeared the money for that purchase had come from the funds Gordon Construction Labour Hire had paid for the cleaning company.

He was surprised to learn that the vehicle Falter and Bennett had been driving the night they were arrested was registered in the name of Gordon Fleet Services, which appeared to own all of the vehicles associated with Gordon Construction Labour Hire, including the Mercedes sedan Steve Gordon had driven to the golf course on the morning he was shot.

Carl noted, that beyond establishing that Sean Moore had provided garden services to Con and Steve Gordon over the years, and that Steve and Sean had been fellow punters until Steve had discovered golf about fifteen years ago, the investigators had been unable to find any evidence of any business dealings between Kieran and Sean Moore and the Gordons.

If any links existed, thought Carl, they were not tangible or ones that had been recorded.

Next, Carl read the summary of the investigation into the business dealings of Sean and Kieran Moore. The report stated that Sean's garden services business had looked profitable, until it became apparent that around fifty percent of the customers on his books did not actually exist. Apparently, Sean had been reporting income, and paying taxes on it, from sources that could not be verified. Although the contents of his safe certainly suggested he had been distributing ecstasy tablets and handling a lot of cash, the investigators had been unable to determine who he had been dealing with, or whether the cash had come from drug sales or winnings at the track.

Kieran Moore's books revealed that the income he had derived from his courier business was enough to keep his vehicle on the road, and support a modest lifestyle. Interestingly, at least as far as Carl was concerned, he'd received the lion's share of his income from one customer - Bob Butterfield, who had been coded as BB in the books. Of course, there was no way of proving that as whatever records Bob Butterfield had kept, had gone up in smoke the day Bennett and Falter had sterilised his farmhouse.

The team that had looked into the record keeping of Michael Murphy's bookmaking partnership with Charlie Boyle and Chris Morris, uncovered a pattern showing losses by one punter being matched by winnings for another punter at each mid-week race meeting. Not in the same race but always on the same day. With on course bookmaking being a cash game, the records were based on ticket stub numbers, not names of punters. To Carl, the pattern suggested an organised money laundering operation involving at least three parties: the loser, the bookmaker and the winner. He had a good idea who the winner was, and going on what Terry Moore had told him, suspected that Sean had played the role of both winner and loser, and the occasional break in the pattern was obviously how the bookmakers got paid for their role in the game. Too bad he couldn't talk to any of them, thought Carl as he closed the report.

Carl closed his eyes and was wondering if he'd ever find her, when a little thought popped into his head. He went out into the Incident Room. It was all but empty, except for Harry, who was sitting at his desk reading the same report on his computer screen.

'Harry, I wonder if our girl used a company car to leave town.'

Harry looked mystified. 'A company car, Boss?'

'Didn't you notice that Falter and Bennett were driving a company car on the night they were arrested?'

Harry flicked back to that page in the report.

'See what you mean. Are you suggesting that she might have had access to a company car?'

'I recall Falter saying that Clare had organised the safe

houses they had been hiding in. What if she'd also organised some back up transport?'

'I suppose that's possible.'

'Anything is possible, Harry. Get on to Gordon Fleet Services and see if any of their vehicles are missing.'

Harry looked up the number and placed a call while Carl went down to the cafeteria and bought them both a coffee.

When Carl got back with the coffees, Harry's eyes told him he'd found something.

'Spill the beans, Harry.'

'A grey Mercedes van. It's been missing since the week Steve Gordon was killed. It was supposed to have been delivered to a workshop for repairs by MG Cleaning Services, but it never turned up.'

'Did you get the registration number?'

'Yes.'

'Get it out to all patrols and send the details interstate. Might be how she left town.'

The excitement of a possible lead to the elusive Clare lasted barely forty-eight hours.

The van was located by a patrol responding to the armed holdup of the drive-through bottle shop of a suburban hotel, when the over-zealous getaway driver, high on dope, collided with a bus as he sped from the scene. The driver was killed, but his accomplice was very much alive when pulled from the vehicle by paramedics, and confessed to stealing the van from the workshop where he worked.

Clare's trail was cold.

CHAPTER 26

NINA RETURNED to work and became part of DI Reid's team, while the Bennett and Falter trials were in progress. She was restricted to light duties, which DI Reid translated into preparing case summaries for Chief Inspector Rankin.

'Even if we can't let you get your hands dirty, Sergeant, at least you can bring yourself up to date and review these reports for me in the process. DI West tells me you have a sharp eye for detail, and I always like a second opinion,' said DI Reid, as he assigned her the task.

'I hope you're not expecting speed, Inspector. My brain might be back to normal operations but my typing skills are still limited,' said Nina, pointing to the plaster cast that still encased her left arm.

'Nina, I've got HR breathing down my neck to make sure you don't get stressed, so there's no pressure. Just do what you can, at whatever pace suits you. If the typing side gets too much, no big deal. What I'm really interested in is your opinion, and you can give that to me verbally. Understood?'

'Yes. Understood, and thank you, Inspector.'

DI Reid left her to it, but it wasn't long before Harry came to see her.

'How's life with the new boss?'

'It's okay. It's not like I haven't worked with DI Reid before. Besides, the way the chief has structured the unit, I think the only differences will be who I report to, and who I take into the field with me, when they let me out of the office.' Nina smiled. 'We're all going to be working on cases together, from what I've heard.'

'That's certainly been the case with the Moore investigation,' said Harry.

'Guess that will scale back now that it's gone to trial,' said Nina.

'Yeah. The focus has shifted to the Gordon murder, but the only part we have is overseeing the search for Alicia Brown, and that seems to have to come to a dead end at the Crazy Dragon. We've had no confirmed sightings of her since she was seen coming back into the motel after the shooting.'

'It might look that way, Harry, but, between you and me, it's keeping a certain inspector awake at night trying to figure out where she went, and how she did it,' said Nina.

'Catch you later. I'm supposed to be doing something for that particular inspector. Great to have you back.'

Nina was liberated from her casts on the same day Stephen Falter learnt that he'd be spending up to twenty five years in prison.

To celebrate her release, Carl picked her up in a limousine and took her out to dinner at Massimo's, her favourite restaurant.

'So, how's it feel to be a woman with no visible means of support?' asked Carl, as he escorted her to the waiting limousine.

'A little unsteady, to be honest. They gave me a walking stick, but it doesn't go with this dress,' said Nina.

'Feel free to lean on me if you have to. We can't have you

falling flat on your face in public on your first big outing, can we?'
Carl placed a supportive arm around her slim body.

'Thank you, sweetheart,' said Nina, leaning in to let him keep her upright.

At Massimo's, the waiting staff made a big fuss of her return and Max, one of Carl's mates from his childhood days in the city, presented her with a large bunch of red roses and opened a bottle of her favourite champagne.

While they drank champagne and waited for their food, they talked about the one outstanding issue preventing the closure of the Moore case.

'Enough about work,' said Carl, when he spotted the waiter carrying their meals approaching. 'I think we need to talk about us.'

Nina waited while their meals were placed on the table.

'That sounds interesting.'

Carl took a bite of his smoked salmon.

'I was wondering whether you were ready to move to that next level, you know, the one we were discussing before your accident.'

Nina put down her fork and knife.

'Are you proposing to me, Carl West?'

'I suppose I am. What do you say?'

She watched as the smile spread across his face.

'I should have known with the limousine and the flowers. What else have you been up to?'

Carl put his right hand into the inside pocket of his coat and pulled out a small, black, soft-covered box. He opened the box and slid it over to Nina, who looked at the diamond engagement ring displayed in the open box.

'Oh, Carl, it's beautiful.'

Carl watched as she slipped the ring onto her finger and examined how it looked.

'I guess that means you're accepting my proposal, then,' said Carl.

'There's no way you're getting this back,' said Nina.

As if on cue, Max arrived with a camera to record the happy occasion, and joined them in a toast to the future Mrs West.

'How long have you been planning this?' said Nina, once the atmosphere in the restaurant returned to normal, following the eruption Max created by encouraging the evening's patrons to toast the happy couple.

'As soon as I knew you weren't going to die on me,' said Carl.

'I love you, Carl.'

'I know. That's why I want to marry you.'

'And when do you want to do that?'

'As soon as we can arrange it,' said Carl.

'You're not giving a girl much time to get ready,' said Nina.

'Take as much time as you want. We can discuss the details once you've gotten used to the idea, and given some thought to what sort of wedding you want.'

'That sounds like a plan I can work with.'

They spent the rest of the meal talking about possible wedding scenarios, and were looking at the dessert menu when Max escorted a couple to their table. Nina didn't recognise the woman, and had to look twice before she realised the man in the tuxedo was Harry.

'Harry, what are you doing here?' said Nina.

'We were at the Law Society Ball, but it wasn't half as exciting as what's been going on here. Congratulations!' Harry kissed Nina on the cheek.

'Nina, this is Jessika Walsh,' said Harry.

'Congratulations. Isn't it exciting to be getting married?' said Jessika.

'Thank you,' said Nina. It occurred to her that Carl must

have planned this as well. 'I'm a bit overwhelmed, actually. I had no idea he was going to do this tonight.'

Harry and Jessika joined them for dessert and coffee, and Carl told Nina how he had met Jessika, and discovered that Harry had some interests outside of work.

'So, Harry,' said Nina, smiling at Jessika. 'I thought we were friends, and now I find out you've been keeping secrets from me all this time.'

Harry blushed.

'We go back a long way,' said Jessika, coming to his rescue. 'We met at uni, but we've only been seeing each other as more than friends for the last few months.'

'Jessika's been trying to get Harry to see the light,' said Carl. 'Apparently, he needs saving from the likes of people like me.'

'I can understand that,' said Nina, laughing. She touched Jessika on the arm. 'Good luck with that but let me warn you, I think that's a lost cause.'

'He does have some other uses,' said Jessika, winking at Harry.

Now that Carl had proposed, Nina realised she was the one with the cold feet. She wanted to marry him, and had said she would, but she couldn't see her way through her inner turmoil to setting a date and planning a wedding.

She knew she didn't want a big wedding. They'd both already done that, but she realised that even a small wedding would take some planning. They'd have to decide on the guest list, the wedding party, where they'd get married, where they'd celebrate, and where they'd go for their honeymoon.

Carl had offered to arrange the wedding but they still needed to set a date to get things underway, and they were required to give the wedding celebrant at least a month's notice of their intention to get married.

She knew Carl was keen to get on with it, but each time they talked about it she ended up in tears, because she always thought about how her parents wouldn't be there.

Although she wasn't particularly religious, Nina arranged to see Father Mulligan, a priest she had met on the Ford case, who seemed to know a lot about grief, and who was highly recommended by Carl's friend and colleague, Marie Wood.

Father Mulligan answered his own door when she rang the bell.

'Hello, Father. I'm Nina Strong.'

'Nina. I remember you now. Call me Frank. Come in.'

Frank Mulligan led her down a corridor to his study at the back of the house. The book lined study looked out onto a garden, whose flower beds were overgrown by a green creeping plant with bright yellow flowers. Nina thought the garden looked like it could use some help from someone like Terry Moore.

Frank directed her to sit in one of the two armchairs in the room, which turned out to be surprisingly comfortable.

'So, Nina, what can I do for you?'

'Father, I mean, Frank, as I mentioned on the phone, my parents were killed a few months ago and I'm having trouble moving on from that.'

'Yes, I remember reading about that in the paper, and if you don't mind me saying so, you look a lot better now than you did when I last saw you in the hospital,' said Frank.

'You saw me in the hospital?'

Nina's expression told Frank that he'd surprised her with his admission.

'I'm one of the hospital chaplains, Nina. No-one knew what faith, if any, you belonged to, so we all prayed for you. It was touch and go when you first came in. I'm glad you decided to stay with us, and I gather so was your boss. What's his name? Ah yes, Inspector West. I saw him sitting by your bed on numerous occasions.'

'Carl. He's part of the reason I'm here. We're getting married.'

'Well, congratulations. That would certainly explain his anxious bedside vigil. I hope he knows how lucky he is.'

'He knows. I've told him.'

'Good for you. So, what's bothering you?'

'I feel so guilty. I know I should be grateful, but I can't help feeling guilty about surviving, when everybody else in the car, even the dog, was killed.'

Frank passed her the tissue box and waited while Nina pulled out several tissues and dabbed at her eyes.

'That's perfectly normal, Nina. The trick is to let yourself feel it and not push it away. It's painful at first but, if you let yourself feel it, the pain will diminish.'

'I miss them so much it's clouding my thoughts. I don't seem to be able to think clearly, and every time I think about the wedding, I end up crying because they won't be there.'

'Maybe you need to allow a little more time before going ahead with the wedding. Is Carl understanding or is he pressuring you?'

'He's very understanding. It was one of his friends who suggested I come and talk with you. Do you remember Marie Wood?'

'Marie. Yes, I see quite a lot of her. She'd be good to talk as well. You probably know her story.'

'Yes, Carl's told me a lot about Steve. They were the best of mates before Steve was killed.'

'I guess you are exposed to death a lot in your work.'

'Yes, but not as much as you, Frank, and most times, thank

God, it's not someone you know. Maybe that's what I'm finding the hardest. This time they're people I love.'

'Grieving is a process, Nina. There are no set rules but there do appear to be a few phases to go through, and talking about how you feel while you're grieving seems to help. Give yourself permission to grieve. You don't have to be strong.' Frank smiled at her and took her hands in his. 'You're allowed to fall apart if you want to, but there is no point in allowing yourself to sink into a black hole and staying there. After all, you're alive and you have a life to live. One of the traps I've noticed is people try to hold on to the past. If you're going to live, you need to let go of the past and focus on the here and now.'

'How do you do that?'

'Do you know anything about meditation or mindfulness?'

'Not really.'

'Okay, let's do a little experiment.' Frank let go of Nina's hands. 'Sit back and get comfortable, and then close your eyes.'

He waited while Nina got comfortable and closed her eyes.

'Now just focus on your breath. You can either notice it moving through your nostrils as you breathe in and out, or place your hands on your belly and feel it rise and fall as you breathe.'

He watched as Nina placed her hands on her belly.

'Just stay with your breath. If the mind goes somewhere else, when you notice, just bring it back to the breath.'

Frank let Nina focus on her breathing for around ten minutes.

'Now, take a deep breath in, and on the exhalation, slowly open your eyes.'

Nina opened her eyes and smiled.

Frank thought Carl West was indeed a lucky man; he could see the beauty of her spirit radiating through her eyes.

'How did you find that?'

'That was very relaxing. Is that how meditation works?'

'Basically. The secret is to do it every day.'

'How long?'

'Doesn't matter really. It's the frequency that's important. Start with ten minutes and go from there. You'll know when to increase it and when to stop.'

'I always thought meditation was something only religious people did,' said Nina, feeling a little embarrassed by her ignorance.

Frank smiled. 'My bishop thinks it's something only Buddhists do, but then again, he and I move in different circles.' Frank chuckled to himself. 'When you get home, google 'Full Catastrophe Living', it's the name of a book that explains mindfulness meditation. There's nothing religious about it.'

Frank wrote the title of the book on a piece of paper for her.

'Now, would you join me for a coffee and a piece of cake? Alice likes to spoil my guests.'

'Thank you, that sounds good.'

Frank left the room to speak to his housekeeper and came back in after five minutes with a tray. Alice had obviously been waiting for him, thought Nina.

'So, have you organised a marriage celebrant?' asked Frank, as he poured the coffee.

'Not yet.'

'I'd be happy to do it for you.'

'Neither of us are Catholics, Frank, and we've both been married before,' said Nina. 'I thought that would be outside your ambit.'

'The bishop might agree with you, but it doesn't have to be a church wedding. I'm registered as a marriage celebrant with the State. In this country, you get married under the powers of the State, not the Church. Besides, I love garden weddings.'

'I think I'd better bring Carl to meet you, then.'

'You do that. Have a chat with him, and then give me a call to arrange a time.'

'Perhaps we can have you over to dinner. Carl's a great cook.'

Nina bought the book Frank recommended, and started a daily meditation practice of ten minutes in the morning, before going to work, and another ten minutes in the evening when she got home.

'You should try this,' she said to Carl, as she opened her eyes. 'It's really relaxing. It's a great way to leave the office behind when you get home.'

'How does it work? You don't seem to be doing anything,' said Carl, as he headed to the kitchen to start on the night's meal.

Nina walked in behind him. 'Show me what you're doing in here, and I'll explain it to you.'

'Okay.'

'What are we having?'

'I'm making that seafood pasta dish you like. It's real easy. The only hard part is remembering to take the mixed seafood out of the freezer to put in the fridge before you go to work.'

'Show me.'

Carl opened the fridge and took out the bag of thawed mixed seafood.

'Where do you get that stuff?'

'I buy it at the seafood shop in the market,' said Carl. 'Now, get the large saucepan out of that cupboard and half fill it with water. Then add a couple of teaspoons of salt and put it on the stove.'

Nina did as he asked while Carl watched her.

'What are you doing?'

'Watching a beautiful woman in her natural environment, the kitchen.'

He laughed, but that didn't save him from a poke in the belly.

'Now, when the water's boiling, we'll drop in this packet of pasta and let it cook for around ten minutes. The only thing you have to do is turn the flame down and give it the occasional stir.' He handed her the pasta and a long handled wooden spoon.

'Once you have the pasta going, you do the seafood in this. He placed a medium sized frying pan on the stove. 'You put in some olive oil, cold pressed virgin, of course.' He held up the bottle. 'Turn on the heat, add some crushed garlic. I cheat on that bit by buying it already crushed.' He retrieved a jar of crushed garlic from the fridge and spooned a teaspoon of the contents into the heating oil. 'Then you can either add some freshly cut up tomatoes or some of these sliced ones you can buy in a can.'

Nina watched while he spooned in some of the sliced tomato pieces from the can.

'You stirring that pasta, sweetheart?'

Nina used the wooden spoon on the pasta.

'Then you add the seafood mix and give it a stir.' He took the wooden spoon from her and stirred the mix in the frying pan. 'Then you turn down the gas and put the lid on. By the time the pasta's ready, you're done.'

'Think I could do that,' said Nina.

'The secret is to get the sequence right and pay attention.'

'That's basically how the meditation works,' said Nina. 'All you do is breathe and pay attention to your breathing.'

'I thought there was supposed to be some mantra or some other mumbo jumbo,' said Carl.

'Well, not according to Frank Mulligan and this Jon Kabat-Zinn guy.'

'Who's he?'

'He wrote the book I'm reading, 'Full Catastrophe Living'. I think you should read it.'

'Okay, lets drain the water from the pasta and eat.'

After eating, they watched the TV news and sat down to read.

'How does this meditation thing work?' asked Carl.

'You just close your eyes and focus on your breathing,' said Nina.

'That sounds pretty simple. How can just breathing with your eyes closed do any good?' said Carl.

'According to this book, it's got something to do with paying attention, instead of getting sucked into whatever you're thinking,' said Nina. 'Why don't you give it a go? I can talk you through it.'

'Okay.'

Carl relaxed into the armchair and closed his eyes.

'Just breath in and out, and notice how you can feel it in your nostrils or how your belly goes up and down. Try resting your hands on your belly, and just focus on how it feels to breathe.'

Nina watched as Carl placed his hands on his belly.

'If you notice that your attention has drifted to your thoughts, just gently bring it back to your breathing.'

Nina smiled, when she realised Carl had fallen asleep, something which was quite common with first time meditators, according to what she had read. She let him sleep.

Carl slept, until he startled himself awake with a loud snore. He opened his eyes and looked around, not quite sure where he was or what he had been doing. When he realised he was sitting in his own living room with Nina, he looked at his watch. Thirty minutes had gone by.

'What happened?'

'You went to sleep.'

'What does that mean?'

'Means you need to meditate a lot more,' said Nina. 'How do you feel?'

'Like I need to go to bed.'

'And, I was planning to stay over for a cuddle,' said Nina.

'If you want a cuddle, you'd better come to bed now before I fall asleep on you.'

In mid-October, they decided on an early December wedding and invited Frank Mulligan to dinner.

Frank arrived with a bottle of shiraz, and the paperwork required for recording their intention to get married.

While Carl was completing dinner preparations, Frank talked with Nina.

'How are things going for you, Nina?'

'I'm feeling a lot better. I've spent some time with Marie Wood. She's really supportive, and Carl and I have talked about it too. I keep forgetting that he had to cope with not having a father, and his mother dying when he was only a teenager. He knows a lot about grieving. I feel rather blessed to have so many supportive people around me.' Nina smiled at Frank. 'Thank you for caring.'

'You're welcome, Nina.'

'Shall we eat?' said Carl, coming in with the roast lamb and vegetables he had cooked.

'Let me open the wine,' said Frank.

'We're thinking of late afternoon on the first Friday in December, in the Botanic Gardens. How does that fit with you, Frank?' said Carl.

Frank took out his iPhone and looked at his calendar.

'When you say late afternoon, what time do you have in

mind?' asked Frank.

'Well, it's daylight saving then, so six o'clock?'

'Okay, I can make that fit. Let's get this paperwork out of the way, shall we?'

'Okay.'

'Do you have your divorce details?'

Nina fetched the folder holding their papers and they spent the next half hour completing the form.

'Now that we have that done, how about coffee?' said Carl.

Over coffee, they discussed the format of the ceremony and the sort of vows they wanted to exchange. Frank gave them some examples to consider.

'We have plenty of time. As long as you have it sorted out a week beforehand, we should be fine. And if these aren't enough, there are plenty of examples on the internet,' said Frank.

'I think you have given us enough to choose from,' said Carl.

'How's the meditation going, Nina?' asked Frank, as he was standing to leave.

'Good. I've settled into a regular routine and that book you suggested has been really helpful. I've even got Carl meditating.'

'Took me a while to get through the going to sleep step,' said Carl.

'And, how are you finding it now?'

'Wish I had found out about it earlier. It's really helping me separate work from home. It's a great way of making that break, but I've also found it helpful at work, being able to take a moment to check in and get myself in the here and now. Makes it so much easier to see what's actually going on.'

'Guess that must be helpful in your line of work.'

'Makes me wonder how much stuff I've missed over the years.'

'Better not to go there, Carl,' said Frank. 'That's living in the past.'

CHAPTER 27

CHIEF INSPECTOR RANKIN looked up from reading Carl's leave application.

'Didn't you just have a month off, Carl?'

'That was carer's leave, Chief. I was looking after Nina.'

'Well, you must have done a good job, I see she's back at work. Why do you want more leave, and not just four weeks this time? And, right across the silly season as well, I see.'

Carl placed a white envelope on the chief's desk.

'Perhaps you'd better read this, Chief.'

The chief inspector looked at the envelope and noticed the embossed flowers in the top left corner. He picked it up and felt the expensive paper.

'Is this what I think it is, Carl?'

'Better open it and see.'

Chief Inspector Rankin inserted his letter opener under the flap of the envelope and slit it open. Dried rose petals fell onto his desk and scattered across it, as he pulled out the wedding invitation. He took a moment to read it. A broad smile spread across his face.

'Creative way of solving your 'Nina problem', Carl.'

The chief inspector stood up, came around from behind his desk and shook Carl's hand.

'Congratulations! You make a great couple. I'm really happy for you, Carl.'

'Thank you, Chief. I hope you and Mrs Rankin will be able to come.'

'Wouldn't miss it for the world. And, Carl, leave approved.'

While Nina was spending her days writing reports and doing her rehabilitation exercises, Carl was drawn into another murder investigation.

The day after Chief Inspector Rankin had approved his leave, the body of a teenage girl was found under some bushes in City Park, a short distance from the park's main gates on North Terrace.

Seventeen-year old Cynthia Reynolds had been reported missing by her mother, when she hadn't come home from a night out in the city. Her partially clad body had been found the following morning, by two park rangers performing the routine opening of the gates to City Park.

Carl and Harry went to see Mike Jonas in his office, after coming back from the crime scene.

The autopsy examination revealed she had been sexually assaulted, and that her attacker had left enough evidence at the scene to convict himself, assuming they could find him.

'Obviously not someone interested in safe sex, Inspector,' said the pathologist.

'So, what do you think killed her, Mike? I didn't see any obvious wounds or marks on the body,' said Carl.

'I'll know for certain when I get the toxicology report, but my initial assessment is a drug overdose. I couldn't find any needle marks, so probably something she ingested, like ecstasy,' said the pathologist.

'What's the probable time of death?'

'I'd say between midnight and one in the morning, Inspector.'

Carl and Harry interviewed Mrs Reynolds, who lived with her daughter in a house, north of the city, adjacent to the local railway station. Both the house and Mrs Reynolds had seen better days.

The interview did not go well. Mrs Reynolds was distraught, and kept repeating to herself that she should never have let Cynthia go into the city on her own. According to Mrs Reynolds, Cynthia had insisted on going into the city to meet a girlfriend for a night out. Mrs Reynolds didn't know who the friend was, except that she was some girl Cynthia had met at work. When Cynthia did not come home on the eleven o'clock train, her mother had tried to reach her on her mobile, and when she hadn't come home by two o'clock, she'd rung the police.

The only new information the interview provided was that Cynthia worked as a checkout operator, in the Target store in the City Centre Building, and that her father had left the scene when she was still in primary school.

On the way back from the interview, they called into the Target store in the City Centre Building, where they learnt from Cynthia's friend, Suzanne Whyte, that after the movie, she had taken a taxi, while Cynthia had left to catch the eleven o'clock train home.

As they walked back into the office, Carl suggested to Harry that he start with the CCTV cameras covering the bus stop located outside the gates of City Park, and the CCTV from the railway station.

'You'd have to be an idiot to drag someone into the park from there, Boss. It's lit up all night.'

'Who knows how bright this guy is? He didn't bother with a

condom. What's to say he has any idea there are cameras outside the gate?'

Harry spent the rest of the morning reviewing CCTV recordings. His initial suspicions appeared to be correct. There was no sign of the girl being taken into the park through the area by the main gates, which were more of a symbolic than an actual barrier to entrance into the park after dark. The recording did, however, contain images of a group of three young men leaving the park through the main gates just before one o'clock in the morning.

There was no sign of Cynthia entering the railway station to catch the eleven o'clock train, so it looked like she must have been intercepted somewhere between the cinema and the station.

By the time Harry had determined that the killer had not used the front gate to get into the park, the Forensics team studying the crime scene had read the message in the footprints around the area where the body had been found. After eliminating the boots of the park rangers who had found the body, they decided that there were at least three different sets, and none of them matched the victim's shoes.

'That semen left behind could be quite a cocktail,' said Carl, when Harry passed on the update he had received from Forensics. 'Better see if we can locate that group you spotted. They were in the area at the time. If they aren't the killers, they may have seen or heard something. In any case, I want to speak to them.'

Harry extracted the best still shots he could from the CCTV recording, and then released both the video of the group coming out from the park and the stills to the media, with a request for public assistance.

While they waited for the public to respond, Harry and a small team of uniformed officers, visited the shops along the most likely route Cynthia would have taken from the cinema to the railway station, and reviewed any security camera recordings from the night Cynthia had been killed.

Harry got lucky. The camera covering the entrance to a bridal shop, located around the corner from the cinema where the girls had gone to the movies, had captured Cynthia's interception by the same group of young men he'd seen in the recording from outside the gates to City Park. The recording from the bridal shop revealed an initial tense stand-off between Cynthia and one of the men, who had attempted to put his arm around her, an exchange of words, followed by Cynthia going with them, on the arm of the man she had initially baulked at letting touch her.

By the time Harry had returned to the office with a copy of the video, Crime Stoppers had received a call from Sonia Tante, a friend of the victim, who had told them that one of the men, Eddie Burton, had been Cynthia's boyfriend, before she had broken off with him.

When Carl and Harry interviewed Sonia, she told them that Cynthia had broken off the relationship because Eddie had turned violent and threatened her, when she'd said no to sex with him.

Carl showed her the still photograph of the group.

'That's him. That one there.' She jabbed her finger on the image of the man in the middle of the shot. 'And that one is his brother, William,' she said, pointing to the man behind him.

'Do you know who the other guy is?' asked Carl.

'I can't be sure, Inspector, but it looks like Cynthia's half-brother, Ronnie Edwards. They're always hanging out together.'

'Do you know where we can find them?' asked Carl.

'They have a flat in the city. I don't know the exact address, but I'm pretty sure Cynthia's mum would know. Ronnie's her son from her first marriage. She thinks the sun shines out his arse.'

After their interview with Sonia, Carl and Harry went to interview Mrs Reynolds again.

Mrs Reynolds went into shock when they showed her the photograph of the three men coming out of City Park, and it was several minutes before she was calm enough to speak.

'I don't understand. Are you telling me that you think these boys killed Cynthia?'

'Mrs Reynolds, I don't know if they killed her but we do have a recording, from a security camera in Huxley Street, showing Cynthia meeting up with them after the movie,' said Carl. 'All I'm saying is I'd like to speak to them; they might be able to help us work out what happened.'

'I can't believe they'd hurt her, Inspector, not with Ronnie there. He wouldn't let them hurt her. And that Eddie, he's such a nice young man, always so polite, and protective of Cynthia.'

'Can you give me Ronnie's address, Mrs Reynolds?' asked Carl.

Mrs Reynolds looked up, startled.

'I need to speak to him,' said Carl.

Mrs Reynolds hesitated.

Carl waited.

'The boys live in Huxley Street, Inspector, at number 286. In flat 3B.'

'Do you know where they work?'

'They're all working on the new hospital. They're builders' labourers.'

'That sounds like hard work.'

'The pay's good. They always seem to have plenty of money, Inspector.'

'Mrs Reynolds, one of Cynthia's friends told us that she had recently broken up with this Eddie Burton. Can you tell me anything about that?' asked Carl.

'If it was Sonia Tante, Inspector, anything she told you about Cynthia and Eddie would be a lie. She's nothing but a jealous bitch!'

Carl thanked Mrs Reynolds for her help and promised he'd let her know as soon as he knew anything.

As Carl and Harry made their way to their car, Mrs Reynolds called Ronnie and warned him that the police were coming to speak to him about Cynthia's death.

'Strike you as a bit strange that Ronnie wasn't there to comfort his mother, Harry?'

'I've given up trying to work out what's normal behaviour and what's strange, Boss. Where to?'

'Let's go visit the new hospital.'

Carl's mobile rang as Harry pulled out from the kerb.

'Carl, I've got the toxicology report,' said Mike Jonas. 'Looks like my original assessment was correct. I'd say there's a bad batch of ecstasy out there. She's the third one this month.'

'When do you think you'll have the DNA analysis, Mike?'

'By the end of the week.'

'Thanks.' Carl ended the call.

'Mike says she's another ecstasy victim,' said Carl, as Harry negotiated the traffic.

As they parked in the car park near the construction site for the new hospital, their call-sign came over the radio. The Operations Room dispatcher informed them that the Burton brothers and Ronnie Edwards had turned themselves in at Police Headquarters.

'Guess we won't be getting the guided tour after all,' said Carl. 'Home, James.'

Harry backed the car out of the parking space they had just entered and headed for the office.

The Burton brothers, Ronnie Edwards and a man in a suit, who Carl assumed was their lawyer, sat in the waiting room on the ground floor of Police Headquarters.

'I'm Detective Inspector West,' said Carl, as he and Harry entered the room, 'and this is Detective Fuller. I understand you want to talk to us about the death of Cynthia Reynolds.'

The man in the suit stood up.

'Peter Fitzsimmons, Inspector. I'm with Ratten and Brown. We've been retained by Misters Burton and Edwards, who wish to make a statement.'

'Mr Fitzsimmons,' said Carl, shaking the lawyer's offered hand, 'would you like to introduce your clients?'

'Edward Burton, his brother William, and this is Ronald Edwards, Inspector.'

Each of the men nodded as they were introduced.

'Gentlemen, if you'll follow me, we'll move to a room upstairs where you can make your statements.'

On the second floor, where the interview rooms were located, Carl decided to interview Edward Burton first. William and Ronald were asked to wait in separate rooms, under the supervision of a uniformed officer.

Eddie Burton admitted to giving Cynthia an ecstasy tablet and to having sex with her. He claimed it was consensual.

'Why did you give her the ecstasy if it was consensual?' asked Carl.

'She liked to relax before we fucked.'

'Had you given her ecstasy before?' asked Carl.

Eddie looked at his lawyer. 'Do I have to answer that?'

'You don't have to answer any questions, Mr Burton, but it's up to you how much information you choose to divulge,' said Peter Fitzsimmons.

Eddie rubbed his hands on his jeans.

'As long as I'm confessing to stuff, I may as well get it off my chest. She was one of my regulars.'

'You're a dealer, then?' said Carl.

Eddie looked at his lawyer again.

'Yeah. I'm a dealer. I didn't know it was bad shit. We've been using for a couple of years. Never had any trouble with the stuff before.'

'Get this lot from your regular supplier?' asked Carl.

'Yeah. I get the stuff from a guy at work.'

'Who do you work for, Mr Burton? Cynthia's mother told us you were working on the new hospital.'

'Gordon Construction.'

Carl looked at Harry.

Okay, we'll want to talk to you about that later. For now, can you tell us what happened with Cynthia?'

'We'd had a fight. She wanted to pay for her stuff with cash instead of sex. I liked fucking her, so I said no.'

'How did you know where she was?' asked Carl.

'Her mother told me.'

'When was that?'

'I called around to see her. Her mum said she'd gone to the movies with some girl from work, and that she was catching the eleven o'clock train home.'

'What happened when you met up with her?'

'I said I was sorry and offered her a hit for free. We went back to the flat. We all had a hit and she wanted to fuck, so we did, and,' Eddie started crying, 'and, she went limp when I was in her. She just stopped moving. I thought she'd passed out but she was dead.'

'What did you do when you realised she was dead?'

'I freaked out.'

'Did you call an ambulance?'

Eddie shook his head. 'I didn't see any point. She wasn't breathing. There was no pulse.'

'You're an expert on those things?' asked Carl.

'I'm the first aid officer in my work team. She was dead.'

'Okay, so how did her body end up in City Park?'

'I put some clothes on her, and then Bill and Ronnie helped me carry her down to the park. It's only a couple of blocks. We put her under some bushes near the front gate.'

'So, what made you change your mind?'

'I realised I'd panicked. I didn't kill her. I know I did the wrong thing hiding the body, and I've pulled Bill and Ronnie into it as well. I didn't kill her, but I know I'm the one that gave her the shit that did.'

'You've done the right thing coming forward.'

'Are you going to charge me with murder?'

'That will depend on what your brother and your friend tell us,' said Carl. 'Now before I speak with them, what can you tell me about who supplies you with the ecstasy, and is that all you get from them?'

Eddie looked at Peter Fitzsimmons.

'Mr Burton, I'd suggest that answering these questions would be seen as helping the police with their inquiries. Would I be correct, Inspector?'

'Yes. You may not be aware, Mr Burton, but there's been a spat of ecstasy related deaths this month, so we're keen to locate the source of the bad shit, as you called it.'

'Jock Harding. He's the guy who decides who gets a job on whatever building site we're working on.'

'And, he works for Gordon Construction Labour Hire?'

'They call it Gordon Construction now. He can get you anything you want.'

'How long have you worked there?'

'About three years. I got a job there straight out of school. My dad works there.'

'Okay, Mr Burton, we'll just get the transcript typed up for you to sign. If you wait here, we'll go and speak to your brother and Mr Edwards.

Carl was not surprised when the statements of the others corroborated Eddie Burton's story.

At the end of the interviews, Eddie and Ronnie were charged with dealing, and all three were charged with concealing a body. At the hearing in the Magistrates' Court they were committed for trial, and then released on bail.

While they were appearing in the Magistrates' Court, Jock Harding was arrested and brought in for questioning. Despite initially stonewalling, he agreed to make a statement about the distribution of drugs through Gordon Construction, in exchange for not being charged with the murders of three young girls, who had died after taking ecstasy tablets he had supplied to Eddie Burton and Ronnie Edwards.

Jock Harding told Carl that he'd been with Gordon Construction from the start. In fact, he'd been one of Con Gordon's right hand men, when the firm was created to represent the pool of workers disaffected by the exploitive practices of the big construction firms.

According to Jock, Con Gordon got what he wanted by promising his workers anything they wanted to keep them happy, including access to a range of illicit substances. In his statement, Jock revealed that Con had supplied Kieran Moore with the ingredients required to make the stuff, in the lab Kieran had up the river, as a way of maintaining quality control of the output. He told Carl that Con had bragged about having an industrial chemist running that laboratory, and was a little surprised when Carl confirmed that he had.

Apparently, the quality of the stuff had dived when Kieran

Moore's operation had been shut down, and he'd been forced to seek out alternative suppliers to keep his people happy. Jock claimed the stuff was made available to workers for personal use. They weren't supposed to be peddling it outside the workplace but, he admitted, some of the newer workers, like Eddie and Ronnie, had screwed up ideas about loyalty.

Harding refused to divulge details of his current supplier, claiming his life wouldn't be worth living, and that the lives of his wife and kids would be at risk.

Harding was charged with dealing in illicit substances and taken before a magistrate, who remanded him in custody when Carl opposed his bail application.

Once Carl had advised him that he had confirmation of his long held suspicions, Chief Inspector Rankin took direct charge of the investigation, releasing Carl to go on leave and get married.

CHAPTER 28

Nɪɴᴀ's first wedding had been a full-blown church service - white wedding dress, two flower girls, three bridesmaids, and a lavish reception with over a hundred guests. The short marriage that followed had ended in disillusion and heartache.

Nina had no intention of revisiting that story and Carl, with a similar story of his own, offered no resistance when she proposed a small, simple ceremony.

The late afternoon sun was streaming through the trees of the Botanic Gardens, located in the north western corner of City Park, when their limousine pulled into the parking bay next to the spot they had reserved for their wedding ceremony.

Frank Mulligan, dressed in a plain grey suit, stood with Harry and Jessika, Chief Inspector Rankin and his wife, Evelyn, Bob Reid and his wife, Joan, Marie Wood with her partner, Paul, Robert and Nancy, and Mike Jonas, the pathologist, with his cameras.

Frank led them through their marriage vows, while Mike recorded the ceremony on video. Harry and Marie were the witnesses when they signed the register. After twenty minutes the official part was over. They were married. Everybody kissed the bride.

After the brief ceremony, Mike indulged his passion for photography, creating an extensive digital record of the happy couple against the backdrop of the gardens - Carl, in his charcoal grey suit, white shirt and sky blue silk tie, and Nina, in a flowing, full length, silk gown that matched Carl's tie.

When it was time for the group photographs, they all laughed as Mike set up the camera and scrambled over to his chosen spot, to ensure he would be in the record of those who had attended.

By seven thirty, the members of the wedding party were ensconced in Massimo's, where, except for Frank, who had to leave early, they celebrated into the wee small hours.

The taxis outside Massimo's enjoyed good business that night, when the wedding party finally went home.

On the following Sunday morning, Carl and Nina boarded a Qantas flight to Hawaii, intent on spending the five weeks of their honeymoon relaxing in the sun, and catching up on all that sex they had missed while Nina was encased in plaster.

CHAPTER 29

CLARE KNEW that no-one disappeared without careful planning, and she'd been planning ever since taking on the role as Steve Gordon's assassin. Not only did she not trust men like Steve Gordon, who went about re-organising their world by eliminating the people that stood in their way through hired killers, like herself, she did not trust thugs like George and Malcolm, who only thought about themselves.

In a way, she was grateful that George and Malcolm hadn't been able to do what they should have done, when Toby appeared on the scene as they were despatching Kieran Moore. That failure had redeemed them a little, as human beings, in her eyes, and had, truth be told, helped her make the decisions she had made. If they'd done the right thing, and simply slit the kid's throat, she knew she'd probably still be doing whatever it was that Steve had planned.

Steve's offhanded order to get rid of the kid, as if he held no value, had opened something inside her that she thought had been taken away forever - her heart.

Toby was such a beautiful child, doing his best to be brave, even though he had worked out his probable fate. Clare had fallen in love with him.

After what she had been through while on active service, Clare believed she'd never be able to feel anything like love, ever again. She had participated in so much killing she had defined herself as a ruthless killer with no emotions. Ever since crossing the line to paid assassin, each victim had just been a target. Shooting Sean Moore had been nothing more to her than a business transaction.

Removing the bookmakers had been the first time she had worked with George and Malcolm. Her part had been easy. One shot in the head for each. George and Malcolm, famous for their clean up skills, had been given the job of making sure the bodies would never be found. Steve had really liked their hospital solution.

George, the more talkative of the two, had told her how they cleaned up sites where industrial accidents had happened, before inspectors were called in, on projects where Gordon's people were doing the work. They seemed to know their stuff and they had access to all the required equipment.

Apart from working for Steve Gordon, Clare was also dealing with the fallout of her mother's stroke. She now knew that one of the downsides of living in a cottage at the end of a track in a remote valley was that people didn't visit very often. Clare had been going to see her mother once a week, usually on weekends.

Her mother had loved living in the wilderness, where she could withdraw into herself, and escape the traumas she had not known how to let go of - her son's death in a helicopter crash, not long after he had realised his dream of becoming a Special Air Services soldier, and the final act of her husband, who had blown off his head to silence the demons that had tormented him since Vietnam.

Her mother had suffered a stroke, and lain on the floor of her little cottage for three days, before Clare had arrived for her Sunday afternoon visit. By the time she had delivered her to City

Hospital, her mother was little more than a breathing vegetable. Since then, her weekly visits had been made to the Seaview Nursing Home, and she had appropriated the cottage as her safe house.

Once she had decided, she took Toby to her safe house and allowed herself a week of loving him, while she initiated her plan for disappearing. As a sniper, one of the things she had learnt about camouflage was that, with the right choice of clothing and accessories, you could hide in plain sight, even with a rifle.

The initial picture the police had released to the public was of a tall, slender woman with short, blonde hair, dressed in body hugging motorcycle leathers.

After dropping Toby off at his parents' house, Clare returned to her hideaway in the hills and packed her bags, with the items she had chosen for her last mission, before disappearing. She knew she would have a week, thanks to Steve's regular routine - he played golf every Tuesday morning before work on the public golf course, just north of the city centre. In Clare's opinion, that golf course with its tree lined fairways was perfect for a sniper.

The following morning, she caught the local commuter bus into the city, carrying her equipment in a black sports bag and her clothing and accessories in a black backpack, wearing the loose-fitting clothes she generally wore when in the role of Alicia Brown.

Once in the city, she checked into the Crazy Dragon Motel, where she knew cash was king and no-one would ask questions. After securing her weapons, she ventured out into the city wearing a dress, high heels, black rimmed glasses and a wig of shoulder length dark hair. She walked around the city using cash to buy what she needed to make good her disappearance.

Each morning, she got up early and went into the gym next door to the motel, and paid the barely awake girl sitting by the cash register, the daily rate in cash.

On Sunday, she made a night excursion to the golf course and selected the spot from which to take out Steve Gordon.

On Monday, she risked travelling on public transport, as Alicia Brown in a hoodie, to visit her mother and say goodbye.

She followed the case on the TV news but did not buy a newspaper, seeing no sense in leaving what would amount to a smoking gun for the housekeeping staff.

On Tuesday morning, she left the motel wearing the black tracksuit and carrying the black sports bag, as she had done every other morning. But on this morning, instead of going to the gym, she made her way to the golf course and climbed into position in the tree she had selected. From her perch, she had a perfect line of fire on the path players used between the third and fourth fairways, and she could see the green of the third through the trees.

Clare had been in position for just over thirty minutes when Steve Gordon and his playing partner came into view on the green. With practiced care, she removed her rifle from the sports bag and, while Steve sunk his putt, assembled the weapon, clipped on the magazine, adjusted the laser guided sight, attached the bag that would catch the spent round as it was automatically ejected, and made herself ready to fire.

Steve crested the small rise between the two fairways and moved into the crosshairs in her sights that marked the centre of her killing zone. Clare squeezed the trigger and heard the loud report of the rifle discharging its deadly missile. One shot in the centre of the chest. She knew she had taken him out.

By the time Steve Gordon had toppled back over his golf buggy, Clare had broken down the rifle and returned its parts to her sports bag. She glanced in the direction of the mayhem she had caused. Steve's playing partner was flat on the ground trying to work his mobile phone, and not looking in her direction at all. She dropped out of the tree and silently made her way through the line of trees back to the footpath that would take her to the city centre.

Mr Ming, the manager of the Crazy Dragon, waved to her as she entered the motel foyer and made her way to the elevators. She went up to her room and had a shower, as if she had just come in from the gym. After the shower, she dumped the sports bag holding her weapons onto the bed and changed into the outfit she had chosen for her trip out of town.

Keen observation during the week, had revealed that Mr Ming was usually overwhelmed by people checking out around nine o'clock. Clare waited until five to nine to exit the motel, when the crowd of people in the lobby was large enough to block Mr Ming's view, so that he did not see the tall, pregnant woman, with dark shoulder length hair and black rimmed glasses, wearing sensible flat black shoes and a grey overcoat with a yellow lining, pulling a small wheeled cabin bag and carrying a yellow handbag, leave the motel.

Once outside, Clare crossed the street to the line of taxis in front of the railway station.

The driver of the first taxi in the line got out and helped her with her bag.

'Where to, love?'

'Airport, thank you.'

She got into the back of the taxi for the twenty minute ride to the airport. Fortunately, the driver was not one of those drivers that wanted to talk.

At the airport, she paid the taxi fare in cash and walked into the check-in area to find a ticket kiosk. At the kiosk, she keyed in the booking number from her online booking and the machine printed out her boarding pass, in the name of Julia Redmond.

With her boarding pass in hand, she was cleared through security and into the departure lounge to await boarding, where she spent a nervous half hour reading a book on the wonders of breastfeeding, before passengers were invited to board the flight.

Clare knew that only fools relaxed their guard when it looked like they were in the clear. Having no idea whether she had been spotted or whether she would be identified from the CCTV recordings before they landed, she stayed in character until the shuttle she had taken from the airport dropped her off at the interstate bus terminal. Before entering the terminal, she went for a walk, deflated the pregnancy bump she was wearing and turned her overcoat inside out, so that it was now a yellow coat with a grey lining.

When she entered the terminal, she walked up to a ticket vending machine and used the cash option to purchase a ticket.

ACKNOWLEDGMENTS

Every author needs a support team to turn a manuscript into a book. I owe a debt of gratitude to Toni and Francesco, my in-house team, for their help with editing and proof-reading.

Thank you to my friends and colleagues in the Indie Publishing world for their advice and support.

Murder. Arson. Revenge.

Detective Inspector West investigates the grisly deaths of two elderly priests: one in a suspicious fire; the other obviously murdered.

The inspector is not the only one hunting the priest killer.

If you like murder mixed with mystery and conflict, you'll probably love the suspense and intrigue in Holy Death, the third book in the Inspector West series.

CHAPTER ONE

Fr Maurice Skinner opened the door at the back of the old church. A stream of pale yellow light escaped into the night and bathed the solitary vehicle standing in the car park behind the building. Darkness reclaimed St Frank's minibus when he closed the door behind him.

Fr Skinner had no need for a light to guide him on his way. The pale moonlight penetrating through the low cloud was more than sufficient to illuminate his path. Besides, Fr Skinner knew all there was to know about walking in darkness.

Dressed in priestly black, the old priest stepped into the night and merged with the darkness. He walked across the expanse of the yard separating his residence from the old church on autopilot. His head was still locked in the discussion he had been having with Robert Sturm, the supervisor of the men's shelter located in the old church.

He was still ruminating on his impending enforced retirement when he reached the side door of his house. He was not happy that Bishop Kerry had turned down his plea to stay on as the chaplain of St Frank's. He'd devoted the last ten years of his life to the men who used the shelter, and couldn't see why he had to stop just because of some stupid rule.

Even though he was turning seventy-five, the Church's compulsory retirement age, he'd argued that at least he was available to do the job. The bishop had insisted that there was no way he could allow him to stay on, as their insurance didn't cover priests beyond seventy-five.

He was furious, but what could he do? The bishop held all the power. After his meeting with the bishop, he'd sulked all the way home and spent the evening complaining to Robert.

As far as he could tell, the bishop had no-one else to look after the needs of the poor souls that called St Frank's home. It wasn't as if the seminary was bursting with new recruits to the priesthood. God, if things don't improve Robert will be right, he thought, and we really will be importing more priests from Africa and India.

On the threshold of his residence, Fr Skinner rummaged in his pockets for his keys. Standing in the dark, he silently rebuked himself for not having replaced the spent bulb in the security light that usually illuminated his approach to the door. He'd meant to replace it earlier in the day but had forgotten all about it, thanks to his meeting with the bishop. Too late now, he thought, as he felt for the keyhole.

After a couple of fumbled attempts, he managed to slip the

key into the lock and turn the handle. As he opened the door, he felt a firm push in the middle of his back, and stumbled into the dark interior of the house.

He crashed onto the floor, hitting his head on the leg of the hat-rack standing in the hallway. He heard the door close behind him, and blinked as the light came on. A pair of firm hands grabbed him by the collar and roughly dragged him up into a kneeling position. With his head locked between two strong hands smelling of cigarettes, he couldn't turn to see his assailant.

A cold fear rose up from deep within his gut. He thought he was going to wet himself.

'What do you want?'

The silence was broken by a voice that Fr Skinner did not recognise.

'I hope you've said your prayers, Father.'

CHAPTER TWO

Detective Inspector Carl West sat at his desk with his hands wrapped around a cup of hot coffee. His head hurt. He wished he'd exercised a little more restraint during the previous night's celebration of Harry Fuller's promotion to detective sergeant, and hoped he'd only have to manage a quiet day of paperwork in the office. Detective Constable Lisa Templar was due to join them tomorrow to replenish the ranks of his diminished team and, despite his headache, he was determined to have things ready for her.

He took a sip of his coffee and started work. He'd only managed to log on to his computer when the telephone on his desk rang. He listened as Operations gave him the details, and then went out into the squad room where, like Carl, DS Harry Fuller was nursing both a cup of coffee and a hangover.

'You look like death warmed up, Harry.'

'You don't look much better, Boss. Hope we're having a quiet one.'

Carl shook his head and immediately regretted it.

'Our luck's just expired. That was Operations. That fire at Gladesview House last night is looking like arson, and they've discovered a body in the ashes. Mike Jonas is already there. Grab your coat, we need to go take a look. I'll drive. You don't look like you're up to it.'

'Thanks, Boss.'

Novella

The New Girlfriend

Everyday Business Skills

Everyday Project Management

Everyday Productivity

Everyday Money Management

Writings of the Mystic

Sharing the Journey: Reflections of a Reluctant Mystic

A Question of Perspective

My Life is My Responsibility: Insights for Conscious Living

I Am Affirmations: The Power of Words

Beyond the Words: Reflections on I Am Affirmations

Mystical Journey: A Handbook for Modern Mystics

Sharing the Journey Coloring Books

Mandalas

Mandalas by 3

Sharing the Journey Coloring Journals

Sharing the Journey Coloring Journal

Discovery

Reflection